A "Gaston" The Poodle MYSTERY

Murder Is as Easy as

Pie

Janice Detrie

Murder Is as Easy as Pie
Copyright © 2022 by Janice Detrie

ISBN: 978-0-9987342-2-4
Printed in the United States of America

This is a work of fiction. Names, characters, places, and incidents are either a product of the author's imagination or are used fictitiously. Any resemblance to actual events, or persons or locales, living or dead, is purely coincidental.

Published by
Janice Detrie

Cover design by Eric Labacz
www.labaczdesign.com

For Frances Milburn who lights the way

Chapter One

When Vlad Chomsky staggered off the Tilt-A-Whirl, he thought his day at the county fair couldn't get any worse. Little did he know the worst was yet to come.

"Daddy, please can we go on the Tilt-A-Whirl one more time?" pleaded Kaitlyn, his five-year-old daughter, widening her eyes in a pitiful expression. "Pretty please, Daddy."

Vlad Chomsky had eaten only dry toast for breakfast and, after the dizzying ride on the midway attraction, his stomach was still revolving. Scanning the dusty pathway for the nearest trash can, Vlad exhaled slowly, then swallowed hard to force the bile back into his flip-flopping stomach. Holding onto the metal exit railing to steady himself, he took a few more deep breaths.

"Are you all right, Dad?" said Nicholas, his eleven-year-old son, staring at him with big, worried eyes rimmed with thick glasses.

"I'm fine, son. Just give me a few seconds to catch my breath. I haven't gone on a carnival ride in such a long time. I forgot how disorienting it can be." Vlad finally straightened up and raked his thinning hair back into place with his fingers. Then he tucked his wrinkle-free shirt into his Bermuda shorts.

"Daddy, you promised I could go on any ride I wanted. I want to go again," Kaitlyn grew more strident. "The Tilt-A-Whirl is the only fun ride I'm big enough to go on."

When they first arrived at the county fair, Vlad tried to interest Kaitlyn in the kiddie rides. His ex-wife, Maria, had warned him she'd be difficult. When he led her to the little helicopters that went up and down, she protested.

"No! I want to go on that ride," she said as she pointed to a ride that looked like two giant hammers welded together.

Vlad watched as each arm of the hammer rose high above the fair, turned upside down, then dove toward the earth. Luckily, a size chart was next to the ride that read: "You must be this tall to ride the attraction." Kaitlyn tried to stand tall, rising on her tippy toes, but her head still was below the line.

"Sorry, Sweet Pea. Maybe next year," Vlad said.

Nicholas looked relieved and said, "I'll go with you on the helicopters. I'll let you pull the bar to make it go up and down."

"No, that's a baby ride. I'm a big girl now." said Kaitlyn, then ran to the Gravitron, a flying saucer look-alike that spun around with the riders standing up. Too short again. She was too short for all of the scary looking rides—except the Tilt-a-Whirl.

Both Nicholas and Vlad deemed the ride tame enough for all of them until Vlad actually twirled around in the darn thing. His head was jerked into the metal backboard so violently he feared whiplash. Just when the ride seemed to be slowing to a standstill and he relaxed, it pivoted in the opposite direction and spun wickedly again, faster than before. Once safely on solid ground, Vlad checked his watch.

"It's almost time for the pie judging. We promised Beatrice we'd be there to cheer her on," he said.

"Boring!" Kaitlyn yelled. "I hate pie, 'specially when I don't get to eat some. I want to go on a ride."

"Now, Kaitlyn. You promised you'd cooperate. If you're a good girl, I'll buy you some cotton candy." He searched the crowd, hoping to catch a glimpse of his oldest daughter, Erin, who had run off with her friends from high school the second they had passed through the gates.

"No, ride. Tilt-A-Whirl again."

Vlad frowned, tugging on his mustache nervously. He dreaded dragging a screaming Kaitlyn into the adult exhibition building. *Let's try to avoid that scene,* he thought.

"Do you see Erin anywhere?" He shaded his eyes with his hand and peered into the bright sunlit midway.

"I can take her on the ride again, Dad," Nicholas said. "I'm eleven. Mom lets me babysit once in a while. I can take her on the ride."

Vlad looked at Nicholas's earnest face and the long line forming at the ride's entrance, then sighed. "I suppose you're old enough to take her for a while. I'll give you some money for cotton candy and soda. Please bring her over to the adult pavilion when you're done."

Vlad bent down and pulled Kaitlyn's face between his hands, forcing her to look him in the eyes. "You are to listen to your big brother. He'll take you on the ride again, and then for a treat IF you're a good girl."

"I'll be good, Daddy. I promise."

"If Nicholas tells me you're good, we'll get corn dogs on a stick for lunch. Maybe a nice souvenir, too."

"Okay, Daddy, I'll be good. I'll listen to Nicky." She grabbed her brother's hand and tugged him toward the queue. "Let's go."

Vlad opened his wallet and handed thirty dollars to Nicholas. "That should be enough for ride tickets and a treat. Don't let her out of your sight."

As the two children joined the throng at the ticket booth, Vlad watched them with trepidation. Fluttering her arms overhead, Kaitlyn danced in and out of line as her pigtails swished about. He could hear Nicholas say, "You need to stand right next to me. Stop bothering the other people." Checking his watch again, Vlad hurried to the pavilion and scanned the crowd, spotting Beatrice's pixie haircut immediately.

Sitting in the second row of spectator chairs, Beatrice waved to him the minute he entered the crowded building, as her grey eyes shone with excitement. She gestured to the empty seat next to her and cleared away her purse so he could join her. Her powder blue bag matched the tiny flowers on her sundress, the spaghetti straps exposing her toned arms and shoulders. Catching his eye, she smiled, and he marveled again that she had agreed to marry him, especially after the disastrous river cruise when a ring of international jewel thieves interrupted their romantic getaway. But with the help of his elderly landlady and her irascible poodle, they solved the case, and Beatrice accepted his proposal.

"Excuse me. Pardon me." He apologized as he stumbled past the audience, mostly ladies, and ignored their annoyed looks.

She slipped her hand into his, and he ran his thumb over the diamond ring glinting brightly on her finger, a symbol of their hard-earned happiness.

"Some people are so rude!"

In the front row an angular woman dressed in a stiff linen shift shot a death ray glare at him. Her mouth curved down in a perpetual frown. When she caught Beatrice's eye, she snapped, "I might have known he belonged with you," then twisted to face the small stage.

A flustered-looking lady hastily set up a microphone near the judging table where an assortment of pies stood waiting to be tasted and evaluated.

Vlad arched a quizzical eyebrow and jerked his head toward the grumpy woman. Beatrice's face grew flush as she whispered in his ear.

"Don't pay any attention to her. That's Florence Heidt. Her strawberry chiffon pie won Best of the Fair for five years in a row, until my cherry berry peach pie won last year. She's still mad about it. Claims I cheated. She's come up with a new chiffon recipe this year. She's sure it will beat mine."

"I never realized pie baking was so cutthroat," Vlad whispered back.

Beatrice rolled her eyes. "Only if you're Florence Heidt. She can be vicious. But, then again, so can the judges, especially Alexandria Adams. No one wants to work with her. I should know. I'm on the County Fair Board."

"Is she the woman who scheduled Garden Club meetings during the workday and then kicked you out because you missed too many meetings?"

"That's her! And there she is, in the flesh."

What imposing flesh! Vlad thought. A titan of a woman swept onto the stage like the *Queen Mary 2* sailing into port. Crimson and purple splotches embellished her pink dress. Meant to be airy and flowing, the gown on Alexandria's solid build assaulted the eyes with hurricane force. A pink and red flower petal hat completed the look of a hand grenade tossed into a flower bed. Wisps of auburn curls lacquered into place outlined her broad face while her laser sharp eyes swept over the stage.

"This isn't the right chair." She pointed an accusing finger at the metal chair. "I need a cushioned chair if I'm expected to sit for any length of time. You of all people should know better. How long have you been running this? I'd expect a modicum of competence by now."

The frazzled woman turned beet red. "I'm so sorry! I brought you an upholstered one from home but, with all the commotion, I left in it my van. I'll send someone to get it right away."

"My husband can get it for you." Alexandria snapped her fingers. "Earl, get the chair from Donna's van. The judging is about to begin."

"Yes, dear. I'll get right on it."

A tall man, skinnier than the starving dogs in the SPCA ads, hurried over to the stage. Donna brushed her fingers through her tangled hair and smiled wanly before she handed him some keys and he disappeared into the crowd.

"I suppose I can make do with this one for a while," the haughty woman sniffed.

She perched on the chair like an emu settling on a sparrow's nest and stared arrogantly at the audience. Vlad's eyes were drawn to her brightly painted toenails crammed inside hot pink patent leather sandals. Even her toes loomed larger than life.

Donna, aka Ms. Frazzle, spoke into the microphone, "Welcome, ladies and gentlemen, to the Madison County Fair Pie Contest. We are most fortunate to have Alexandria Adams on board today. Alexandria has been the mainstay of our bakery judging for fifteen years. She truly takes the cake!"

The audience politely applauded as Alexandria slowly nodded her head in acknowledgment. Then she turned her attention to the dozen or so pies spread out on the table in front of her, inspecting each as if she were choosing the only genuine ruby from an assortment of fakes. Alexandria waited until all eyes were on her before she spoke.

"Here are the standards of a good pie. The building block of a prizewinning pie, the crust, must be tender and flaky, with subtle layers of buttery goodness and a perfect blend of salt and sugar. The filling is the heart and soul, presenting delightful flavors using only the freshest ingredients of the highest quality. The topping is the pièce de résistance, whether it be a fluffy meringue or a crumb topping, or a simple top crust sprinkled with sugar. It must provide the finishing touch of the pie eating experience."

Ms. Frazzle added, "Alexandria will judge on these merits. One pie will be chosen as the Grand Prize Winner, the Best of the Fair. Who will be the lucky baker this year?"

"The Grand Prize Winner is determined by skill and creativity. Luck has nothing to do with it." Alexandria shot a look of disdain at the wretched woman, whose face crumpled into near tears.

None of the first few pies met Alexandria's exacting standards. The first pie, a two-crust cherry, had the misfortune of a tough, leathery crust. She spat the offending pastry into a napkin and deemed it a "dishonorable mention." The coconut custard fared only slightly better.

"Too much coconut and not toasted to a nutty flavor." She slapped a pink ribbon on the entry card.

Just then her husband appeared with the new chair, complete with cushioned seat and arm rests. Donna whisked away the offending chair, and Alexandria tested the spongy softness of its replacement with her hand before she settled back down. She dismissed her hovering husband with a wave of her hand and stared expectantly at her harried assistant.

Vlad leaned closer to Beatrice and said, "Perhaps a more comfortable chair will improve her disposition."

"I wouldn't bet on it," she replied, shaking her head.

Alas, the lemon meringue had not been sealed properly to the edge of the crust and had emerged from the oven flat as a pancake. The meringue atop the banana cream pie was fluffy and high, but the vanilla cream filling turned curdy, not creamy. She wrinkled her nose and gave them honorable mention ribbons.

The crumb-topped apple fared better. She said, "At last, a pie that's appealing rather than appalling," then attached a red ribbon to the entrant's card.

The judging continued until only two pies remained. Donna slid a chiffon pie to the center of the table. A fluffy green pastel cloud alighted on a perfectly fluted crust.

Alexandria arched her eyebrows and exclaimed, "What is this? I've never seen a chiffon this lovely color."

She leaned closer to the entry card and read aloud: "Buttermint chiffon pie. How delightful! A truly unique creation."

Florence Heidt glanced over her shoulder and gave Beatrice a smug smile before turning her attention back to the judge. Ignoring her, Beatrice sat poker-faced with a straight spine. Vlad reached over and gently squeezed her hand. She squeezed his back.

After cutting a sliver of the foamy chiffon pie, Donna placed the airy concoction in front of the judge.

Alexandria inhaled deeply and said, "What a delicious, minty aroma! A feast for the nose as well as the eyes."

She picked up the fork, then paused to say, "A chiffon pie is a fragile creature. The egg whites must be whipped into stiff peaks but not allowed to get dry, then folded into a custard mixture that's cooled to the perfect temperature. Let's see if the baker has achieved this delicate balance."

The green froth disappeared in her mouth as she slowly chewed, then swallowed. "Ah, melt-in-your-mouth goodness. Perhaps the crust is just a tad mushy, but the light fluffy taste more than makes up for it." She attached a blue ribbon to the entry card.

With excitement in her voice, Donna spoke, "The first blue ribbon of the day goes to this incredible pie. Will it be the Best of the Fair?"

A loud murmuring swept through the audience, and several heads turned to look at Florence, seated proudly in the front row. She had pleated the judging timetable into a makeshift fan and was waving it in front of her face. Once more she flashed a nasty smile at Beatrice.

"Last but not least, another lovely fruit pie," Donna said, moving Beatrice's pie in front of the judge.

Red and blue bits of fruit bubbled through the lacy lattice top, the rich jewel tones peeking through the diamond shapes.

"Nicely done. The twisted lattice work is exquisite. It surely took much time to create such perfect strands," Alexandria commented. "We shall now see if it tastes as good as it looks. Pretty is as pretty does."

As Donna cut a small wedge of pie and lifted it onto the plate, the judge continued, "Look how the pie held its shape. No runny juices. What a perfect scalloped edge to the crust!" She inhaled deeply. "And a delicious aroma. A suggestion of the scent of summer."

Vlad gave his mustache a few tugs, tapping his foot with a staccato beat. Reaching again for Beatrice's hand, he felt like biting his nails. She sat Zen-like, the corners of her mouth turning up in a slight smile.

"How can you stay so calm?" he whispered.

"The pie guru on YouTube says to keep everything chilled as you make a pie—including yourself," she answered.

Alexandria lifted the fork to her mouth and savored her first bite. "A perfect crust. Well-constructed of flaky layers. Dissolves into delectable buttery shards in the mouth."

She chewed slowly, then swallowed. She thoughtfully tilted her head before she spoke. "The baker has captured all the succulent flavors of summer as well. I detect cherries and peaches and some other fruit. Donna, what's the name of this pie again?"

"The entry card reads: Cherry Berry Peach Pie," she said.

Florence whispered loudly to her companion. "Some people bake the same old pie year after year. Just because they won once, they figure the recipe is a sure thing."

Glad that Beatrice still held tight to his hand, he really wanted to make a rude gesture with his middle finger at the back of the nasty woman's head, but that would be sinking down to her level. Beatrice always made him choose the high road.

Alexandria knotted her eyebrows and said, "Ah, berries. But what kind of berries? Blueberries? I must have another bite to be sure." She shoved a bigger bite into her mouth. "Yes, certainly blueberries, perhaps wild blueberries, a subtle bitter taste. There's just a hint of some spice to enhance the flavor. It's a bit tangy. Perhaps just one more bite and I'll be able to tell what it is."

"Your taste buds must be very sensitive," Donna commented.

"The ability to distinguish the addition of even the slightest dash of spice is developed over years of training. A true gourmand is worth her weight in gold."

"We'd have to raid Fort Knox to come up with her weight in gold," Vlad whispered as Alexandria took a third bite.

Beatrice shook her head at him with a little frown.

"What can the unusual flavor be?" The judge knitted her brows with an intense expression as she slowly savored the bite.

Suddenly, she made a strangled sound and clutched her throat. As she opened her mouth in an attempt to speak, globs of fruit spewed out. Three or four gurgling noises emanated from her throat before the volcanic eruption of vomit spread across the plastic tablecloth like flowing lava forming a Jackson Pollock likeness of pie ingredients.

The entire audience looked stunned as her eyes bulged with the effort of expelling the pie. She half-rose from her chair, but immediately flopped back down like a limp rag doll. She grasped the edge of the table in an attempt to pull herself up, her mouth like a gaping wound.

"My mouf...numb.., can't feel my hands, my legs," Alexandria struggled to speak. Suddenly, her body went rigid, her back arched, her legs splayed sideways, jerking and shaking, as though currents of electricity coursed through them. If not for the padded arms of the chair, she would have toppled to the floor.

Vlad turned to Beatrice and said, "What the hell?"

Her face drained of all color as she stared in disbelief at the scene unfolding before them. She clasped her hands together in a prayerful pose and muttered, "I don't understand."

Writhing in pain, Alexandria moved her hands down to press against her chest as if she was pushing her heart back into her body. She emitted a guttural moan that came from deep within, like a wounded bear in the last throes of death.

She managed to choke out a few words. "The pie…"

Those were the last words she spoke before she collapsed facedown into the vomit-covered Cherry Berry Peach Pie.

The audience froze in horror and disbelief.

Then Florence Heidt leapt to her feet, a gaunt figure in her shapeless dress. She whirled to face Beatrice, pointed a bony finger, and growled, "What on earth did you put in that pie?"

Chapter Two

The EMTs arrived in under five minutes, entering the chaotic scene with professional efficiency. As they pushed through the crowd, Earl Adams eased his wife off the chair before wiping away pie filling and vomit from her face. Down on the floor, he supported her head in his lap.

Rocking back and forth, he begged, "Stay with me, dearest. Don't leave me. Please stay with me."

Her unseeing eyes stared at the overhead light, and her slack mouth would issue no pronouncement of the Grand Prize Winner. Sprawled out, she covered most of the small stage as convulsion after convulsion rocked her body.

A buzz swept through the unbelieving audience. "Oh my God! What just happened? Is she dead?"

Vlad sheltered Beatrice in his arms, safe from prying eyes. As she buried her head in his chest, tears welled up in her eyes.

He whispered, "There, there. Ignore that nasty woman. Your pie had nothing to do with her collapse."

The two EMTs bent down to lift Alexandria.

"Lift with your legs, not with your back," the older one admonished his partner.

Unfortunately, they managed to lift her head and her feet, but her derriere was fused to the floor. They soon realized they needed help. The younger one whipped out his cell phone.

"I'll call for help. Officer Roberts is manning the emergency tent. We'll get him here to assist."

When the police officer arrived, all three grappled with the unwieldy woman's body. On the count of three, they hoisted her onto the gurney, groaning with the exertion.

One of the EMTs said to Earl, "You can follow us to the emergency room."

They whisked her to the waiting ambulance, sirens blaring as they pulled away.

"Are you able to drive?" the police officer asked the stricken husband.

"I-I don't know. My wife usually does the driving. And she's…oh, God, she's…" He closed his eyes and moaned.

"I can take him to the hospital," Donna jumped in. "My van's parked right behind the building."

"Aren't you in charge of the contest?" the officer said, examining the big purple Organizer ribbon pinned to her chest. "I need your statement of what happened leading up to the incident."

"Let me take him. I'm not needed here. My car is nearby, too," Florence Heidt buzzed onto the stage like an annoying wasp, hovering between Earl and the officer.

"That would be most kind," Earl said. "I'm in no condition to drive." He held out his shaking hands.

Florence grasped him by the elbow and steered him toward the exit. "Come along, you poor man. You must feel horrible. Something surely was wrong with that pie."

"Will she be all right? She looked terrible. All those spasms! I think she's g-g-gone!" He put his hands in front of his face and started to weep. "I can't bear it if she's gone."

"We'll find out at the hospital. Let's hurry." Florence led the dazed man away.

The crowd began to filter out, still chattering about what they'd just witnessed. Vlad heard murmurs of "Did she have some kind of seizure? A heart attack? Maybe a stroke? I heard she had a peanut allergy. Was it something in the last pie?"

The officer waited until most had left, then surveyed the scene. "So what happened here?"

Donna wrung her hands as she spoke. "We were just about to finish the pie baking contest. Alexandria was tasting the last entry when she made a horrible sound and vomited like there was something wrong with the pie. Then she started having some convulsions."

"And this is the pie she was eating?" The policeman nodded his head toward the red and blue mess.

Globs of smashed pastry mixed with bits of cherries, blueberries, and peaches were scattered on the judging table under a film of partly digested pie.

"It's my pie, officer." Beatrice moved to the foot of the stage. "I baked it this morning. All the ingredients came from the Farmer's Market yesterday. Nothing out of the ordinary."

"But Alexandria did notice something unusual. A flavor she couldn't identify. She was eating her third bite when she collapsed," Donna interjected. She gave a sideways glance at Beatrice and clutched the ends of her purple ribbon with both hands, twisting it round and round.

"Maybe she had an allergic reaction?" Vlad suggested.

"We'll know more when the doctor examines her. No sense jumping to conclusions until we find out if the pie is the culprit." Hands on hips, the police officer frowned at the offending pie, as though it belonged on a wanted poster in the post office.

"She's been judging pies at the county fair for fifteen years. I organized each one of those contests. She's never had a reaction like this before," Donna said with a quiver in her voice.

The officer's cell phone rang. The voice on the other end crackled as the policeman solemnly nodded his head.

"I see. Heart arrhythmia, respiratory problems. Maybe something she ingested. Quick acting. Okay, we'll wait until then."

Returning the phone to his back pocket, he cast his eyes upon Donna and then Beatrice. "That was the ER doc. Alexandria Adams has all the hallmarks of poisoning. They're doing some bloodwork to see if they can determine the source. We'll have to test samples of all the pies. This is now a crime scene."

"A crime scene? Oh, my goodness! What will the fair association say?" Donna's hands fluttered about like a moth trapped in a backyard lantern. "And Earl, that poor man! He must be devastated."

"I'll need both your names and phone numbers before you leave and the names of anyone else you can think of to interview as a witness. We'll be contacting you down at the station shortly for a formal statement." He pulled a notepad and pen from his breast pocket and looked expectantly at Beatrice.

In a numb voice, Beatrice gave the officer her information, her worried eyes betraying her dismay. She bit her lower lip as the officer jotted down the information. Vlad also volunteered his name and number, keeping the interchange business-like and hoping he displayed a confidence he didn't feel. When the officer turned his attention to Donna, Vlad veered closer to Beatrice and held out a comforting hand. She slipped her hand into his, and they moved toward the exit.

"If that's all for now, Officer, we'll be leaving," Vlad said.

Just then Vlad's two kids burst through the door.

"Dad, we saw an ambulance leave the fairgrounds!" Nicholas said.

"The siren went roo-a-roo," Kaitlyn clamored. "It was so loud I covered my ears." She brought her hands up to her head to reenact the scene.

"And the lights were flashing. Everyone got out of the way," Nicholas added. "I wonder who got hurt?"

"One of the judges here in the pavilion got sick so they had to call the EMTs to take her to the emergency room," Vlad said.

"Is that why that cop is here?" Nicholas pointed to the police officer still talking to Donna. "Darn, we missed all the excitement. You just had to eat caramel corn before we came here," he accused his sister.

"I was real hungry. You said cotton candy is too messy. See, clean hands." She held them up for Vlad to see.

"It took you forever to eat your caramel corn," Nicholas said, clearly annoyed. "One little kernel at a time."

"Mom always tells me to chew my food. I don't wolf it down like you." Kaitlyn stuck out her tongue at her brother.

Vlad intervened. "Please, children, don't squabble. Can't you see Beatrice is a bit upset?"

"Why? Didn't she win a prize for her pie?" Nicholas asked.

"It's not that, Nicholas." Beatrice's voice shook. "I knew the judge quite well, and I didn't want her to get sick." She bit her lower lip, holding back tears.

"Did your pie make her sick?" Kaitlyn looked at the mess on the table. "That looks like your pie."

Vlad quickly answered, "Don't be silly. Beatrice's pie did not make anyone sick." He added with fake heartiness, "Who's ready for lunch? My treat."

"I think I'll take a pass and head home. I was up at four-thirty, rolling out pie dough and cutting fruit. I'm exhausted." Beatrice's body slumped forward like the air slowly leaking from a pinprick in a balloon.

"Should I stop by your place once I take the kids to their Mom's?"

"Yes, I'd like that. I have some leftover chicken salad we can have for supper," she said with a forced smile.

"I'll pick up a bottle of wine on the way," he said as he gave her a kiss on her cheek and watched worriedly as she trudged out the exit.

"I'm still hungry, Daddy. I want a corn dog." Kaitlyn tugged fiercely on his arm. "Let's go eat."

"Can I have chicken tenders and cheese curds?" Nicholas asked.

"Of course."

"And a root beer float?" Nicholas added.

"Whatever you kids want."

His cell phone rang. It was Erin, his missing in action teenage daughter, asking if she could catch a ride home with her friend's mother. He gladly gave her permission to stay longer.

By the time the kids ate and finished deliberating over which cheap souvenir to buy, it was almost three o'clock. Maria, his ex, was weeding in the flower bed when he dropped the kids off. She looked up, face partly hidden by her sun hat, and gave him a wave. Kaitlyn scampered over to her, brandishing her laser sword and striking Star Wars poses. Nicholas sauntered into the house, wearing his new Space Force baseball cap. Vlad waved back, glad that Maria seemed too distracted to chat.

First, chilled white wine from the Kwik Stop store, then a drive across town to Beatrice. The only noise in the car was the hum of the air conditioner. Vlad finally allowed himself to relax. As he turned onto her street, he thought of all the ways he could comfort her: draw her a relaxing bath, bring her a glass of wine as she soaked, put on some uplifting classical music.

He spotted the two figures on Beatrice's porch swing from a block away. A male wearing a Green Bay Packers baseball cap, a dingy white t-shirt, and motorcycle boots propped up on a large flower planter. His companion wore a wide-brimmed hat with peacock feathers tucked into the band, a turquoise boa flung around her shoulders, and a shimmery dress adorned with sequined flowers, the kind of thing only a geriatric burlesque queen would wear. When he pulled up, a chubby poodle emerged from behind the large planter and started yapping incessantly.

Now he knew the day was heading from bad to worse. Anytime his eccentric landlady and her not-so-handyman showed up, Vlad knew it was going to be trouble. Not to mention her obnoxious little dog.

Vlad stepped out of the car, clutching the wine bottle and trying not to hyperventilate. He greeted them through clenched teeth, "Sandra Tooksbury and Norm Clodfelter. What a surprise to see you here!"

The elderly lady scrutinized him over the tops of her oversized glittery sunglasses and said, "We heard what happened at the pie judging. Possible poisoning! Right here in Crawford, Wisconsin. There's not a moment to lose. Gaston is eager to solve another mystery."

As though to demonstrate his enthusiasm, Gaston dashed up to Vlad and gave his ankle a little nip.

Norm cracked his knuckles and chortled, "So, Doc, when can we get started on the case?"

Chapter Three

Beatrice stepped onto the porch bearing a tray with a lemonade pitcher and three glasses, a plate full of snickerdoodle cookies, and a bowl of water for Gaston. She set them on a small table next to the glider and placed the bowl of water in front of Gaston. He quickly slurped up the water, then stood on his hind legs, front paws on the table, pitifully eying the plate of cookies. Sandra broke one in half and tossed a small chunk a little distance away to distract the dog from the tray, then reached for a second cookie for herself. Norm grabbed a handful and noisily munched as he talked.

"No lemonade for me, thank you. I'll have a cold brewskie, if ya got one," Norm said

"I think I have a few beers left over from the end of the year picnic at the college. I hope a lite is okay?" Beatrice raised her eyebrows in a question.

"Gotta have something to wash down these cookies. Very tasty, by the way." Norm also threw a chunk of cookie to Gaston, who leapt up and caught it midair.

"I'll have a glass of wine, please," Sandra said. "You can just pour it into that tumbler. Don't dirty a special glass for me."

Beatrice took the Chardonnay bottle from Vlad and asked, "Would you like a glass of wine, too?"

"No, thanks. The lemonade looks delicious. I'll pour myself a glass." He filled the tumbler and sat down on the top step while Beatrice went back into the house.

"So how did you find out about Alexandria Adams so fast?" Vlad inquired.

"Juanita Edwards' daughter works in the hospital cafeteria. It was all the tittle-tattle with the lunch crowd." Sandra brushed cookie crumbs off her boa as she spoke. "She called Juanita, and Juanita called me, especially when she heard it was Beatrice's pie that did her in. Tsk-tsk. Who'd ever think of someone keeling over judging pies at the Madison County Fair? People are saying it was poison." Sandra threw the remaining piece of cookie to Gaston.

Norm chewed slowly on a cookie. "That's the most excitement at the Madison County Fair since my Uncle Bud and Aunt Vivian finally took that helicopter ride over the fairgrounds."

Sandra chimed in. "I remember when that pilot drummed up money by giving people a ride in his helicopter. Wasn't it fifty dollars for a ride?"

"Yep. Fifty bucks a pop. Year after year, Uncle Bud would ask Aunt Viv if she'd go up on the helicopter with him. He'd really like to take a ride in that helicopter. She said no. Fifty bucks is fifty bucks. Every year Uncle Bud would beg to ride in the helicopter, they'd bicker for a while, and she always said no. Fifty bucks is fifty bucks.

"Finally, the year Uncle Bud turned eighty, he begged Aunt Viv to spring for the ride. Told her it was on his bucket list—probably never have another chance."

Sandra commented to Vlad, "I know how that feels. Carpe diem, I always say."

Norm continued. "This time the pilot overhears them bickering and said, 'Look, I'll give you a free ride on one condition. If either of you makes a peep while we're flying, you owe me the fifty dollars.' They argued about it for a minute but finally agreed and climbed in behind the pilot.

"The pilot, dead set on making them at least gasp, took off as fast as he could and started doing some crazy maneuvers, rolling, turning, diving. After fifteen minutes without hearing a sound from them, he gave up and landed. When he looked behind him, only Uncle Bud was there.

"The pilot asks, 'Where the hell is your wife?'

"Uncle Bud tells him, 'She fell out a few minutes after you took off.'

"The pilot shouted, 'Why the hell didn't you say something?'

"Uncle Bud says, 'Well, I wanted to, but fifty bucks is fifty bucks." Norm smiled broadly.

Sandra giggled and said, "That's one of my favorite stories."

Vlad groaned, "I should have known."

"Should have known what, love?" Beatrice asked as she appeared with the open bottle in one hand and wine glass in the other. She filled a tumbler and the empty glass, then settled down on the top step next to Vlad.

"Nothing." He pressed his lips tightly together and shrugged. "Just another one of Norm's yarns. I almost fell for it."

"What about the case?" Sandra questioned. "Shouldn't we be talking about where to start? Gaston is more than ready."

Gaston returned to his shady spot behind the planter and looked expectantly at the dwindling plate of cookies.

"Maybe we should take him to the scene of the crime and let him sniff around," Norm said. "He's better at finding clues than any bloodhound."

"There is no case. Right now murder by poison is hypothetical. We don't have a victim because the last we heard Alexandria is still alive. Besides, the police are better equipped to handle it than Gaston." Vlad thoughtfully ran a finger down his mustache.

"You sang a different tune when that terrorist snuck into your apartment and held a knife to your throat. When he threatened to hurt your family, who came to the rescue? This little feller, that's who." Norm patted the poodle on the head.

"Are you forgetting who captured the leader of the ring of jewel thieves? Thanks to his timely attack, the police were able to nab the thief before he could escape," Sandra added. "I admit the two of them had me fooled with their father and son from Pennsylvania act, but Gaston pegged them as phonies right from the start, didn't you, my clever love dog?" She tossed him another chunk of cookie. "He didn't like either of those crooks."

"All right. I confess Gaston appeared at the opportune moment in each case, but that doesn't make him another McGruff, the crime fighting dog." Vlad looked to Beatrice for confirmation. "It was just a coincidence."

"There's no coincidence in crime solving. There's just a detective waiting to make the connections. And Gaston the Wonder Dog is the Sherlock Holmes of dogs," Sandra insisted.

Beatrice spoke up. "Gaston certainly is an exceptional dog. But Vlad's right. We don't know that a crime has been committed. I certainly didn't put anything untoward in my Cherry Berry Peach Pie. I can't imagine who would want to poison Alexandria Adams."

"I can't imagine who wouldn't. I've had a few run-ins with that terrible woman myself," Sandra wrinkled her nose in disgust. "She had the nerve to complain about Gaston sharing my dinner at Ronny's Supper Club. She called him a dirty mutt and threatened to call animal control when he growled at her. The manager made us leave before we even had dessert."

Norm wiped the beer foam from his upper lip with the back of his hand before he spoke, "She was in the Super Saver getting groceries one day and arguing with the checkout girl over a store coupon that expired. Insisted she still get the sale price. Didn't care about the huge line of customers behind her. When she didn't get her way, Alexandria got so mad she walked off screaming she'd never shop there again. Left all her stuff on the counter. What a battle-ax!"

"Beatrice, didn't you have some disagreements with her as well?" Vlad asked. "Didn't she try to exclude you from the Garden Club and try to disqualify you from participating in the annual home garden award? Said you weren't an active member."

"I'd prefer not to discuss the incident. She is a mainstay of many clubs besides the Garden Club. There's the County Fair Board and numerous charities. Let's not speak ill of the woman while she's struggling for her life," said Beatrice as she swirled the remaining wine in her glass before setting it down and staring at it. "I keep thinking of her poor husband—so devastated by her collapse."

"All right, dearie. It's been a difficult day for you. You started with such high hopes for a second blue ribbon. And it all came to naught. You need a little loving to cheer you up." Sandra snapped her fingers at the recumbent pooch, who stared hopefully at her hand for more cookies. "Gaston, give Auntie Beatrice a kiss. She needs a little puppy love."

The poodle waddled over to Beatrice, stood on his hind legs, and gave her face a sloppy lick. She tried to move away from his tongue as he aimed it toward the crumbs on her lips.

"Good boy," she said as she gave him a gentle push.

Back on his four paws, he stuck his nose in her wine glass and sniffed at the contents. No cookies there. He ambled back to his spot and rested his head on his front paws.

Norm drained the beer bottle, set it down on the table, and leaned forward, elbows on knees. "I know what'll cheer ya up. Let me tell ya another Uncle Bud and Aunt Viv story. I gotta million of 'em."

Vlad stifled a groan and reached for the wine.

Chapter Four

The sun was setting by the time Sandra and Norm took their leave. Beatrice's face was etched with worry lines and pale with exhaustion. She pulled a scruffy black cardigan over her shoulders, after shivering for a while in her blue sundress, and carried the tray of dirty dishes into the kitchen. Slumped over the kitchen sink, she began to fill it with soapy water.

Vlad gently took her hands in his and offered, "I'll take care of cleaning up. Why don't you run yourself a nice, relaxing bath? When I'm done here, I'll light some candles and turn on some soft music. I'd be happy give you a back rub. Maybe I can find something else to take your mind off the pie contest."

He turned off the gushing water, picked up the dishcloth, and began to scrub the glasses. Beatrice stood silently watching him for a few moments, then she spoke.

"If you don't mind, I'm so exhausted. I'd just like to crawl in bed and forget about today for a little while."

Vlad did mind but couldn't add to her stress level so he agreed to call it an early evening and go home.

"I'll take a rain check for tomorrow," he said. "Can I take you out for breakfast?"

"I'm sorry, I have to work at the library tomorrow. I only hope Florence Heidt has off this week. I can't face her just yet," she answered, biting her bottom lip.

"I forgot Florence is the assistant librarian at Memorial. She isn't just your rival at pie making."

"No, she's a thorn in my side at work, too. She's been resentful of me ever since I got promoted to head librarian. She applied for the position and was so angry the committee selected me that she filed a grievance. I try to schedule us on different days, but sometimes our schedules overlap," she sighed with a shrug.

"What a bummer."

"If you thought her cattiness was bad yesterday, you should see the evil looks she gives me when we cross paths at work. At least at work I'm her supervisor so she's forced to control her mouth in front of me." Beatrice played with a loose button on her sweater, eyes focused on the work schedule clipped to the refrigerator.

"Would you like me to heat some milk for you or fix a nightcap?" Vlad dried his hands on the towel and reached for her, kissing her tenderly. She melted into his arms and leaned into his chest for a minute before she pulled away.

"No, darling, nothing tonight. I'm sorry." Her face was saddened with regret. "You've been my strength and support today. I don't know what I'd have done without you. Tomorrow I'll cook something special for supper, in appreciation, just the two of us."

SLEEPING ALONE IN HIS small apartment, Vlad experienced a dreary reminder of what his life was like without Beatrice, without her sparkling grey eyes and spritely smile to greet him in the morning. The unfortunate incident at the pie judging had left her uncharacteristically dispirited. Hopefully, a good night's sleep would set things right.

The next day dawned with glorious sunshine streaming through the crack where the shade didn't quite reach the windowsill. Vlad threw back the covers on the Murphy bed in his one-room efficiency and stumbled to the kitchenette to make coffee. Lifting the shade, he enjoyed the morning sunlight, reveling in the possibilities of a summer day. The reward money from the capture of the international jewel thieves meant financial worries were a thing of the past. No teaching the summer session at Crawford College for the pittance that, in his newly divorced state, kept the two households afloat. No digging into his teaching bag of tricks trying to motivate disinterested students. No trying to cram a semester's worth of information into six weeks. Instead, he planned to spend his summer waking up next to his new fiancé, cooking breakfast in her cozy kitchen, lazing on the porch reading. This was meant to be his summer of easy joy. But yesterday's disaster at the fair changed all that.

While the teakettle was heating up water for the French press, he shuffled into the bathroom to wash up. His dark, thin hair stuck out at forty-five-degree angles so he brushed it lightly into place, hoping it looked fuller, and used a tiny comb to groom his mustache. He peered closely at his eyes in the mirror, not too many dark circles underneath. It's amazing what a summer off can do for chronic fatigue. Even his posture improved greatly from the usual hunched position he developed after correcting the multitude of papers.

The shrill ring of his cell phone interrupted his reverie. He rushed to answer it, hoping Beatrice had changed her mind about breakfast. But alas, it was Maria, his ex.

"Are you busy this morning? I know that's a foolish question, considering you're not teaching this session."

"No, nothing on the calendar today. What's up?"

"I need your help, ASAP. I have to show a house to a hot prospect in thirty minutes, a last-minute appointment. They've been dithering about buying for weeks and want to bring their parents from out of town to look it over. Even took off from work to meet me."

"Erin's not around?" he asked.

"She is, but she has to work the concession stand at the pool at ten. Nicholas has baseball practice at ten-thirty, and he's refusing to get dressed. It's been the morning from hell, and it's not even nine o'clock."

Vlad could hear the rising frustration in her voice.

"Why is that?" The teakettle's whistle cut short his reply.

"I didn't have time to do the laundry so Erin's work t-shirts are all dirty. Kaitlyn insisted the ducks and geese were starving at the park and she has to feed them. I tried to discourage her, but you know how stubborn she gets."

Vlad turned off the whistling kettle and set the phone on speaker on the counter as he poured water into the French press. "Sounds pretty stressful."

"Stressful is putting it mildly. When I got the call to show the house, Kaitlyn threw a fit, yelling 'You promised to take me to the park.' I swear the neighbors on the next block probably heard her. Then Nicholas started acting up. God, I get so sick of this shit sometimes."

Maria's strident voice sent a shiver down his spine.

"I'll throw some clothes on and be right there."

He poured his coffee in a to-go cup, sipping as he dressed into his shorts and button-down shirt. He gave the Murphy bed a push. No time to straighten the bedding before it slid into place against the wall. He slipped on his socks, then his sandals. Wallet, keys, phone. Check. Out the door in a flash, he tiptoed quietly down the stairs.

But not quiet enough. The creak on the stairs going down alerted Sandra Tooksbury, who stepped out of her apartment. Dressed in her pink satin bathrobe and furry pink slippers, hair matted on one side, she clutched an empty leash in her hand.

"You're dressed bright and early. I thought you weren't teaching this summer." she said.

"I'm not, but I got a call from Maria. She needs me to take the kids this morning. I'm driving over to the house," Vlad said, holding up the car keys.

"I was hoping you'd be able to take Gaston for his morning walk. I forgot to set my alarm last night, and I overslept. He really needs to go out but I haven't even put on my face yet."

Without blush and make-up, the wrinkles in her face looked like a topography map with faint traces of white cold cream lingering in the ridges. Her eyes were as faded as old blue denim, and the network of veins in her legs disappeared into her slippers.

"I'd like to help, but Maria is waiting," he said as he rushed past her, his hand reaching for the outside doorknob.

"Perfect! You can take Gaston along. He'd love to play with Katy and Nicky."

She snapped the dog's leash to his collar, hauling him into the entryway, front paws stick-straight with resistance. "You'd like to take a car ride with Uncle Vlad, wouldn't you, Lovey Puppy? You'll see your little buddies, Katy and Nicky."

"But... but... Nicholas has baseball practice, and Erin is going to work," Vlad said.

She dragged Gaston over to Vlad. "Katy will love to have Gaston all to herself. She can practice all the tricks we taught him."

She handed him the leash and the gadget that held the plastic doggie doo bags. "Here you go, dearie. No rush to bring him back. I'll be here all day. I'll fix us a few martinis when you return."

She swished back into her apartment, leaving behind the scent of lavender and Noxzema face cream. Gaston stared balefully at Vlad, then lay down on the door mat. He refused to budge and gave a warning growl when Vlad reached to pick him up.

"Lovey Puppy. My ass." Vlad muttered. "I don't have time for this shit, either."

He snatched the dog up and carried him growling to the car. Gaston emitted a deep-throated warning on the drive across town. Vlad reached for the classical music station. When a Vivaldi concerto came on, he turned the volume full blast. The Baroque violinists drowned out the dog and put Vlad in a calmer frame of mind. Until he stopped and opened the car door.

Gaston hopped out, squatted in the middle of the freshly mowed lawn, and did his job. Who knew such a little dog could produce that much excrement? Vlad scooped up the deposit with one of the plastic bags with one hand, grabbed the leash with the other, then led the reluctant dog up the walkway. Before he reached the door, Kaitlyn burst out, arms open wide in greeting.

"Yay! You're here!"

Vlad expected her little arms to wrap around his waist but instead, she dropped to her knees and flung them around Gaston. The poodle's excited yips matched Kaitlyn's cries of joy as he gave her a doggie kiss, then began to run in little circles before her. Vlad juggled the bag of poop and the leash holding the frenzied dog as Maria appeared in the doorway.

"Oh my God! Don't tell me you brought that mangy mutt with you?" She stepped onto the driveway, Coach purse flung over her shoulder and a set of keys in her hand. She wore her red draped suit and meticulous make-up like a four-star general reviewing the troops.

"He's not a mangy mutt!' Kaitlyn protested. "He's a highly trained show dog. Auntie Sandra says so. And he's real smart. Shake hands, Gaston."

The poodle sat down and raised his front paw.

"See, Mom. See how smart he is. Do you want to see more tricks?"

"Sorry, I don't have time." Maria threw up her hands in surrender. "I can see I was wrong. He's a smart dog."

Kaitlyn stood up and reached for the leash in Vlad's hand. "Can I take him to the backyard?"

"Of course you can, Sweet Pea." Vlad handed over the leash. "Just hang on tight. We don't want him to run off."

"C'mon, Gaston. Let's play Dora the Explorer. You can be Boots." She led the yipping dog away.

Maria shook her head as she watched them disappear around the house. "I don't understand why you let that crazy old lady manipulate you like that. Conning you into bringing that dog with you, even on your 'trip of a lifetime' down the Rhine." Sarcasm dripped from her voice.

"She isn't conning me into anything. I find the dog amusing," he lied. "And the kids love him. Look how happy Kaitlyn is to see him."

"Go figure!' Maria shrugged. "Honestly, that old lady could con a deaf person into buying an audiobook."

"She's a little eccentric, but she's a great landlady. She never complains if I'm a little late with the rent." Vlad stopped before he said something he'd regret like *when you go over your budget and I need to bail you out.*

"I don't understand why you're still living in that dinky studio apartment. Now that you came into a little extra money and my real estate job is finally taking off, you could upgrade yourself to a larger one." Her voice took on a persuasive tone. 'I could steer you into some beautiful new condos going up at the edge of town."

"You know I'm Mrs. Tooksbury's court-appointed guardian. I'm responsible for her well-being. I need to live close enough in case of an emergency. She is almost eighty-two."

"That's just what I mean—more manipulation. Why can't that handyman of hers assume some of the responsibility? Doesn't he live in her basement?"

"I don't care to discuss this anymore! The matter is closed." Vlad glared for a moment before he said, "I'm here to help with the kids. Does Erin need a ride?"

"She's planning on walking. And I need to leave this minute." She slid into the car, checking out her make-up in the mirror before starting the engine. "Thanks for covering at the last minute. There's a box of mac and cheese on the counter for lunch. I hope you don't mind staying longer. I have a ton of paperwork to catch up on."

Not waiting for his answer, she backed the car out of the driveway. When she reached the street, she rolled down the window. "See what you can do with Nick. He's been impossible all summer. He's still not dressed for baseball practice. Maybe you could toss a ball around with him?"

Vlad flung the plastic bag of poop in the garbage can next to the garage, wishing he could get rid of all the shit in his life that easily.

Chapter Five

Erin greeted him at the door, her face one storm cloud away from an outburst. She wore a crumpled blue t-shirt with Crawford Aquatic Center emblazoned across the front, black extremely short shorts, and black flip-flops on her feet. Vlad knew better than to suggest sensible shoes for work or more modest attire.

"This place is falling apart," she complained. "Mom's so busy with work and dating Gordy, nothing gets done. Look at my shirt!" She twirled around so he could take in the full effect of the wrinkles and smudges "I had to dig it out of the clothes hamper. Can't you do something?"

"I'm here for today. What would you suggest?'

"If you weren't a klutz, I'd suggest doing a load of laundry, but I remember the last time you 'helped' with the wash." She used finger quotations to emphasize *helped*. "You shrunk my fav shirt. Poor Nick had pink underwear."

"I've learned a lot since then. I'll tackle some of the wash," he assured her, trying to look more confident than he felt. "I think I can handle towels and underwear."

"And I'm worried about Nick." Her angry expression changed into concern. "I think he's getting bullied again. Maybe at baseball. He hates it even more than soccer, but Mom insists he go because she and Gordy got him a new glove for his birthday."

A car horn tooted out front.

"That's Jessica. She's picking me up for work. Gotta run." She headed for the door.

"I thought you were walking to the pool?" Vlad said.

"I just told Mom that. She doesn't like me to ride with teenage drivers. See ya." She slammed the door before he could protest.

Vlad stood for a moment in the entryway, torn between heading toward the basement laundry or climbing the stairs to his son's room. A memory surfaced from his elementary school days in Phys. Ed. class. The two best baseball players were the team captains, and they alternated choosing their teams. One by one the other boys were chosen until just he and Howard Herman were left. Howard, a skinny anemic-looking boy with continual scabs on his knees and elbows, couldn't throw straight. Vlad, nicknamed the strike-out king, was a fast runner but seldom got on base. They eyed each other warily, each hoping they'd be picked next so as not to win the title of the biggest loser. Vlad crossed his fingers, hiding them behind his back, desperately thinking, *Pick me. Pick me.*

No matter which boy was selected, the hurt feelings festered, an inner scab formed as chronic as Howard Herman's outer ones, just waiting for a cruel jab to ooze once more.

Slowly ascending the stairs, Vlad rehearsed a pep talk to deliver to his son. Being on a team helps you learn cooperation and social skills. Makes you feel a part of something bigger than yourself. Health benefits. Exercise. An opportunity to play outdoors in the sunshine. Make friends.

He knocked on Nicholas's door. "May I come in?"

He heard a muffled "I don't care."

Still in pajamas, Nicholas was lying on his stomach with a Harry Potter book propped up against the headboard. His room was decorated with wizard posters and a banner from when they went to the Renaissance Fair. A framed picture of the Discovery space shuttle had a prominent place above his desk. Not a sports figure or major league baseball pennant in sight.

Vlad sat down on the bed next to him. "Do you want to talk about what's wrong?"

"I don't know," Nicholas answered, refusing to take his eyes off the page,

"Well, if you did know, what would you say?" Vlad waited until the silence in the room grew so heavy it threatened to crush him.

"Carson is a bully, and I hate him!" he finally blurted out.

"Is Carson on your baseball team?"

"Yes, he's on my team." Nicholas sat up and met Vlad's gaze. "He was in math and social studies and my gym class last year at middle school. I thought I'd have a break from his torture this summer but then he showed up in baseball."

"What did he do that's made you so upset?"

Nicholas spoke barely above a whisper. "He's always saying mean things about me, like how much I suck at baseball and how I throw like a girl. He loogies on the ball before he throws it to me."

Vlad felt his anger rising but managed to keep his voice calm and level. "Did you talk to the coach?"

"No. That would just make things worse. I tried talking to my teachers last year. He stopped for a while but then started being sneaky when he did things, like put gum on my chair before class and stick embarrassing cartoons about me on the bulletin board when nobody saw him," Nicholas said, his face sad at the remembrance.

Vlad felt a pang in his heart. "Why didn't you tell me? I'd have talked to the principal."

"He'd just deny it. All his friends would back him up."

"I understand why you don't want to go to baseball practice with him." Vlad knew trying to hug his son would embarrass him so he rubbed his back gently instead. "Did you try talking to Mom about it?"

"No. Gordy always says, 'Boys will be boys.' I don't want her to think I'm a wuss. Besides, she's the reason I won't go back," he spoke with a hint of rebellion.

"Please explain."

"Mom made me ride my bike to practice on Tuesday. She said the park is only a few blocks away and it's good exercise. I'm eleven now and should be more independent. I didn't mind. A lot of the guys ride their bikes to the park. When I went to go home, someone stole my seat so I couldn't ride my bike. I told the coach, and he wouldn't let us leave until we found it. He made everyone help look. I could tell Carson did it by the way he snickered."

"So what happened?"

"Matt found it in the boys' bathroom, in the toilet. Everybody laughed. Coach was mad, but no one owned up to it. He helped me dry it off. Told the kids he was disappointed in the unsportsmanlike behavior. We are a team, and teammates look out for each other." Nicholas thrust out his lower jaw and glared. "They all hate me, and I'm not going back. You can't make me!"

"I'm not going to make you today. But you have to talk to Mom about this. Promise?" Vlad said firmly.

"I guess." He refused to meet his gaze.

"Let me talk to your coach if it doesn't get better."

"Maybe." His eyes remained focused on the rocket pattern in his bedspread.

"I brought Gaston today, and Kaitlyn and I are going to take him to the park to feed the ducks. Want to come along?" Vlad said with a heartiness he didn't feel.

Nicholas's face brightened up at the mention of Gaston.

"Did Auntie Sandra come, too?" he asked.

"No, just Gaston. You'll have to get dressed quickly if you want to join us."

Ten minutes later the four of them were happily strolling in the park, Kaitlyn holding Gaston's leash on the way. She agreed to allow Nicholas to be in control on the way home. Gaston frequently stopped to sniff at interesting shrubs and lifted his leg a few times to water the foliage. Vlad had gathered a few bread crusts for the ducks and geese in a ziplock bag. The bright July sun turned the river into a ribbon of sparkling ripples. As they drew nearer to the riverbank, numerous little families of mother ducks with fluffy ducklings and geese with gangly goslings waddled along the shore.

"Wow! There's a lot of babies," Nicholas observed. "And a lot of goose poop."

He pointed to the ubiquitous black piles on the shoreline. "Watch where you step," Vlad warned.

"I'm going to count the ducklings," Kaitlyn began. "One. Two. Three. Four. Five. Six. Hold still, dummies. I can't keep track."

Some of the hungrier or braver ducklings flocked toward them. Gaston took this as an invitation to play tag. He darted toward the ducks so suddenly he jerked the leash out of Kaitlyn's hand. He yipped, and they scattered in all directions, quacking frantically.

"Come back, Gaston!" Kaitlyn shouted.

"Bad dog! Stop chasing the little ducklings." Nicholas dashed after Gaston.

The poodle chased one adult toward the river until the duck dove out of reach in the water and paddled harmlessly downstream. Then he turned his attention to a goose family retreating to the water's edge. While Gaston barked fiercely from the riverbank, a mother goose pivoted and bore down on the little dog, hissing and honking.

"I'll get Gaston," Vlad yelled. "Kids, stay where you are." He hurried toward the dog.

But it was too late. Nicholas had already bolted after Gaston. He hit a patch of goose poop, slid along the grass, and landed on his backside, letting loose a string of curses. Vlad snatched the leash trailing behind the fleeing dog and pulled him up short. Kaitlyn grabbed a loose stick and waved it threateningly at the riled goose.

Vlad sprang between her and the angry mother, shouting, "Go away!"

Finally, the goose backed off, returning to her alarmed goslings. Clutching the leash firmly, Vlad reined in the yapping dog. Then he helped Nicholas to his feet while Kaitlyn held her nose.

"Ew, goose poo."

"It's your fault. You let go of the leash, dumbhead." Nicholas glared at her.

Kaitlyn skipped around in a circle, singing, "Nicky fell in goose poo. Nicky fell in goose poo."

Gaston chimed in with frenzied barking.

"Shut up, brat. Shut up," Nicholas yelled and scurried after her. "I'll smear goose poo on your face."

Vlad's cell phone rang. As he struggled to retrieve it from his back pocket, he scolded, "Stop it, you two. Settle down. I'm talking on the phone. Hello," he barked into the mobile.

"It's me, Sandra. It's been a hell of a morning," she said reproachfully. "While you're fooling around with Gaston and the kids, I've been fielding calls from all the ladies at the senior center. Alexandria died last night, and now there's going to be an investigation into the cause of death. Everyone thinks it was the pie. Beatrice's Cherry Berry Peach Pie. We need to get to work. How soon can you be here?"

Chapter Six

By the time Maria finally returned, Vlad had a load of laundry in the dryer including the poop-stained shorts, both kids fed, and Nicholas showered and dressed in clean clothes. Gaston and the kids were settled in front of the TV, happily absorbed in a Disney movie, a modern-day fairy tale featuring the offspring of several Disney villains. The sweetly sinister teenage protagonists appealed to both kids with no arguments about what to watch. Vlad was cleaning up the kitchen when Maria strolled in.

"Do I hear the dryer running?" she said.

"I did some laundry for you, trying to get you caught up."

"Thank you. I wasn't expecting you to do all that." She smiled gratefully. "I really appreciate it."

She sank down into a chair and kicked off her heels. "How did Nick's practice go?"

Vlad sat down across from her. "He didn't go." He put his hand up to stop her from speaking. "Before you protest, you need to hear him out. He's being harassed by a bully. He promised to talk to you about it. Please listen with an open mind. He's very unhappy."

"I knew something was up. He's been so moody lately. I figured it was early onset adolescence. Erin acted the same way when she was in middle school."

'It's more than that. I'll let him tell you about it. It's been going on for a quite a while. He doesn't want you to think he's a wuss."

Maria looked stricken. "Is that what he thinks of me? That I'd call him names?"

"You two need to talk. And I need to leave. Something important has come up" He stood up and headed for the family room. "I'll pick up the kids Saturday morning."

"Thanks again. By the way, the couple bought the house."

"Congratulations."

In the family room both kids were engrossed in the video. Nicholas slouched on the couch, and Kaitlyn lay on the floor her arm flung around the snoozing poodle. Vlad bent down beside them.

"Gaston and I need to leave," Vlad said, snapping the leash to the dog's collar, "but I'll see you this Saturday."

"Will we see Gaston?" Kaitlyn asked. "I love Gaston." She gave the poodle a hug.

"Maybe. Do I rate a hug, too?"

"Silly Daddy. I love you, too."

Both kids paused the movie and said their good-byes.

"Nicholas, Mom's in the kitchen all alone," Vlad hinted. "It's a good time to talk." He watched his son slowly rise and walk like a condemned man to the kitchen.

Instead of going straight home, Vlad decided to stop by the library and inquire if Beatrice had heard the news about Alexandria. He hoped she hadn't. He'd rather she heard it from him than the gossips at work. Then he remembered he had Gaston. He couldn't leave him in the car on a hot summer day. He'd have to tie him up to the bike rack outside the library for a few minutes. He pitied anyone who tried to steal him.

Luckily, the bike rack was in the shade. "You stay, Gaston. Stay. I'll be right back."

The little dog sat on his haunches waiting expectantly for his next command.

"Maybe you are a highly trained dog." Vlad said as he patted the dog's head.

The dog licked his hand and gave him such a pitiful look, he suddenly had a stab of remorse.

"All right, I won't leave you out here. You can come in with me, but you have to behave. No tugging on your leash and trying to escape. If you're a good boy, I'll give you a doggie treat. I have Greenies in the glove compartment. C'mon, Gaston."

The toy poodle obediently trotted beside him into the library. No lifting his leg or snuffling around. He held his little head high like he was entering the ring at the Westminster Kennel Club Dog Show.

Unfortunately, Beatrice was not in her office.

"She's been in a tech team meeting all afternoon," said the young work/study student processing books outside her door. She gave Gaston a questioning look, but Vlad's scowl silenced any protest.

"Could I leave her a note? I'll just be a minute. Will you make sure she gets it?" Vlad picked up the notepad on the desk and a spare pen. "I'll just sit over there and write." He gestured toward a study carrel near the reserve stack.

"Sure thing."

As he sank into the chair, Vlad pondered how to word the note so it sounded urgent but without alarming Beatrice. Gaston curled up under the carrel and immediately fell asleep. Soon little doggy snores invaded the quiet. Nervously pulling on his mustache, he carefully wrote:

Dearest Beatrice, Please call me immediately. I'm on my way to Sandra's. Are you still free this evening? We need to talk.

Before he could sign his name, he overheard female voices in the stacks.

"Did you hear Alexandria Adams died? She collapsed at the County Fair judging pies. My cousin works at the hospital, and she called me at lunch time." An unidentified female spoke in a confiding tone.

"I was there. It was awful. She started gagging and vomiting. Then she had these spasms like convulsions. She said her hands and feet were growing numb. She managed to gasp out 'the pie' in her fading breath. Then she collapsed facedown into the pie."

A second voice chimed in, the voice of a drama queen, Vlad noted.

"The pie! She blamed it on the pie? Whose pie?" The first speaker exclaimed.

"Our esteemed leader, Beatrice Krup, baked the pie." The second voice dripped with sarcasm. "You know there's been bad blood between the two for ages. Alexandria kicked her out of Garden Club for cheating in the Most Beautiful Home Garden Contest."

Vlad thought, *I've heard that voice before. But where?*

"Really? I never in a million years would have thought Beatrice would cheat. She's so nice," the first incredulous voice said.

"It's all an act. How do you think she got the library promotion? Pure deception. I am even more qualified. I went through the same interviews. Yet they offered the position to her. I know she lied to Human Resources on her resume."

Bingo. Vlad realized. *It's that nasty woman at the pie judging—*

Florence Heidt.

"I heard you filed a grievance," the first speaker said.

"I did. And that's not all. When she got kicked out of the Garden Club, they said she was so angry she threatened, 'I could kill that Alexandria Adams.' Next thing you know she dies judging Beatrice's pie. Probably put something in it. And she knew Alexandria would be the judge because we know she's always the judge. She's a big shot on the fair board, you know."

Rage filled Vlad at the lies and innuendos that woman spewed forth. He leapt to his feet and propelled himself around the tall bookshelf like a cruise missile. He zeroed in on his target and exploded.

"How dare you spread falsehoods about Beatrice! She would never harm another human being, no matter how unfairly she'd been treated. She's the most honest, kind woman I know. The only thing poisonous is your gossip. Shame on you."

He glared at her, daring her to continue. Gaston unexpectedly appeared at his side, leash dragging behind him, emitting a low growl. When Vlad ordered "Sit! Stay!" he plopped his hind quarters down, showing his teeth in a silent warning.

Florence's face turned as red as Wile E. Coyote's after the Road Runner dropped an anvil on his foot. She opened and closed her mouth, sputtering without saying anything intelligible. Her eyes blazed with fury at being called out as she clenched her fists at her side.

Her younger coworker spoke up. "I told her I didn't believe what she was saying about Beatrice. She's been a super boss, super competent and caring. There must be some mistake."

"The only mistake is listening to vile gossip. I seriously hope you won't repeat this character assassination." He stared at the two women with a look that would admonish even Darth Vader.

The younger one glanced down at her feet, her long hair falling in front of her face. She slowly raised her eyes to his, tucking her hair behind her ears. When she returned his gaze, she had the decency to blush.

"I certainly won't. I better get back to work. These books won't reshelve themselves." She quickly wheeled away the cart filled with books.

He was left in a staring match with Florence, who glowered at him, her eyes sending waves of loathing. She finally found her voice.

"I'm only saying what people are thinking."

"I'll file a complaint with Human Resources if you don't stop. I expect Dr. Andrews would have something to say about your unprofessional behavior."

"Whatever. I'll stop. But I'm not the only one with suspicions," Florence shot back before she followed the young clerk into the stacks.

Still shaking with anger, Vlad led Gaston to the carrel and signed his note, pressing down so hard that he punctured the paper. He folded it in half twice and scribbled her name. After a few calming breaths, he handed it to the young lady.

"Please make sure Beatrice gets this as soon as she returns to the office."

"Of course, Dr. Chomsky. I won't leave until I see her and give it to her personally."

"I'd appreciate that very much."

He stalked out of the library, Gaston still heeling at his side. The little dog trotted obediently all the way to the car, even ignoring a fire hydrant in his eagerness to get to the vehicle.

All the way home Vlad replayed the scene in his head, growing more indignant with each mental retelling. Gaston gave a little woof and settled down on the front passenger seat, sticking his face into the stream of cool air coming from the air conditioner. Occasionally, he shot a wary look in his direction. By the time Vlad pulled into his parking spot, he was ready to turn around and give that Florence another tongue-lashing. He wondered how far she would go to sabotage Beatrice's career. *Did she feel enough malice to tamper with her pie?*

Before he could restart his engine. Sandra Tooksbury appeared in the doorway with a cocktail glass in hand and a pinched expression on her face. Wearing a floor-length duster with splashes of flashy colors and magenta silk capris, she swept down the driveway like Greta Garbo.

"Where have you been? Norm and I have been expecting you. He's two beers ahead, and I have a martini for you waiting in the shaker. Gaston hasn't eaten his lunch, and you know he can't work on an empty stomach."

She opened the passenger side door, and Gaston hopped out with a happy yip.

"Come on, Lovey Puppy. Let's get started. Gaston the Dog Detective—more than ready to investigate a new case. Our biggest yet!"

Chapter Seven

Norm was seated on the flower-covered loveseat, thoughtfully nursing his third beer, the ubiquitous Green Bay Packers cap by his side on the cushion. His graying long hair was neatly pulled back into a ponytail, and his faded Harley Davidson t-shirt seemed fairly clean. His frayed blue jeans and smudged athletic shoes seemed an improvement over the stained sweatpants and mud-encrusted motorcycle boots he normally wore on a workday. He was dressed for adventure.

"Where ya been, Doc? We got the news about that Adams woman hours ago."

Sandra poured the remainder of a gin martini into a cocktail glass and handed it to Vlad. "Here you go, dearie. Made with your favorite Gordon's Gin. Make yourself comfortable while I feed Gaston."

She flounced into the kitchen with the poodle happily scampering behind her.

"You realize it will be days before we know anything. First, there'll be an autopsy," Vlad said. "Then a toxicology report on the pie. They probably have to send everything to the state crime lab because Crawford isn't equipped to handle poison identification—if Alexandria truly was poisoned. What makes you think the police will even share that information with us?"

"Because Gaston helped them solve the other big case, the terrorist attack. They realize he has special talents. Like Sandra says, the Sherlock Holmes of dogs," Norm blustered.

Vlad thought back to that horrifying night when the firebombing agitator broke into his apartment and threatened him with a knife, leaving a slight scar on his throat where the knife nicked him. Gaston charged the terrorist, distracting him long enough for Vlad to bludgeon him with a wooden lamp. The temperamental poodle not only saved him but captured a man wanted by the police in several states.

Sandra returned from the kitchen with a jar of olives and used a toothpick to stab one and plop it in his drink.

"Is something wrong, dearie? Your face looks like Norm just gave you a wedgie."

"Yes." Vlad, with a mental shake of his head, returned to the present. "I had an incident at the library when I stopped by to give Beatrice the bad news." He took another big sip of his drink and proceeded to relate the encounter with Florence Heidt.

"She's an evil, spiteful witch," he finished, his voice, shaking with repressed and uncharacteristic anger, showed just how much he cared about his fiancée. "She's out to cause trouble for Beatrice."

"Aha! Revenge. That's quite a motive for murder." Sandra pointed the jar of olives at him. "If she casts blame on Beatrice, she retaliates for losing out to her for the library job."

"And losing at the pie contest last year," Norm added. "Revenge is a dish best served á la mode."

Vlad took another sip of Sandra Tooksbury's excellent martini. "If we can figure out the *why* of Alexandria Adams' demise, we can figure the *who.*" His voice reflected a new sense of urgency.

Sandra set the jar of olives on the coffee table and picked up her martini. "That's the spirit, Vlad. We need to come up with a plan of action before we start our investigation." She swallowed and spoke again. "Why would someone sabotage Beatrice's pie?"

"Maybe they'd try to call it food poisoning." Norm suggested. "Didja know I got a case of food poisoning on the cruise when we were at the German market? It was the wurst."

"This is serious, Norm. No time for your bad jokes," Vlad huffed.

"Sorry, Doc. I couldn't resist. But I'll knock it off," Norm promised. "It's just that I got a shitload of food poisoning jokes and nowhere to dump them."

Gaston came in from the kitchen and hopped up on the loveseat. Norm snatched his cap from under the dog just before he flopped down. He plunked it back on his head before saying, "Who's your Poppa. little feller? Who loves ya?" Gaston scrambled to his lap and licked his face. "You like my jokes, doncha Buddy?"

Gaston emitted a happy little yip, then settled down for a nap.

"Vlad is right. This is no time for fooling around. Beatrice is on the hot seat." She flashed her blazing blue eyes at Norm. "We've got to help prove she's innocent. Just like we did when you were accused of stealing the diamonds on the cruise ship."

A sharp knock on the door interrupted their discussion. Sandra opened the door to a distraught Beatrice, dark circles under her eyes and a trace of tears glistening on her cheeks. She stumbled into the room, her mouth quivering as she wailed, "She's dead. Alexandria's dead. She died after eating my pie. The police are sending the remains of my pie to the state crime lab for a toxicology report."

Vlad rushed to engulf her in his arms. She sobbed into his neck, her tears dampening his shirt.

He gently rubbed her back, crooning, "It'll be all right. Everyone knows you didn't do anything wrong. I'm sure it's standard procedure after an unexplained death."

"That's right, dearie. We know you're innocent. We'll find the real culprit. Gaston is on the case. Watch."

Sandra snapped her fingers, pointed to her side, and said, "Here, Gaston."

The little dog raised his head, all alertness, sprang down from the love seat, and stood by her side. Sandra began walking across the room.

"Heel"

Gaston trotted obediently beside her.

"Which person here is guilty of stealing old Playboy centerfolds and pinning them up on his bedroom wall?" Sandra motioned with a barely perceptible flick of her finger.

Immediately, the poodle copied the stance of a German Shorthaired pointer, standing motionless, straightening his back and tail, lifting one front leg, and aiming his nose directly at Norm.

Norm laughed and held his hands up. "I confess. Guilty as charged. C'mon here, Sherlock. Settle back down."

He patted the cushion beside him, and the dog curled up for a well-deserved nap.

"Thanks for the reassurance." Beatrice's sobs turned into snuffles. "Everyone at work gave me weird looks when I was walking out the door. Even Megan, the work/study girl, when she handed me your note. They all think it was my pie."

She backed away from Vlad and held his gaze. "I went upstairs to your apartment, but you didn't answer. I panicked for a minute. I was hoping you'd be here."

"I'll always be here for you," he assured her. "We're in this together."

"Let me make another batch of martinis, and we'll get to work. We're going to get one step ahead of the police. While they're twiddling their thumbs waiting on their reports, we're going to start our investigation. Don't you worry, dearie. We'll find the real culprit." Sandra marched determinedly back to the kitchen.

Vlad held her at arm's length and looked into her eyes. "We're brainstorming motives. If we can determine why someone would want Alexandria dead, we can start questioning suspects."

"Totally undercover. They'll never know we're on the case," Norm said. "I can make such a blanket statement cuz I'm keeping it under wraps."

Vlad rolled his eyes as Beatrice managed a weak smile. Sandra reappeared with a cocktail glass and shaker just in time to catch the last line.

"Enough tomfoolery, Normie," Sandra scolded. "We have a murder to solve." She handed a cocktail to Beatrice. "We thought of revenge as a reason to off Alexandria."

"You'd have to have a lot of hatred to poison someone. She wasn't the most popular person, but murder? Seems pretty drastic." Beatrice shook her head. "She was extremely rich. Could money be a motive?"

"Does her husband stand to inherit everything?" Vlad asked. "You'd think he'd have access to her bank accounts by virtue of being married to her."

Vlad's comment ignited a spark in Beatrice, and the words tumbled out. "Alexandria was very controlling. She may have used her purse strings to keep Earl in line. She also had a daughter who moved away the minute she graduated from high school. She's some kind of theatrical producer in New York. Seems there's some sort of estrangement between the two, although Alexandria would never admit it."

"Revenge. Hatred. Greed. Anything else come to mind? I should write this down." Vlad looked at Sandra. "Got a pen and a notepad I can use?"

"Of course. Here in the desk drawer." She wandered over to a small writing desk and pulled out a pen and notebook.

Vlad flipped to a fresh page and started writing.

"A couple of years ago that astronaut lady was gonna murder her ex's new girlfriend. Drove from Houston to Orlando nonstop with the murder weapons in her car. Wore Depends so she wouldn't have to stop for a potty break. What did the news reporters call it?" Norm snapped his fingers. "Crime of passion! That's it!"

"Crime of passion? Have you had a good look at Earl Adams? He would fit right in with the Addams Family's Uncle Fester." Vlad scoffed.

"Still waters run deep." Sandra replied. "Don't judge a book by its cover. Look at the Laci Peterson murder. She and her husband, Scott, seemed like the perfect couple, handsome and beautiful. Until she disappeared on Christmas Eve. Then her body and the body of her unborn son wash up months later. Police catch her husband in a bunch of lies, and he gets convicted of murder."

"Ok. Crime of passion." Vlad sighed as he jotted it down. "We may be stretching it with the passion angle. This is Crawford, Wisconsin, we're talking about. The most passion people feel around here is for a twofer deal at the Super Saver."

"Who knows what hidden demons lurk in the hearts of those foiled by love? Don't you ever watch old movies? Peyton Place was a small town, too. Plenty of passion there." Sandra swirled the olive around in her drink before she took another sip.

"We have motives. Now we need some suspects. We need to decide who will do the investigation." Vlad looked expectantly at each of them.

"The husband is always the prime suspect in a murder." Norm tapped the beer bottle with his index finger. "I say Earl Adams is the first person to investigate."

"I'll find an excuse to visit Earl," volunteered Sandra. "The bereaved husband always needs some feminine sympathy. Home cooking. Fresh baked bread. That sort of thing. I'll use my feminine wiles, and Gaston will help."

"What about Donna Kloostra? She had access to the pies. She could have tampered with them. Can we connect her to a motive?" Beatrice suggested.

"Alexandria certainly treated her with contempt at the contest. Let me google her." Vlad whipped out his phone. "Let's see. She owns the bookstore. A professor is a natural for a bookstore visit. Maybe I can dig up something."

"Who else had access to Beatrice's pie?" asked Sandra.

"I suggest Florence Heidt. Her pie was next to mine, and she sat in the front row." Beatrice began pacing the room.

"You can't investigate Florence. She saw us together so I can't, either." Vlad said, adding to himself, *After the confrontation at the library, I'm on her shit list. I can't get anywhere near her.*

"I'll figure out a way to meet Florence." Norm stood up and struck a body-builder pose. "A lot of women find a guy like me hot. Look at what happened in Germany. Helga still calls and texts me. You think this Florence likes motorcycles?"

The movement woke Gaston, and he hopped down to trot behind Beatrice.

"What about me? What can I do? My reputation is on the line until the police remove my Cherry Berry Peach Pie as a possible murder weapon." Beatrice dropped the hands to her sides and clenched them into tight fists.

Gaston stood on his hind legs and gave her hand a comforting lick.

"You can go to Alexandria's funeral with me," Vlad offered. "We can pay our respects to the grieving husband and check out the mourners in case anyone there seems suspicious. Murderers often attend their victims' funerals, you know, deflect suspicion while admiring their own handiwork."

Beatrice raised her eyes to his and smiled. "When you vowed to travel with me to the ends of the earth, I bet you didn't have a funeral home in mind."

Chapter Eight

A heat wave engulfed the town on the day of Alexandria Adams' funeral. Decked out in his navy suit and tie, Vlad was already wishing he hadn't suggested casing the funeral home for suspects. As he walked to his car, his white shirt became drenched in sweat, and he tasted perspiration on his upper lip. He slipped out of his suit jacket and tossed it in the back seat. Cranking up the air conditioning as high as possible, he drove slowly to pick up Beatrice.

She sat primly on her front porch, on the same glider that Norm and Sandra occupied after the pie fiasco just two weeks ago. Her funeral attire consisted of a black sleeveless sheath with a simple silver and onyx necklace. Vlad wished he felt as cool as she looked.

"Still no word from the state crime lab," Beatrice spoke grimly. "My appointment with the police detective is the day after tomorrow."

Neither spoke much on the drive to the funeral home. The visitation was scheduled from ten until eleven-thirty, with the memorial service immediately after it. Vlad reached over and gave Beatrice's knee a gentle squeeze. She grasped his hand, raising it to her lips for a brief kiss. Just the touch of her lips sent a wave of pleasure through him. What if he swerved to the curb and gathered her in his arms, turning her innocent kiss into a full-blown embrace? *To hell with the funeral!* he thought. A sideways glance at her worried face told him to keep his mind on his driving. *We're detectives today; making love comes later.*

After parking the car Vlad and Beatrice joined the line of mourners paying their respects to the family. Entering the lobby, the funeral home director designated where they could sign the guest book and drop their sympathy cards and/or memorial checks in the slot of the brown box. Alexandria's face, younger but still unhappy, frowned at them from the memorial card. Beatrice picked up the card and clutched it in her hand.

Unfortunately, Alexandria was one of those women whose disposition was remarkably improved by death, Vlad reflected.

As the line curved into the visitation room, the cloying sweet smell of flowers assaulted Vlad's nostrils. The oppressive heat followed him into the crowded room, surrounding him like a bath of split pea soup. Just walking through it took so much effort he wanted to lie down in front of the anemic air conditioning vent and close his eyes. Prerecorded organ music of unrecognizable hymns permeated the air, making him wish for a moment of dead silence. If not for Beatrice beside him, he would have swerved toward the nearest exit and spent the morning in a quiet bar swilling ice cold beer.

Then he got his first glimpse of the grieving family. A middle-aged woman in black, similar in stature to Alexandria, stood first in line. She loomed over Earl, his long face formed by the relentless gales of life chiseling away any softness. He mechanically shook hands or endured hugs. Lastly came a tall, slim young woman, hair pulled back in an amethyst clip, wearing a mauve dress, perfectly cut to flatter her figure. No mourning rags for her.

"That must be the daughter," whispered Beatrice. She glanced at the In Memorium card. "Her name is Gillian Adams so obviously not married. The obituary says she's from New York City. The older woman is Alexandria's sister from Pensacola, Victoria something."

"We can probably scratch them from the list of suspects," Vlad remarked.

A collage of photographs was pinned to a trifold bulletin board. Vlad saw various Alexandrias at different ages. A toddler holding a stuffed bunny. A little girl in a Brownie uniform. A high schooler in debate club. A stiff family portrait. Even a picture with the perpetually frazzled Donna Kloostra. Some older photos pictured a thirty-something man and woman, not her sister, with a younger Alexandria and Earl in outdoor settings, at the beach and at a backyard barbecue with two children, a boy and a girl. The two couples seemed unlikely friends, for the Adams were dressed so conventionally while the unknown couple bordered on hippie attire. The woman's auburn hair cascaded below her shoulders in tight Pre-Raphaelite waves; the man's neatly trimmed beard and long hair drew attention to his intense dark eyes.

"Who are they? They seem to be close friends," Beatrice observed.

"At least in younger years."

Vlad glanced around. "Let's watch for them, see if they turned up."

"Will we be able to recognize them from the old photos?"

"He might shave, and the hairstyles might change, but that woman's nose is forever." He pointed at the tiny turned-up nose in the photos.

After offering condolences to the family, they filed by the coffin with a waxy Alexandria laid out, her hands folded across her chest. Vlad scarcely recognized her as the pie contest judge. Her hair rippled with unnatural waves, her lips bloomed with cranberry red color, and the perpetual scowl on her forehead was gone.

"She looks so peaceful," Beatrice remarked as they drifted away. She added in a whisper only Vlad could hear, "for someone probably burning in hell."

As they drifted toward the back of the room, they saw the couple in question seated near the last row of chairs. The woman still retained the distinct nose and flowing hair. She wore a gypsy-print flowing dress, her male companion in a loose button-down shirt. Vlad felt a twinge of envy at the man's relaxed attire as Beatrice led the way to the seats directly behind them. Before they sat down Vlad proffered his hand.

"I'm Vlad Chomsky, I teach at the college. This is my fiancé, Beatrice Krup. We've been on several boards with Alexandria. She was so public-minded. And you're...?"

"Sid and Shar Fredricks, next-door neighbors," the man answered.

"I teach yoga classes at the house," Shar said. "Sid also teaches meditation classes at home and at the Mindful Meditation Center in Madison."

"I take it you've known the Adams' a long time," Vlad said.

"Ever since we built our houses on the same cul-de-sac back in the '90s," Sid replied. "But we haven't seen much of them lately. Alexandria was a very busy lady."

"Too busy to make her annual Christmas fruitcake and bring it over." Shar sighed.

"You might consider that a blessing." Sid rolled his eyes heavenward.

As the minister stepped onto the dais in front and led them in prayer, Vlad surveyed the room. All he saw were the backs of heads. Even so, he recognized Donna, with her frizzled hair escaping from a black hat perched atop her head. She sat in the front row with the bereaved family.

Obviously, she had a closer relationship with Alexandria than just the county fair. He swore he saw Earl reach into his suit jacket while everyone's heads were bowed, pull out a small silver flask, and tilt his head back for a surreptitious swig.

The minister launched into a eulogy so universally applicable that Vlad was reminded of the Mad Libs game. When Erin was in middle school, they filled in parts of speech to a generic narrative, often with hilarious results. The eulogy could have been from a page ripped out of Erin's game pad. Alexandria was a _____ (fill in with an adjective) *caring, loving, devoted* _____ (fill in a noun) *mother, wife, sister*. She was a pillar of the_____ (fill in a place) *community, Garden Club, church*. None of it truly fit the irascible woman from the pie judging contest, but it followed funeral etiquette: Don't speak ill of the dead.

All were invited to the graveside service and a funeral luncheon afterwards. As they rose to file out, Vlad said to the couple, "Do you have a schedule of classes somewhere? I've been considering a yoga class or tai chi. I heard it helps with stress."

"We have a webpage. Google Yoga With Shar. I'd be so happy to have a man in the class. It might inspire the women to bring their partners." She gave him a warm smile. "It was nice meeting you. Too bad it was under such sad circumstances."

Vlad and Beatrice watched as the two walked past Earl and his family. The sister averted her eyes, and Earl gave them a curt nod. Only the daughter seemed grateful to see them as she took their hands and gave them a squeeze.

"Not too neighborly anymore," Beatrice commented.

"Can we please take a pass on the graveside service? I'll die in this heat." Vlad loosened the tie and shrugged off his suitcoat.

"Yeah, I think we got what we came for. I imagine Sid and Shar Fredericks will know some useful tidbits about Alexandria's personal life. They've got to have some inside information on the family," Beatrice commented.

"At worst I'll get some exercise. Hopefully, it'll improve my health and well-being."

Chapter Nine

Soon Vlad found himself driving down Larkspur Lane on Tuesday evening headed to his first-ever yoga class. Despite being rather unathletic, he'd spent almost an hour clicking through yoga classes on YouTube studying the clothes. Males were almost nonexistent, and all the female instructors wore skimpy leotards, leggings, or yoga pants. One especially sylph-like lady just wore an exercise bra and form-fitting shorts. He hoped Shar Fredericks didn't subscribe to her channel. He was stuck wearing sweatpants or athletic shorts. His gym shorts were a disgrace. They seemed to have shrunk in the intervening years since he last wore them. The temperature of the July afternoon had already risen to Dante's Inferno levels so sweatpants were out.

Vlad drove to the Super Saver and bought the longest, baggiest athletic shorts he could find, then stopped at Riverview Park to change in the men's room. Finally, he arrived at the address on Larkspur Lane, parking near a Colonial revival house on a secluded street.

Shar greeted him warmly at the door, her hair pulled back in a stretchy band at the nape of her neck, clad in a loose tunic and yoga pants, with bare feet. "Welcome to class. I'm so glad you decided to join us this evening."

As she ushered him into a large, carpeted room off the foyer, Vlad studied the minimalist décor. A single photo of a Buddhist temple on the stark white walls contrasted with the colorful Tibetan prayer flags hung over the doorway.

Shar noticed his interest. "This once was a dining room, but it's just Sid and me rattling around alone in this big house. So I converted it into a yoga studio. And Sid took over the guest suite for his meditation classes."

Vlad glanced back at the entryway. "Is Sid around? I had a few questions I wanted to ask him about his Soul Health Coaching. How is that different from his meditation classes?"

"Sorry. Sid had a meeting in Madison tonight. I'm sure he'd be happy to explain. Just send him an e-mail or text."

A few women were already sitting on mats, talking quietly, while waiting for class to begin.

"This is Vlad, our newest student." Shar went around the room, introducing him to the ladies, whose names he promptly forgot.

"Oh, I didn't bring a mat. I didn't know I needed one," he stammered.

"It's fine. The carpet is very cushy," one woman said. "We just prefer our own mats."

He stood awkwardly, trying to gauge where to seat himself. If he sat in the front, they'd know right away he had no yoga experience. He imagined them laughing at his clumsiness. But if he sat in the back, he'd have a good view of their behinds, which would make him feel very uncomfortable like a lecherous old man.

Shar solved his dilemma by gesturing to an open space far off to the right. "I think you'll find this is a good spot for observing my moves."

A lady slid to the side to make room for him, and he sat down.

"Since we're all here let's begin class with some calming breaths," Shar said.

I can do this, Vlad thought, *I've been breathing all my life.*

"Please sit in half lotus, or just cross-legged if you're not there yet."

Vlad tried to sit with his legs crossed in front of him, like the woman next to him. But his right leg seemed to have a mind of its own. It didn't want to cross in front of the left. He noticed how Shar's right foot rested on her thigh. His knee popped up, and he couldn't fold it down like hers. It was starting to cramp ominously.

"Take a deep cleansing breath. Slowly inhale. Feel the air move through your nostrils, down to your lungs. Imagine it traveling all the way down to your feet, bringing energy to the lower part of your body,"

Shar had them take several more cleansing breaths until Vlad felt like his lungs had been through the car wash. His legs hurt so much he shifted them straight in front and bounced them a few times on the carpet to get the blood flowing back into them. The lady next to him raised her eyebrow but said nothing.

"Please come to a standing posture. Next, we'll do a Salute to the Sun."

Vlad clambered to his feet, ready for whatever torture came next.

"Take a deep breath, and stretch your arms high above your head. Stretch to the sky."

Wow, he thought, *the stretch actually feels good.*

"Now drop to a forward fold."

Vlad watched as she bent at the waist and dangled her head down.

"Rest your belly on your thigh, and let your head drop and your hands say hello to the earth."

Vlad glanced at the lady next to him out of the corner of his eye. *I can do this one, too. Just like her.*

That was his last moment of confidence. Shar took them next to a lunge, then something called downward dog, with his butt high in the air, his body in an upside-down V shape. They lifted one leg in something Vlad labeled dog at a fire hydrant. When he tried to swing his leg up like everyone else, he almost toppled over. The class continued around him while he struggled to keep up. After five more of these, Vlad was ready for a snooze in the sun, not a salute.

"Our next pose will be Warrior Two. Arms out, shoulder blades wide, palms down. Step out with your left foot." Shar stretched her arms out parallel to the floor and stepped into another lunge, a savage expression flitted across her usually serene face.

For a second Vlad thought of Morgan le Fay fighting Prince Valiant. Vlad blinked twice, and the fierce expression was gone. *A trick of the light?*

Shar conducted the rest of the class like a maestro in front of an orchestra, all the ladies smoothly floating from one pose to the next. He was sweating profusely in his athletic shorts and tee, a telltale stain darkening his armpit, while the ladies in the class merely glistened. She took them through so many animal named poses Vlad felt like he belonged in a zoo.

"Now it's the time for the last part of class, the time we all enjoy and you so richly deserve. Deep relaxation. Please lie down and find yourself a comfortable position."

Hallelujah! At last.

Vlad lay down and flowed along as she took them through a few deep breaths. That was the last he heard until he felt Shar's hand gently shaking his shoulder.

"Vlad! Vlad! Wake up!"

His eyes fluttered open, and he saw Shar bending over him, a gentle smile on her face. "You fell asleep during the deep relaxation."

"Oh, no. Was I snoring or drooling?"

"A little bit of both. But don't be embarrassed. It happens quite frequently, especially in a class of beginners."

Glancing around, he noticed the rest of the class had left. "Everyone else is gone. I feel like such an idiot for falling asleep."

"It's perfectly normal. I let you rest for a bit, you seemed so relaxed. I know this class wasn't easy for you." Shar continued to smile. "I hope you weren't scared off by all the different poses. You'll catch on quickly. I can tell."

"I'm not so sure, but I need the exercise. I'm not a gym person," he admitted.

"Somehow I guessed weightlifting wasn't your thing, either."

Vlad lumbered to his feet and brushed a hand through his disarrayed hair. "Do you mind if I use your restroom? It's a long drive home."

"Of course not. The bathroom is this way." She led him down a long hallway with a bathroom at the end.

Once the door closed Vlad surveyed the room. *What would Sherlock do?* His eyes rested on the medicine cabinet, and he slowly opened the door to examine its contents. He wasn't sure what he was looking for. The only reason to suspect the neighbors was their long history and apparent falling-out, as evidenced by Earl's reaction at the funeral. He was sure strychnine or cyanide wouldn't show up in a bottle labeled with a skull and crossbones, but he wanted to be as thorough as possible. No poison bottle. Just the usual mouthwash, moisturizer, benzoyl peroxide, Band-Aids, and various beauty products.

Then he noticed a prescription bottle. He read the label, Xanax, prescribed for Shar. Expired three years ago but still on a shelf. *Why would someone who seemed so calm and self-possessed have a need for an antianxiety drug?* He quickly replaced it, closed the cabinet, and flushed the toilet. He turned on the water faucet, washed his hands, and dried them on the fancy guest towel.

As he was walking down the hall, he observed the display of family photos. A wedding picture of a much younger Shar and Sid. Vintage pictures that he assumed were parents and grandparents, dressed in clothing styles from the roaring '20s and the boring '50s. A baby picture of a little boy, followed by a studio picture of the three of them, and more pictures of the boy at various ages of childhood and early adolescence, one happily smiling in a baseball uniform, another holding a trophy and a Pinewood Derby car. Vlad snapped his fingers. *It's the same boy from the photo collage at Alexandria's funeral, the one with both families.* The last picture was a studio portrait of the same teenage boy, probably his high school graduation.

"I can't help noticing the handsome young man in the pictures. Is that your son? I think I saw him with the Adams girl in a picture at the funeral. Is he away at college?" Vlad asked when he returned to the yoga studio.

Shar's face clouded with sorrow, and she paused a moment before she answered. "That's Justin, our son. He passed away in an accident several years ago." Her voice broke and tears welled in her eyes.

"I-I'm so sorry for your loss. I can't imagine how painful it must be," Vlad stammered, taken aback at the unexpected response.

"You never expect to outlive your children. It's the worst thing that ever happened to us. Children who lose their parents are called orphans. Wives who lose their husbands are called widows, and men are widowers, but there's no word for parents who lose their child. The pain is as indescribable as the lack of a proper name for it." Shar brushed away a tear. "We try not to dwell on it."

"If I had any idea, I never would have asked about him. I'm sorry to bring up such a painful topic," Vlad said. "Again, I feel like an idiot."

"You had no way of knowing. Besides, sometimes it feels good to talk about Justin. I can't pretend he wasn't the main part of our lives for eighteen years. The pain never really goes away."

She took a deep, audible breath and said, "Enough of my pity party. Sid and I have worked hard to move past it. We don't even talk about it anymore. Now, please excuse me. I must prepare for my next class. I hope the first class didn't wear you out too much." Shar brought her hands to her chest in a prayerful position, bowed her head, and said, "Namaste."

Vlad echoed the posture and the word. "Namaste."

As he slowly walked to his car, he thought, *Humans are certainly full of contradictions Their first appearances can deceive. Sometimes you have to dig below the surface for what has been carefully hidden.*

Chapter Ten

Sandra Tooksbury critically assessed her make-up job in the magnifying mirror propped up on her antique white vanity. Foundation and blush gave her a healthy sheen. She believed women always needed to hide their age through make-up while men could hide their age simply by marrying a woman who looked young. Although her hands shook just a little, the plum eyeshadow at the outer half of her eyes made them look larger, and the eyeliner was fairly straight. She dabbed some glue along each fake eyelash, waving it about so it dried to just the right amount of stickiness. She pressed it carefully in place. *I don't want it to look like some centipede died on my eyelid,* she thought with a chuckle. An application of mascara blended fake and real together. She blinked coquettishly. *Sandra, girl, you still have the LOOK.*

Choosing the correct outfit required more thought. Earl Adams was a lifelong insurance agent, nearing retirement age, so she didn't want to scare him off with push-up bras and cleavage, even though she could still fit in her fringed bikini bra and sequin panties from her show biz days. She didn't want to dress in mourning clothes, either. She wanted to distract him, put him off guard so perhaps he'd reveal more than he intended.

As she perused her closet, she pulled out the lavender pants outfit, which accented her gray hair. The silk palazzo pants flowed nicely as she moved while the long chiffon jacket atop the purple floral top was the right touch of casual. She accessorized with multiple bracelets, especially her new bangle with the purple rhinestones, and multiple silver chains around her neck, including the one accented with Swarovski crystals

Twirling about to admire herself in the full-length mirror, she told her reflection. "Sandra Tooksbury. You don't look a day over seventy. Well, maybe over seventy-five."

Looking for a treat, Gaston scampered in as she put on the finishing touch of plum lipstick. "We need to dress you up, too, my little love."

She found the well-used harness with the handwritten "Service Dog" lettering and slipped it on the squirming dog. He spent five minutes trying to bite it off, then barked loudly in an attempt to goad her into removing it.

"Stop that, Gaston! I know you're not in the mood for costumes, but you have a role to play in this masquerade, too. You need to look official. If you behave, I'll give you a Greenie," she cajoled.

The poodle followed her into the kitchen and settled down when she tossed him a treat. As he eagerly wolfed down his Greenie, she rummaged through a jumble of plastic containers. She pulled out a plastic food storage box and found the matching lid. Then she called Norm on the phone.

"Could you please drive me over to Earl Adams' house on Larkspur Lane? We need to stop at the Sweet Talkin' Treats bakery first for some of their caramel brownies."

"How do you know he'll be home?"

"My friend Juanita attends his church. When she was there on Sunday, she signed up to bring food over today at eleven. I'm taking her place. I made my famous tuna salad, and I'm picking up dessert at the bakery. No sense in slaving over a hot stove in this heat when I can buy something better than I can make." She tapped the food storage box with her index finger. "I'll put the brownies in a box from home so they look homemade!"

A HALF HOUR LATER Sandra arrived at Earl's with a cloth shopping bag filled with tuna salad and brownies, Gaston at her side. When they drove up the cul-de-sac to the magnificent house at the end, Norm let out a loud whistle.

"That's some big honkin' house! I'd almost call it a mansion. Reminds me of the mansion that was robbed last week. The burglars took all the jewelry, all the valuables, and the electronics. They even took all the bathroom fittings. So the police have nothing to go on!"

Sandra shook her head and sighed. "I should have expected that from you, dearie."

"Yeah, I heard Stevie Wonder is so rich he bought his mansion sight unseen!" Norm chuckled. "I've been waiting a long time to tell that one."

"Please try to mind your manors when you tell rich people jokes," she shot back. "With that bit of foolishness, I'll leave."

She waved Norm off after she got out of the car. "I'll call when I need a ride home, IF I need a ride home," she said. "My mobile is in my purse."

He drove off still laughing.

"Come along, Gaston." She tugged on his leash. "The curtain is about to go up on our finest performance. Canine sleuth and sidekick."

Whenever she experienced stage fright in the past, she tried to imagine all the people in the audience sitting around in their underwear. The image of sunken chests, flabby bellies, and knobby knees never failed to restore her confidence. She rang the doorbell and closed her eyes, attempting to visualize Earl Adams unclothed. The gaunt, cadaverous man who answered the door challenged even her imagination. Still dressed in a dark funeral suit, he looked like he had narrowly escaped a coffin himself. No need to picture him in boxers. He looked terrible enough fully clothed.

"Hello, Mr. Adams," she smiled warmly. "I'm from Good Shepherd, bringing you today's meal. My name's Sandra Tooksbury. I hope you don't mind if I brought my service dog, Gaston."

"Please come in. It is so kind of you to bring food. I confess I haven't felt much like cooking, especially since my daughter headed back to New York. It's been peanut butter sandwiches the past few days."

"We'll put some meat on those bones. Church ladies to the rescue. Perhaps you'd like to put this in a refrigerator. It's my famous tuna salad with my secret ingredient." She lowered her voice to a conspiratorial tone. "I toss in some chopped up fennel. But swear you won't tell a soul."

Earl obligingly took the cloth bag from her, saying, "Your secret's safe with me."

He hurried out of the room without so much as a backwards glance.

"Now's our chance to look around. See anything suspicious, Lovey?" Sandra whispered, surveying the well-appointed living room. A marble-topped fireplace with a painting above it that surely didn't come from the Home Goods store. An elegant pale grey sofa with so many pastel pillows there was scarcely room to sit. A matching loveseat, luxurious oriental rug, and two peach leather chairs. Gaston began sniffing in the corners of the room and under the furniture. He paused next to an ornately carved desk tucked away in a corner with piles of papers and gave a quiet yip.

Before Sandra could take a step toward the desk, Earl returned, empty bag in hand. "Thank you very much. I appreciate your kindness. I wish I had more time to chat."

Handing her the bag, he swept his hand toward the door. Sandra ignored that gesture and babbled on.

"My, what a lovely house you have. Did you hire an interior decorator? I love the artwork, especially the painting of the flower market. It looks just like the streets of Paris." She pointed to the picture above the fireplace of a cobblestone square filled with tubs of flowers. "It looks like one of those paintings by that famous artist—what's his name—something like Monnet."

"We couldn't afford a Monet." He gently corrected her. "Actually, it came from Montreal. We bought it on vacation. Alexandria loved to practice her French so we took a little road trip into Canada when we were first married. Started at Niagara Falls and drove along the St. Lawrence." He sighed. "I always wanted to go back."

"Did you get this in Montreal, too?" Sandra pointed to a blue vase filled with silk flowers.

"Alexandria loved flowers. She liked to fill that vase with cut flowers from her garden all summer. She practically founded the Garden Club." The wistful expression on his face hardened into a glare. "That's why I just don't understand how that woman could carry a grudge. Alexandria came home one night very upset with her. Said that woman had accused her of blackballing her from the Club when all my wife was trying to do was enforce the rules. She had standards to uphold."

"Which woman are you talking about?" Sandra tried to maintain a wide-eyed look.

"Beatrice Krup, that's who. I knew the two didn't get along, but I never thought she'd try to poison my wife," he said angrily.

"Poison? Are you sure Alexandria was poisoned?"

"We're waiting for the results from the state crime lab, but the medical examiner ruled out a heart attack or any underlying physical cause. Alexandria was in excellent physical condition, healthy as a horse."

Sandra thought. *Unfortunately, she looked like one, too.*

A Clydesdale or Percheron. But she only tsk-tsked. "How terrible! Do the police suspect foul play?"

"Why else would a perfectly healthy woman suddenly drop dead? The only possible answer is someone meant her harm." Earl spat the next words out. "It's hard to believe Beatrice Krup would go to that extent, but there's no one else."

"Perhaps you should be more cautious until the police have the results. You don't want to start unfounded rumors. You could ruin that woman's reputation." Sandra reasoned with the distraught man.

"Why? She ruined my life! I always thought we'd have more time together. We were waiting for the day I retired from the insurance business. But our life took a different turn. Now here I am. Alone and grieving!"

Sandra expected the man to raise his hand to his forehead and wail "Woe is me!" like an old-time melodrama.

Suddenly, his whole demeanor changed as he proclaimed, "I'm sorry to cut your visit short, but I really must leave for the office." He looked pointedly at the briefcase standing nearby. "I promised my colleagues I'd be back today. I firmly believe hard work is the best medicine."

"If you ever need someone to talk to, I'm here. My phone number is taped to the Tupperware container," Sandra said.

"It's been most kind of you to offer," he said. "I'll keep that in mind."

They both strolled toward the foyer.

With a flick of her finger, Sandra dispatched Gaston into action. The little dog dashed up to Earl and barked loudly. He put his front paws on the man's leg, halting his movement. The poodle dissolved into a frenzy of noise.

"What on earth is wrong with this animal?" Earl snarled. "Get down." He pushed Gaston away.

"Oh, dear. He's warning you. I'm about to have a seizure," she said. Dropping the cloth bag and her purse, Sandra clutched her forehead with both hands. "OOH! My poor head! The room is spinning. It's starting to go black." She stumbled into Earl's arms.

"I need to lie down until the feeling passes." She made her body go rigid. "The couch, please. Right now! Before I fall over."

She moaned and collapsed against him. All the while Gaston ran in circles around them, barking his warning.

Earl picked her up and carried her to the couch. With a sweep of his arm, he cast all the pillows to the floor, except for a small one he used to prop up her head. Sandra threshed about, slugging him repeatedly with her flailing arms. Earl bobbed from side to side, trying to dodge the blows. All the while Gaston continued barking and running.

"Should I call 911?" Eyes wide with terror, he shouted above the yelps.

"No. I'll be fine in a moment."

Gradually, she stopped twitching and lay still. Gaston drew near and pushed his snout under her limp hand.

"Some water would help," she said weakly.

"I'll get you a glass." Earl rushed out of the room.

"With ice, please." she added.

The minute he left, she scrambled over to the desk and rifled through the papers. She heard him moving about in the kitchen, yelling, "Are you sure you'll be all right?"

"Yes. Just bring water," she moaned.

Some bills, some charity requests, a thank you letter from the fair association. *What's that?* She spotted an insurance policy. Needing to take a closer look, she picked it up and opened the folded document. Suddenly, the footsteps from the kitchen grew louder as Earl approached.

"Gaston, don't let him out of the kitchen yet. Attack." She snapped her fingers.

Gaston ran to the kitchen and began growling at Earl. Sandra heard him take a step back and say, "What the hell? What's the matter with you? I'm just getting water."

The policy insured Alexandria for two million dollars. Earl was the sole beneficiary. Sandra nearly had a real stroke when she saw it. She quickly buried it back in the pile, then dashed back to the couch, flopping down, arms akimbo.

"Something's wrong with your dog. He's trying to bite me," Earl bellowed from the kitchen. "He won't let me out of the room."

She heard him kicking at the dog, saying. "Go away. Leave me alone."

"He gets that way when he thinks I'm in danger of dying. His protective side kicks in. Gaston! Please come here!" Sandra ordered.

Gaston ran to her side, followed by Earl carrying the water. Ice sloshed against the side of the glass as he bent down to hold it to her lips. She placed a trembling hand over his and took a deep drink, then lay her head back on the pillow.

"Thank you. I'm feeling better. If I could just rest a few minutes more until my head clears."

"Of course. Whatever you need to do." He cast a wary eye at the suddenly quiet dog, who still glared at him malignantly as he guarded his mistress. "Just control your beast—I mean dog." Earl stood up and moved toward the desk, reaching for the phone. "I'll call my secretary and let her know I've been delayed."

Abruptly, Sandra sat upright, swinging her feet to the floor. "That isn't necessary. I think I can stand now. If you bring me my purse, I'll call my neighbor Norman to come and get me."

Earl scooped up her purse, holding it in front of him like a shield as he passed by the dog. Sandra dug out her mobile, then clicked on the phone icon and Norm's name.

"I'm ready to go home, dearie," she said into the phone. "I've had one of my spells. So please hurry."

Gaston fetched the cloth bag from where it lay on the floor and dragged it to the couch. Earl took her arm and helped her up. He held onto her, keeping his distance from the poodle who stood peacefully on the other side of Sandra. The three moved slowly in formation toward the foyer. Once there, Earl nervously kept watch from the side window and let out an audible sigh of relief when Norm appeared.

Only when she was safely inside the car, with Gaston ensconced in the back seat, did the deep furrows on Earl's forehead go away.

"Thank you, dearie," she said as he shut the door. She closed her eyes and shrunk back into the seat as Norm steered into the street.

"Well, what did ya learn?" Norm asked as they pulled away from the house.

"I learned Earl took out a two-million-dollar life insurance policy on his wife."

"Whew! That's some moola! There's a million-dollar motive! Good work!"

"A *two*-million-dollar motive, dearie. I learned something even more important. I learned I need to hit harder to knock some sense into that dreadful man."

Chapter Eleven

Vlad was waiting on the porch for Sandra to return from Earl's residence. The minute she stepped out of the car, he peppered her with questions. "Did you find out any information about the medical examiner's report? What was Earl like? Did he act suspicious? Did he say anything about the police investigation?"

"Just a minute, dearie. Let me catch my breath. Come inside where it's cool."

Gaston led the way while Norm brought up the rear. Before Sandra could sit down, the dog again nipped at the harness.

"It's too hot for that, Lovey. Let me take it off you," she said.

She removed the ratty harness and turned to Norm. "I could use something cold to drink. There's iced tea in the refrigerator. And Gaston could use some cold water. Would you mind going into the kitchen?"

She flopped in the nearest chair and put her feet on the cushioned footstool. "That dreadful man announced that Alexandria was in fine health, according to the autopsy. So Earl claims it had to be poison. And he's pointing his bony finger at Beatrice's pie."

"It's too soon to know about the poison!" Vlad exclaimed.

"That's not all, Doc," Norm said, bringing in three glasses of iced tea. "Wait 'til you catch a load of what Sandra found out. Tell him."

Sandra told him about faking a seizure so she could snoop through the papers on the desk. "It was one of my best performances. He looked like he was afraid I'd die on his fancy sofa. He was even more afraid of Gaston. He acted like he was being attacked by a crazed Rottweiler, instead of an adorable poodle. What a coward!"

"Guess what she found on the desk?" Norm asked excitedly.

"What did you find?"

Sandra's eyes glowed as she confided, "He took out a two-million-dollar life insurance policy on Alexandria. He's the sole beneficiary."

Norm whistled. "Can ya picture it? Two million. He'll be rolling in the dough."

"He writes insurance policies for a living. He'd know all about the legalities and the payouts," Vlad pondered. "I wonder if his daughter knows."

"She's out of the picture. She went back to New York," Sandra added.

"If he wanted to bump Alexandria off, why didn't he do it at home?" Norm asked.

"Then he would be the main suspect. But if he slips poison into a pie at the county fair, then he could cast suspicion on whoever baked the pie. Now there are several suspects, with most of the suspicion falling on Beatrice." Vlad tugged on his mustache. "Could he be that diabolical?"

"Now I really wish I'd slugged him harder!" Sandra exclaimed. "That scoundrel!"

Vlad's cell phone interrupted the conversation.

"Dad, are you busy this afternoon?" It was Nicholas. "Can you take me to my baseball game? Mom has to work, and I don't want to ride my bike."

Vlad hesitated to answer. *Just when we're starting to get somewhere on this murder case. Evidence of an actual motive. A "who" to connect to the "why." Two million dollars is a hell of a motive. Now we have to figure out the "how" after the crime lab finds out what the poison was.*

"Please, Dad."

Vlad couldn't ignore the desperation in his son's voice.

"Of course I can. What time should I pick you up?"

"At two. Thanks, Dad." Nicholas sounded relieved. "Bye, Dad." The boy hung up.

Vlad looked at the time on his cell phone. One o'clock.

"I promised Nicholas I'd take him to his game. I'm sorry. I have to leave in a few minutes. Let's figure out our next steps."

"We need more evidence on Earl Adams than just an insurance policy," Sandra said. "If Earl doesn't call me, I'll drop by his place to pick up my containers. This time I'll go all out. It's time to bring out my hoochie-coochie clothes. That man needs to liven up, really let loose. And I'm the dynamite that can blow him up. I might ask one of you to dog sit Gaston when I go again. He's petrified of the pooch."

"I don't think we should forget the rest of our investigations. On *Father Brown*, the police always arrest the first suspect, and they're always wrong. We don't want to make the same mistakes." Vlad said. "We need to keep digging deeper."

"I've got a surefire way to hook up with Florence Heidt. She's gonna come out of work tomorrow and find a flat tire that kinda develops a slow leak. Then it's Super Norm to the rescue."

"What are you going to say to her? She's not exactly warm and friendly. I'm speaking from personal experience." Vlad shuddered as he recalled the expression on her face after their encounter in the library.

'Ya don't think she'd go for something like 'Hey, baby. I'm your power source, and you're the kinda resistor I'd like to deliver my load to'?"

"Are you crazy?" Vlad exclaimed. "What kind of woman would fall for that trashy line? She'd probably slap you in the face. You're going to have to come up with something smoother."

"Yes, dearie. You've been hanging around too much at the Thirsty Rhino."

"I'll work on it. What about you, Doc? You still got some detective work to do."

"I suffered through three yoga classes, but I need to talk to Sid. Shar's opened up to me, but Sid's pretty elusive. I still need to interview Donna Kloostra, the pie contest woman. Her relationship with Alexandria doesn't add up. I've got to check out her bookstore. But Nicholas comes first."

BASEBALL GLOVE IN HAND, Nicholas ran to the car the minute Vlad drove up. When he settled into the passenger seat, he turned off the classical music and found a station with pop. He tapped his hand on his thigh in time to the beat of some tune that seemed to repeat the words "Girl, you are so yummy, yummy" ad nauseum.

Vlad commented, "You seem to be in a good mood today."

Nicholas paused with the drumming and said, "Erin played catch with me this morning before she left for work. She gave me some pointers. I feel like I'm getting better."

"And you talked to your mom?" Vlad asked.

"Yeah. She said I had to finish the season, but I never had to do baseball again if I didn't like it. And we only have the rest of July scheduled for games."

"I think Mom just wants you to be active and not sit with a book or be on the computer all day. Did you ever consider a different sport?"

Nicholas slouched in his seat and stared out the car window before he replied. "I tried soccer and didn't like it. I hate baseball. What else is there?"

"I was thinking about something in the martial arts or jujutsu. You'd only be competing with yourself. We could check out the martial arts academy downtown before school starts."

"I'll think about it."

Vlad could almost see the neurons firing as Nicholas grew quiet. Finally, the boy spoke.

"Do you think I'd learn some moves like on *The Avengers*?"

"I'm sure of it."

Vlad found himself a spot on the bleachers near the top so he had a good view of the field. He mostly needed a good view of the bench because that's where Nicholas spent most of the game until the last inning. The game dragged on. Vlad couldn't stop thinking about driving to the bookstore and striking up a conversation with Donna. *How can I dig into Alexandria and Earl's life without arousing suspicion?*

His son's team was ahead by two runs, and the coach decided to give the benchwarmers some time on the field. He put Nicholas out in right field. Vlad watched his son chew his lip in intense concentration.

The first batter hit a blooper and beat the throw to first base. The pitcher threw two strikeouts in a row. The last batter came up and hit a pop-up to right field.

Vlad shouted, "Come on, Nick. You got this!"

Miraculously, he did it. He held his glove up and positioned himself under the ball. It plopped right into his glove, and he used his left hand to hold onto it. Nicholas stared at the ball as though he didn't believe it was still in his glove.

The boys in the dugout were cheering, "Yay, Nick." For the first time ever. All except one frowning teammate, who Vlad assumed was Carson, the bully.

Nicholas left the field with an incredulous smile.

"Do you want to go somewhere to celebrate?" Vlad asked when they got back to the car. "I know somewhere you'd really enjoy."

"Okay. Some of the guys are going for ice cream."

"How about we go somewhere new? I know a place called Cool Beans and Books,' Vlad suggested. "You can pick out whatever book you want. And I'm in the mood for an iced latte."

And some major sleuthing with Donna Kloostra.

Chapter Twelve

Norm sauntered through the deserted parking lot behind the library, hands in the pockets of his freshly laundered cargo pants, jingling the loose change, while casually glancing about. Not a soul in sight. As he strolled next to the grey Prius that Beatrice identified as Florence's, Norm pulled his hand out of his pocket, scattering the coins under the car. Kneeling down ostensibly to pick up the change, he deftly removed the cap from the pressure valve. The small blade of his pocketknife, pressed against at the valve stem, made quick work of deflating the back tire. He picked up the coins and made his way to the shade of the nearby overhang, practicing a few of his pick-up lines.

"Know what would look great on you? Me," he said to himself. "Nah. Probably too forward.''

He snapped his fingers. "How about 'You must be a campfire, cuz yer so hot and I want s'more.' Nah. Too cheesy. She's a grown woman, not some flaky chick."

"Or I could say, 'Would you like to feel my shirt? It's made of boyfriend material.' Hm-m-m. Maybe?"

Fortunately, he didn't have to wait much longer for Florence to appear.

"What the hell?" When she saw the flat tire, she let out a string of curses that would put the bikers at the Thirsty Rhino to shame. The ordinary frown she wore on her face deepened to a scowl.

She walked back and forth like a caged tiger, muttering barely audible threats to the Toyota gods. She clicked the unlock remote and lifted the hatchback. Norm watched her struggle with moving shopping bags around to get at the spare tire. She took a step back and reached into her purse, pulling out her phone. Time to make his move.

"Wow! Looks like ya got a flat." He ambled next to her and shook his head. "Ya must have picked up a nail or something. Want some help changing it?"

"Yes, please. I had a hell of a day at work, and the last thing I need is a flat tire. I'm still dressed in my good clothes. I hate to ruin them by changing a tire." She smoothed the loose-fitting navy and pink cardigan over a pair of crisp navy slacks, front pleat in place. "I was about to call Triple A for assistance."

"No probemo. Glad to help a damsel in distress." Norm pulled out the spare tire and a jack, then jacked up the car, talking as he worked. "Aside from taking my breath away, whaddaya do for a living?"

"I'm a media specialist for the college library," Florence said coolly.

"Work at the library, huh? Wish I had my library card with me cuz I'd be totally checking ya out." He prattled on. "What kinda gas mileage ya get with this baby?"

"Around fifty miles to the gallon," she sniffed. "Just trying to do my part for climate change."

"I hear ya. We haven't found a solution to climate change but we're definitely getting warmer. I know my temperature's rising just being around you." He looked up and flashed his most engaging smile.

She rolled her eyes. "There's just no discouraging you, is there?"

"No, ma'am." He turned back to changing the tire.

Norm stood up, carried the car jack back to the trunk, and placed it back in the stowaway compartment. Then he put the flat tire on top, closed the hatchback, and wiped his hands on his pants.

"Ya probably should get that checked at the service station. They can probably fix the leak," he advised. "I'm Norm Clodfelter. What's yer name?" He held out a friendly hand, which Florence pointedly ignored.

"I'm Florence. Florence Heidt," she answered,

Norm let his hand drop but continued smiling at her. She returned his grin with a half-hearted smile.

"I do appreciate you coming to my rescue. I'm sorry I was so abrupt with you. There are some things going on at work, and it put me in a bad mood. I can see it's hard to stay in a bad mood with you around."

"That's cuz a small part of life is what happens to us, but it's how we react that's ninety percent of living. I'm determined to live in a way that makes someone smile, even if it's only myself," Norm said.

Florence surveyed the Green Bay Packers cap, the Grateful Dead shirt, and the baggy cargo pants before she spoke. "May I offer you twenty dollars for your help?"

"No, but ya can offer me something cold to drink at the local establishment," Norm gestured to the nearby diner. "and ya can join me for a quick one."

"I suppose. Just a quick one. I want to take the tire into Super Saver automotive before they close."

They walked past Norm's Harley as they left the parking lot.

"That's my bike," Norm said. "Have you ever ridden on one?"

"No. Too dangerous." She shook her head.

"Ya might be right about that. I had a buddy who got into a bad motorcycle accident. While he was hospitalized, the doctor amputated one of his feet." He had a woeful expression on his face.

"That's horrible. Poor man," Florence clucked sympathetically.

"That's when I found out something very important about myself." Norm gave a long pause.

"You need to ride more cautiously?" she suggested.

"No. I found out I'm Lack-Toes intolerant." He chuckled.

Florence groaned. "No more bad jokes, please!"

When Norm held open the door for her, Florence pushed past him and seated herself at the closest booth, her back to the entrance. She slunk down, fidgeting with the trifold advertisement touting the new summer coolers in flavors of mango and pomegranate. Norm waved to the waitress who brought two menus.

"The menus aren't necessary," Florence said, handing hers back to the waitress. "We're just ordering a beverage. I'll have a glass of club soda with a twist of lime."

"I'll have a beer, please. Ya got any Budweiser?"

"Yes, we do, in bottles." The waitress stood poised with the pen on her order pad. "Anything else?"

"Ya got any fried cheese curds? Changing that car tire perked up my appetite." Norm smiled at Florence. "I'll be happy to buy them."

"No, no. You saved me from an unpleasant task. I'll get the drinks and cheese curds." Florence snapped. "Could you speed up the order? I need to get my car to the service station today."

As the waitress scurried off to get their drinks, Norm leaned back in the booth and drawled, "Now, pretty lady, what happened at work to get you so keyed up?"

"I don't care to talk about it." She thrust out her chin defiantly.

"Sometimes it helps to get things off your chest. It's better than rerunning bad things in your mind. That just gets you all stirred up with nowhere to let off steam. Ya can tell me what happened. I don't know nobody from the library."

Florence stared at him for a moment, then spoke. "I suppose you're right. It might help to talk to someone. You certainly aren't a regular at the library so there shouldn't be any repercussions."

The waitress brought the drinks, and Norm waved away the glass. He took a swig from the bottle before saying, "Go ahead. Spill it."

"The network was down today so the only way students could check out materials was by hand. We had to write everything down, then enter it when the system was back up. It took forever."

"I can see how that would be frustrating but ya still seem pretty angry."

"It's my incompetent boss. Instead of having the work/study girl do all the menial work, she made me enter it in. I have better things to do with my time. Book orders to process. Fall reserve lists to pull from the stacks. Work that requires some thought." She tucked her pageboy hair behind her ears and took a sip of her club soda.

"Yer too sharp for that."

"Exactly!" She snapped her fingers. "I've been at that library longer than she has, yet she got the promotion to staff supervisor. That job should have been mine. I earned it over all the years. I always deferred to the former supervisor, made myself practically indispensable to him. Stayed late to accommodate his schedule. I should have been a shoe-in for the job."

"So why weren't you?" Norm raised a quizzical eyebrow.

"Because Beatrice Krup is a conniver, that's why. She ingratiated herself with the interview team with all her flattery. Her professional development classes. Her master's degrees. She tried to impress them with her cutting-edge ideas for improvement. Her embrace of technology." She spat the next words out. "See where technology got us today! It's only good when it works."

Florence clammed up when the waitress brought the cheese curds. Norm pushed the basket toward her and said, "Have one. They're delicious."

She shook her head no and leaned forward to whisper

conspiratorially, "But I'm going to fix all that. She'll discover she's not so high and mighty."

Norm knotted his brow. "How do you plan on doing that?"

"Part of my plan is already in play. Promise not to tell anyone?"

"I promise. Cross my heart." Norm made an invisible cross over his chest.

"You heard about the judge who dropped dead after eating some pie at the county fair?"

"Yep. Who hasn't? That woman dropping dead after a pie contest is probably the biggest excitement Crawford has seen since the terrorist firebombed the Super Saver."

Her voice rose excitedly. "And I was there with a front row seat to the whole incident. It was no accident. Alexandria Adams was poisoned. Guess what pie she was eating when she collapsed? Beatrice Krup's Cherry Berry Peach Pie!"

"H-m-m. That pie sounds kinda yummy."

"That's beside the point. Either Beatrice put something in the pie to get revenge on Alexandria—they were sworn enemies, you know—or someone else tampered with it. Doesn't matter which." She picked up the lime wedge and twisted it hard. "Beatrice is in big trouble. I'm making sure everybody knows it."

"Aren't the police investigating the suspicious death?"

"Yes, but there's also the court of public opinion. And that's where Beatrice Krup is going down for murder." Florence threw the mutilated lime into her drink and continued. "I just keep repeating that Beatrice is guilty. People are starting to believe it. Eventually, Human Resources will hear the rumors and get involved. Due to the number of benefactors who fund endowments to the college, they can't allow any hint of scandal to become public knowledge. The donations would quickly dry up, and the college would be in serious financial trouble."

"But what if she's innocent?"

"So what? People love to believe the worst lies. One good conspiracy is better than a thousand truths."

She left a twenty-dollar bill on the table and stood up to leave. "You were right. Talking about my difficulties to a complete stranger was most helpful. I'm not angry anymore. In fact, my misfortunes pale in comparison to Beatrice Krup's. Here's some language you'll understand. When the shit hits the fan, I'm going to be looking good, and she'll have it all over her face. Thanks again for changing my tire."

As Norm watched her leave the restaurant, he couldn't shake the feeling of disgust. He'd been saving his best line for last, but she was so repugnant, he refused to use it. There was bound to be some normal woman at the Thirsty Rhino who would appreciate him saying it to her:

"Are you my appendix? Because you give me a funny feeling in my stomach that makes me feel like I should take you out."

He wondered if Florence Heidt was so filled with hatred for Beatrice that she'd do anything to destroy her. Did she hate her enough to poison her prizewinning pie?

Chapter Thirteen

Cool Beans and Books was located just off Main Street in an old store built during the early 1900s. Made of Cream City bricks, the decorative trim reminded Vlad of a gingerbread house with its swirls and tulip shapes. A hanging sign, more like a medieval guild sign with a wrought iron frame, featured the image of a book. The shop's bay window was packed with colorful book displays while a black and white cat curled up between the books napping in the afternoon sun.

A welcoming smell of coffee beans and old books greeted Vlad and Nicholas as they entered. A rail that ran along the whole length of a balcony exhibited old hardcover books. The balcony held a few armchairs and small tables that overlooked the street and more shelves filled with books. Downstairs, next to a display of current best sellers, a glass case filled with vintage collectible children's books drew his eyes to first editions of *The Velveteen Rabbit, Charlie and the Chocolate Factory*, and *The Phantom Tollbooth*—titles he remembered enjoying as a child. Even older titles—including *The Wizard of Oz* and *The Five Little Peppers and How They Grew*—joined them. Someone surely loved all kinds of books.

"I'm in sixth grade, and I like to read fantasy books. Where can I find them?" Nicholas asked Donna Kloostra, who was sitting on a stool behind the counter perusing a magazine filled with new titles. Her reading glasses slipped down her nose, and she pushed them back as she looked up, her curly auburn hair escaping from the banana clip attempting to corral it.

"The middle grade and young adult sections are upstairs. You should find lots of fantasy novels there." She gestured to a set of stairs at the back of the shop.

Nicholas scurried through the shelves of adult books and disappeared up the steps.

"He certainly knows what he wants," Donna said with a smile. "What can I get for you?"

Vlad studied a glass case filled with muffins, scones, cookies, and bars. "I'll have a decaf iced latte made with half and half and two of those large chocolate chip cookies."

"For here or to go?"

"For here. Do you have any juice or milk for my son?"

"I can pour him a glass of milk or make him an Italian soda with flavored syrup and sparkling water. I have raspberry, strawberry, and vanilla flavors. Vanilla makes a cream soda type drink."

"Let's go with that. He'll probably be a while choosing a book."

"No problem. I'll get your latte." She set the magazine down, gliding over to the small refrigerator and coffee making appliances.

Vlad surveyed the small cases of books. Best sellers. Local authors. Book Club Picks. Cooking. Gardening. Self-Help. Literature.

"Your bookstore is very nice. I can't believe I've never been here before. I guess I always just pop into the college bookstore because it's close to work, but yours has much more character."

"Is there anything special you're looking for?" She asked over the hum of the coffee grinder.

"I'm just browsing. I came here mainly for Nicholas. He made a game saving catch at baseball today so we're here to celebrate," he said with pride. "First time all season he had a chance to show his stuff."

Vlad wandered over to the How-To section. *I don't suppose there's a book on how to poison your wife*, he thought. *Probably have a hard time keeping that one on the shelf.*

He sifted through the exercise and diet guides, then the woodworking, needlepoint, and jewelry making. Maybe he should take up a hobby besides solving crimes.

Donna set the drinks and cookies down on the counter. "I won't ring you up until your son brings down his book."

As if on cue, Nicholas poked his head down the stairwell. "Do you have the third book from Philip Pullman's *Book of Dust* series?"

"No, sorry. But we do have *The Secrets of the Immortals* series. It's been very popular."

"I saw it up here. Thanks." He disappeared again.

Vlad took a sip of his coffee before he spoke. "I saw you at Alexandria Adams' funeral. What a sad occasion!"

"I remember you from the pie baking contest as well. One of the worst days of my life." She took off her glasses and wiped her eyes. "Alexandria and I were friends for a long time. Since childhood, really. She moved here when I was in seventh grade. I was her first friend in Crawford."

"So you knew her before she married Earl?"

"I've known Earl even longer. He was my next-door neighbor growing up. Poor man. Life's not been good to him," she sighed.

"Really? He's a successful insurance agent, living in one of the nicest houses in town. Seems like he's done pretty well for himself," Vlad protested.

"It wasn't always that way. Earl and I lived on Houghton Street, just north of downtown. My dad was a janitor for the bottling plant, and Earl was raised by a single mom. She waitressed at the Good Eats place and sometimes helped my dad clean at night. It wasn't easy for them."

Vlad tugged on his mustache. "It seems hard to believe Alexandria would be attracted to someone who was poor."

"Earl was a star basketball player. He had an athletic scholarship to the University of Wisconsin. That's how good he was. And he was popular, too."

"I guess he has the height for basketball, but he doesn't have the build of an athlete." Skepticism was written all over Vlad's face.

"Oh, he was really something back then." She leaned on the counter and seemed to be taking measure of him before she spoke. "Tell you what. Come back tomorrow. I'll bring in my old yearbooks. You can see for yourself."

"I'll be glad to, if it's no bother."

"It's no bother. He had so much going for him back then until his affliction…"

Nicholas bounded down the stairs before she could finish. He held two books in his hands. "Dad, these are the first two books in the series. Can we get them both? I really want to read both of them. Please, Dad, please. I'll pay you back from my allowance."

Vlad looked at the latte, the Italian soda, and the two giant cookies, and thought of the last twenty-five dollars in his wallet. "I'm sorry, son. You can only have one book today."

Donna jumped in, "Tell you what. I'll reserve the second book for you until you can save up for it. I'll keep it here under the counter with your name on it. Okay?"

"I suppose." He gazed longingly at the second book before slowly handing it over to her.

As she plugged the amounts into the cash register, Vlad dug out his wallet and laid the money on the counter. Nicholas was already sitting at the table with their drinks, eagerly reading his new book. He sipped on the cream soda, oblivious to the cookie on the plate in front of him.

Vlad smiled and said, "Thank you for your kindness. Hopefully, we can talk more tomorrow."

Looks can be deceiving. Earl Adams is a perfect example of that. Maybe his deception goes beyond his appearance. Tomorrow you'll tell me what terrible affliction struck Earl Adams.

Chapter Fourteen

Vlad waited until ten minutes to five to walk into Cool Beans and Books. He figured there would be fewer customers so he would be less likely to get interrupted right before it closed. Donna paused, counting out her cash register, and gave him a friendly wave.

"Can I get you anything?"

"No, thank you. I'll just take a seat here until you're done."

Vlad sat down at an empty table. The black and white cat suddenly appeared from behind a stack and ambled over. Sniffing his bare leg, it rubbed against him. When Vlad reached down to pet it, the cat pivoted away, flicking its tail at him, head held high in the air.

"That's Maximilian, Max for short. I wouldn't advise petting him. He's as likely to nip your hand as he is to purr," she laughed.

"I seem to bring out the worst in pets. My landlady has a dog with a similar personality." Vlad watched the cat wander over to the kitchen area, probably looking for a snack.

Reaching under the counter, Donna pulled out an old high school yearbook. She strolled over to the table and plopped it down in front of him.

"This is from our senior year. You might want to browse through the pages while I finish closing out the cash register." Then she wandered over to the front door and flipped the hanging sign to Closed.

He began thumbing through the pages. Senior pictures. Lots of bangs and bushy, long permed hair, both boys and girls. Hair spray and comb teasing prevailed during the '80s. Earl Adams was on the first page of the Class of 1989. Vlad almost didn't recognize him with the disheveled mullet—short hair in the front, long in the back. The bangs had pretty much receded by now. The high nose was still the same, slightly aquiline, and his thin lips curved into a smile. A quote—"Stature is a sign of greatness"—and a list of activities spanned eight lines, including Prom King and All-State Basketball.

Curious to discover who was queen to Earl's king, Vlad barely recognized Donna Kloostra's elfin face when he turned to the prom photos. Vlad double-checked the caption. Definitely Donna, in a formal with an embroidered bodice, off the shoulder straps, and a long flowy organza skirt. The tiara nestled on her upswept hair and a sash declared her Prom Queen.

No Alexandria in sight so Vlad thumbed back through the senior section until he found her. Alexandria Knight. Her quote: "Veni, vidi, vici." Her list of activities was even longer than Earl's, including National Honor Society President, Student Council, and an officer in almost every club available. Alexandria conquered, all right. She wore a blunt bob hairstyle, parted down the middle, with the sleek curve to the chin. An intricate gold chain above the collar of a designer blouse completed her proud patrician look. Before he could find the Athletics section to look at Earl in his basketball uniform, Donna slid in the chair beside him.

"Did you find Earl on the varsity basketball team?" she asked.

"I didn't get that far. But I did find both of you at the Junior Prom."

"The prom was the highlight of my high school existence. Earl was selected for prom court and asked me to go with him," she said with a wistful look.

"Were you two an item?" Vlad looked at her curiously.

"No, nothing like that." Dona dismissed the idea with a wave of her hand. "Earl was a bit shy. He had a huge crush on Alexandria, but she was already going with Sid Fredricks. So I became his date by default. He and I were good friends. He wasn't comfortable asking one of the cheerleaders or the popular girls. I was sort of the comfortable old sneaker."

"Sid Fredricks dated Alexandria!" Vlad quickly turned to Sid's picture. Stylish hair, preppy clothes. "Unbelievable. So different from how Sid looks now. When did Earl and Alexandria start going out?" Vlad glanced again at the yearbook picture of Alexandria, then Earl in the mullet. An unlikely match.

"The summer between our junior and senior year. He was a lifeguard at the pool, and Alexandria stationed herself on a chaise lounge near his lookout chair. Soon they spent every waking moment together. She'd tell her parents she was going to my house and end up at Earl's. They were inseparable all summer. Unfortunately, Alexandria often made me join them so she wasn't exactly lying to her parents."

"Bummer for you," Vlad mumbled.

"Exactly. I can't tell you how embarrassing it was to sit in the last row of the movie theater eating popcorn by myself while Alexandria and Earl made out. I hated it, even though Alexandria always paid for my ticket and snacks," complained Donna.

"Why didn't you say no?"

Donna held up the daunting image of Alexandria in the yearbook. "Would you have the nerve to say no to Alexandria Knight, the richest girl in school? Plus she claimed to be my best friend. I wasn't going to become a social pariah by pissing her off."

Vlad thumbed back to the smiling picture of Earl Adams, so young and carefree. "You said something about Earl and his affliction. What was that all about?"

"During Earl's sophomore year in college, he came down with a bad case of mononucleosis." She frowned at the memory.

"Isn't that called 'the kissing disease'? Did Alexandria get it, too?"

"No, just Earl. He had to drop out for the fall semester. He was so fatigued he couldn't get out of bed, much less climb the stairs to his dorm room," she said bleakly.

Vlad arched one eyebrow as he spoke. "Mono is pretty common among teenagers, from what I've read. I'd hardly call it an affliction. Seems like Earl turned out fine. He's a successful business man now."

"Mono was only the beginning of his problems. He developed hepatitis. His complexion turned yellow, and he urinated black for weeks. He was finally getting over that when he came back to college in January. There was a lot of pressure for him to return to basketball practice right away. During his first game one of his opponents on the court elbowed him in the abdomen fighting over a rebound. When he got confused and made a shot for the opposing team, the coach noticed he wasn't acting right and pulled him from the game."

"Did he still have hepatitis?"

"Worse. He had a ruptured spleen. Nearly died from bleeding in his abdomen. He was saved by emergency surgery, but his basketball career was finished," Donna said mournfully.

"But he was an athlete. Even with emergency surgery, he should have sprung back." Vlad disagreed. "He was only nineteen, twenty years old. I had an emergency appendectomy when I was young, and I recovered pretty quickly."

"Earl wasn't as fortunate. He ended up with chronic Epstein-Barr. He lost a ton of weight. As you can see, he never gained it back. He lost his basketball scholarship. He almost had to leave school completely. Except for Alexandria, Earl's life was spiraling downward," she said, slowly shaking her head.

"Let me guess. She married him, and they lived happily ever after."

"More than that. She was pregnant, and they eloped. Gillian was born that spring. They moved to married housing, she hired a nanny, and both went back to classes. She's supported Earl ever since." Donna made a wry face. "Totally controlled the purse strings. He even hit me up for a loan a time or two."

"I never would have guessed Alexandria Adams messed up once in her life!" Vlad stared at her in amazement.

"That's why I never understood her attitude toward Gillian and Justin when they wanted to go to prom together." She shook her head and sighed.

"Gillian and Justin Fredricks? Sid and Shar's son?" Vlad remembered the family pictures at the funeral of the two young people together.

"Yes. He and Gillian dated in high school, too. Like his father and Alexandria. But I've blabbed enough for today." Donna stood up abruptly. "You'll think I'm a terrible gossip." She blushed.

Suddenly, Max started meowing loudly and jumped up on the counter. He raised his paw to bat at a display of bookmarks by the cash register. He meowed again and watched for Donna to look up. He stretched a tentative paw toward the display, his eyes on his owner. With one bold swipe, the bookmarks were scattered over the floor.

Donna scurried over to the cat and scooped up a pile of bookmarks, plopping them on the counter. "Oh, dear. The hungry beast attacks. I better feed him before he moves to the bookshelves. I'll be picking up books until midnight if he gets frustrated."

Vlad rose to his feet. "May I keep this yearbook for a few days? I still want to see Earl in his prime. He looks so different with a mullet. Hard to believe it's the same man."

"No problem. If you stop by again at closing, I can answer any more questions you may have."

She reached into a cupboard and pulled out a small bag of dry cat food and poured some into a bright blue bowl with a pattern of cat paws on the side. Max nudged her hand out of the way and began devouring the kibbles, not waiting for her to put the bowl on the floor.

"Thanks, Donna. I appreciate the time. I have a whole new perspective on Earl Adams. Poor guy." Vlad felt a pang of pity as he let himself out.

Under Alexandria's thumb. Her stranglehold might drive him to take out a two-million-dollar life insurance policy. Vlad thought to himself as he drove home. *And Sid Fredricks—the meditation guru—was dumped by Alexandria in high school for Earl. What a tangled web we weave!*

Chapter Fifteen

Beatrice willed herself to be calm as she carried the coffee to the car. Every weekday morning for four years she stopped at the Higher Grounds coffee shop for a large coffee with cream. On a first name basis with the two women who worked there, she exchanged pleasantries with them and had a morning chat. One woman, usually Judy, waited on customers while Susie made the lattes, cappuccinos, and other coffee specialties. Beatrice even knew the names and ages of their dogs and children and what hair salons and grocery stores they patronized. That's why the incident not only surprised her, but also filled her with foreboding.

Only a few other customers were in the shop. Two college coeds on their laptops conversed as they ate muffins and busied themselves on their computers. Two middle-aged ladies waited at the pick-up side of the counter. And Beatrice stood at the order spot.

Both Judy and Susie were busy behind the counter, Susie brewing lattes and Judy wiping down the oven area where the muffins and scones were baked. Beatrice quietly waited for one of them to notice her standing there but neither looked up. The two ladies at pick-up stared at her and began whispering, hands raised to cover their mouths. Finally, Susie brought over their drinks but made no move to take her order. Instead, she put a carton of half and half back in the refrigerator and carelessly swiped a towel over the cappuccino maker. Judy continued her cleaning in the back, taking trays down and replacing them in the same spot. Susie wandered over to her, said something, then jerked her head in Beatrice's direction. Both women then turned their backs to her.

"Good morning, ladies." Beatrice cheerfully said.

No response.

Ahem!" Beatrice cleared her throat. "Could I please order a coffee to go?"

Still no response.

She repeated her request a little louder. "Could I please have a coffee to go?"

Susie looked at her with narrowed eyes. "The drip coffee isn't working today. Try the Kwik Stop."

"Could I please have a latte instead? I noticed that seems to be working."

"Skim, two percent, or half and half?" Susie spat the words out while Judy just glared.

"Uh, may I have the two percent?'

Susie slowly walked to the refrigerator and looked inside. "All out of two percent." She turned to Judy and said, "You'll have to make a run to Cullin's Dairy for two percent."

"Half and half will be fine." Beatrice fidgeted with the zipper on her purse and tried to keep her voice calm.

The two college students stopped talking to observe the interchange. Beatrice felt their curious eyes shift from Susie to her and back.

Susie searched again in the refrigerator. She picked up the carton of half and half and shook it. "Almost out of this, too. All we got is skim."

"Skim will do."

Beatrice felt her face getting hot as Susie measured the coffee into the thing with a handle and pressed some buttons on a keypad. Then she placed the to-go cup under the dispenser. After frothing the milk, she poured it into the coffee. Beatrice watched Susie clear her throat and move her head like she was going to spit into the coffee, but she spit into the towel instead.

Without washing her hands, she made a detour past Judy and whispered loud enough for all to hear, "You think you know someone, but you never really know when the devil takes hold of them."

Susie slammed the latte on the counter. "That will be four dollars."

As Beatrice fumbled in her purse to retrieve a five-dollar bill, she met Susie's hostile gaze openly. "Thank you. Please keep the change. And don't believe everything you hear. Trust your heart, not your ears."

Susie looked embarrassed as she mumbled a thank-you.

WHEN BEATRICE ARRIVED AT WORK, she greeted the work/study girl, the library aides, and the scattered students with a cheerfulness she didn't feel. She closed the door to her office and sat at her computer, drumming her fingers on the desk. "I've got to do something. I can't just wait around for the police and I can't interview the suspects, because I'm one myself. There must be something I can do," she said out loud.

She stared at her screensaver, a photo of one of the castles they sailed by on the Rhine. The gleaming white towers rose from the dark green forest. When Norm was in trouble, the team went into action to root out the real thieves. Gaston attacked the fleeing robber before he could destroy evidence and escape from the ship. She knew they were working overtime on her case. This very afternoon Norm would be introducing himself to Florence and surreptitiously questioning her. Sandra and Gaston were onto Earl while Vlad covered both the Fredricks and Donna at the bookstore. Little by little, they were gathering pieces of the puzzle. But a big piece was missing—the murder weapon! What poison had the terrible effects like she observed on Alexandria?

The horrible death was forever etched in her mind. Projectile vomiting, followed by numbness and convulsions. But death was unmercifully not instantaneous. Beatrice shuddered to imagine the scene at the hospital if the pie judging was any harbinger of what had followed.

She began typing poisons into her search engine. Strychnine. Cyanide. Arsenic. These were the common poisons in movies and period detective shows she watched.

"Strychnine starts with spasms and progresses to nearly continuous convulsions until the backbone arches continually. Then death by asphyxiation, by paralysis of the pathways that control breathing," she read. Not strychnine.

"Arsenic is naturally occurring and present in groundwater near highly industrialized areas. Most poisoning is due to long term exposure, and symptoms first appear in red or swollen skin. Odorless and colorless, it could be mixed in food, but death would not likely occur very quickly," according to the next entry.

She read on: "Cyanide could be found in apple seeds and pits of other fruits, but one would have to chew about two hundred seeds to receive a fatal dose." However, she learned potassium cyanide can be purchased from a chemical supply house because it is used in gold and silver plating. Early symptoms include headaches, dizziness, a fast heart rate leading to cardiac arrest. It sounded promising but not a match.

None of these seemed likely.

Beatrice was about to give up when she thought of the Garden Club. How many people present at the pie judging contest were knowledgeable about gardening? Florence, Donna, maybe even Earl if he had access to Alexandria's gardening books. She typed *Poisonous Plants in your Garden* in her search engine. Bingo. *Ten Deadliest Plants in the World* came up first. Some of them were not found in North America—Angel's Trumpet and Rosary Peas grew in tropical regions. That excluded Wisconsin for sure. But as she scrolled down the list, the bright pink oleander bloom caught her eye. This shrub was even planted in parks and schoolyards. Then she saw the light purple flowers of the belladonna with its shiny black berries. How like blueberries in appearance! "The sweet and juicy fruit are tempting to children…As few as 2-5 can kill a child, 10-20 an adult…Even touching the plant can cause irritation." Could it have been slipped into her pie?

The next plant, aconite, also known as monkshood, made her sit up and pay closer attention. The large blue-purple flowers in the picture were very similar to the delphinium she had in her backyard garden. She studied it closely and read carefully. The plants looked alike but were not the same genus.

"Hummingbirds are not known to pollinate aconite flowers." Smart hummingbirds! "Long used in preparing poison-tipped arrows for hunting or warfare." "Fast-acting." "Accidental ingesting can be fatal. All parts are poisonous but the roots are especially toxic." "Documented case of gardener falling ill from touching the roots…Half a tablespoon in whiskey can kill a large man, and can go unnoticed."

Her breathing quickened as she read. "Marked symptoms occur almost instantaneously. Death usually occurs within two to six hours. The first symptoms of poisoning are gastrointestinal, including nausea, vomiting, and diarrhea." *Projectile vomiting fits for sure*, she thought. "This is followed by motor weakness, sensations of tingling and numbness in the mouth and face, spreading to the limbs. Convulsions and ventricular arrhythmia follow, leading to death if untreated." *Oh my God. The first symptoms matched Alexandria's reactions.*

She reached for her cell phone to call Vlad. Her computer screen went dark before she could scroll down to *Favorites*. What the hell? A loud insistent knock interrupted her thoughts. She rushed to answer. A library aide stood there with a panicked look on her face.

"The network just went down. What should we do?"

Beatrice shoved her phone in her cardigan pocket and followed her out the door.

Chapter Sixteen

"You won't believe the day I've had," Beatrice said as she opened the door to Vlad. Her usually polished hair looked like a deranged stylist had worked on it in a wind tunnel. The hem of her blouse hung halfway out, the other half still tucked into the waistband of her skirt. Her espadrilles had been kicked off and lay askew on the welcome mat. A faint trace of peach lipstick clung to her lips. She led him to the couch where a bottle of Merlot stood uncorked on the coffee table, ready to be poured into the two waiting glasses

"What on earth happened?' Vlad asked as he poured them each a glass and sank into the couch, pushing the pillows aside to make room for her. He pulled her next to him and gently massaged the back of her neck as she spoke.

"The ladies at the coffee shop treated me like I was Hannibal Lecter's sister. I swear Susie would have spit into my coffee if I hadn't been watching. Then I was doing some research on poisons on the internet and the whole system crashed. I had to force Florence to actually interact with the students. She gave me snake eyes all afternoon whenever I walked past the check-out desk. I was holed up with the techies until about forty-five minutes ago. They were able to fix the problem. It wasn't hacked, thank goodness. We weren't victims of ransomware, either, but the timing of the crash seems too much of a coincidence—right when I was trying to find out more about poisons that might have been used to kill Alexandria. And finally, when I got home, there's a voice message from the police, a Detective Johnson, telling me to come down to the station tomorrow. My day was hell. How was yours?"

She swallowed some wine, then leaned into him.

"I decided to try the bookstore again today. Donna was most informative about the saga of Earl and Alexandria. I'd almost pity him if I didn't know he's going to cash in on a two-million-dollar life insurance policy. He came down with some kind of chronic debilitating condition in college that ruined his athletic scholarship. Worse luck, Alexandria got pregnant so they had to get married. He's been living under her thumb ever since."

"The daughter we saw at the funeral caused the hasty wedding?" Beatrice raised her eyebrows in astonishment.

"You got it! I would have loved to eavesdrop on Alexandria's wealthy parents when they heard the news about their overachieving daughter and her premarital hanky-panky."

"I imagine she cast Earl as the sex-crazed villain to deflect blame from herself. Alexandria never could accept responsibility for any wrong actions. Always someone else's fault. I don't know how Donna Kloostra put up with her all those years. I would have slipped poison into her cocktail ages ago."

Vlad tweaked his mustache thoughtfully. "Not only that, Alexandria dated Sid Fredricks before she took up with Earl."

"Alexandria and Sid. I don't believe it! They would have been more of an odd couple than Earl and she." Beatrice took another sip of Merlot as she digested this news.

"Sid looked a lot different in high school—almost as preppie as Alexandria. By the way, I have Donna's senior yearbook in my car, if you want to step into the past and see him and a young Alexandria."

"God, no! The old Alexandria was more than enough Dragon Lady for me. The only thing I want to step into is a slinky negligée and your arms. Massaging my neck feels nice but there are other parts of me that feel quite neglected. I could use a little tension release."

She slid her hand along his bare leg and inched her way toward his thigh. She withdrew her hand and swung her leg over his body so she seated herself facing him on the couch. Her sweet verbena scent filled his nostrils as she flung one arm around his neck and slowly unbuttoned the top of his polo shirt with the other. Her tongue parted his lips and thrust deep into his mouth, playfully flicking against his tongue.

Ignoring the kink in his back, he tried to ease them down on the narrow couch but Beatrice hung over the side, and he felt her slipping from his grasp. His passion building, he pushed the coffee table away with his foot, miraculously not spilling the glasses of wine. Then the two lovers plummeted onto the carpet, as he broke their fall with his left arm, and flipped her back on top, with hardly a twinge of pain. The urgency of his desire fought the clumsiness of unhooking her bra with only one hand. *Damn!* he thought. *Why couldn't somebody invent a magnetic clasp for bras?*

The bra somersaulted overhead and joined the growing pile of discarded clothing. Soon shorts, skirt, and undergarments were scattered around the room like leaves before the autumn wind. The unexpectedness of her passion combined with her subtle movements to fill him with delight. Vlad was eager to give Beatrice his best effort to take her mind off her bad day. Soon both forgot every frustrating incident, every obstacle that kept them apart, in the expression of their love.

"What a perfect stress release!" Beatrice laughed and collapsed into his arms.

She stretched out full length upon him. The imprint of her body on his seemed like he was made of clay and would carry her impression not just on his body but on his soul. Her scent flooded his senses, and he felt the rise and fall of her chest matching his own. His happiness knew no boundaries as they nestled there together.

"Thank you so much," she said after a few seconds. "As long as I have you, I can face the police, Florence's nasty glares, the whispers behind my back—anything life throws at me."

"When I asked you to marry me in Amsterdam, I said our love was forever. Nothing has changed. I'm a forever kind of guy." His soothing touch rested in the hollow of her back as he tenderly kissed her, reveling in the sweetness of her breath, the softness of her lips touching his.

"I don't even mind the rug burns on my knees for a moment like this." Beatrice traced delicate circles through the hair on his chest. "There's only one other thing I'd want to make this night perfect."

Vlad wasn't sure he had the stamina for a second round. Her weight began to press down on his lower back, still a little iffy from Shar's last yoga class when he tried to bend backwards into a camel. But if that was what Beatrice wanted, he'd try his best. He hesitated just a heartbeat before he asked, "What's that, sweetheart?" almost dreading her answer.

"I've been picturing it in my mind all day. I really wanted it hot. I don't mind getting sticky. I love it when it's hot," she gushed as she raised herself up and returned to the couch. Another sip of Merlot brought a contented smile.

Vlad joined her on the couch, inhaling deeply and holding his expanded chest for a count of four. A few more deep breaths might restore his vigor. Unfortunately, the deep breathing brought on a fit of coughing. Only a drink of wine brought it to a halt.

"If you give me a few minutes," he stammered.

"I can't stop thinking about it. Been driving me crazy. What I need is a hot fudge sundae from Cullin's Dairy. Let's get dressed and get some ice cream."

Chapter Seventeen

Beatrice paused in front of the hall mirror to examine her appearance. "My God, I look a fright! My hair looks like a hurricane hit it." She had changed into a periwinkle t-shirt dress, which accentuated her trim figure, and strappy sandals. After running a hand through her tousled hair, she grabbed a small brush and began combing it. Then she dabbed on some lipstick, tilting her head left and right for a final check.

"You look beautiful. I love that wild look. I'm the luckiest man in the world because you're mine." He pulled her to him and kissed her passionately.

She kissed him back just as fiercely.

He murmured, "Are you sure you want ice cream?"

"Yes. Ice cream is the perfect complement to Merlot. Let's go." She grabbed his keys from the hall stand and pushed him toward the door.

As Vlad backed out of her driveway, he chatted agreeably. "The kids have been asking to go fishing from the bridge at Tripoli Island. I need to go online to renew my license from the DNR. Maybe go tomorrow or the day after. The poles and tackle box are still at the house. I told Nicholas to find them in the garage. Probably up in the eaves. Not sure why Kaitlyn wants to come along. After five minutes she'll be bored to tears."

"You could always take a walk with her on one of the trails at Tripoli while Nicky fishes," she suggested.

"At this time of year the mosquitoes will drain you dry. The trails are overgrown and nasty. Maybe I'll ask Sandra if we can take Gaston along so Kaitlyn can play fetch with him. He could use the exercise."

"Speaking of exercise, how are the yoga classes going?"

As she spoke, Beatrice gently caressed his bare leg. He removed his hand from the steering wheel and gave her thigh an affectionate squeeze. *Keep both hands on the wheel*, he reminded himself.

"Hard to say after only three sessions. I'm constantly finding excuses to stay after class and ask questions without Shar getting suspicious or thinking I'm hitting on her. Sid's seldom around on Tuesdays. I'd really like to find out whatever happened with Alexandria in high school. He's pretty damn elusive for someone who calls himself a Soul Life Coach."

"What's a Soul Life Coach?" Beatrice knotted her brow.

"My point exactly. There's something off with those two. Constantly preaching mindfulness and personal growth, yet there's always an undercurrent. A dark look that disappears so quickly you aren't sure you really saw it."

The drive to downtown and Cullin's Dairy took them along Jefferson Street, past attractive older homes made of Cream City brick, most lovingly restored to their former glory, featuring wide front porches and an abundance of beveled or stained glass windows. As they neared downtown, the stately houses changed over to clapboard rentals, front yards littered with big wheel trikes, faded Little Tikes cars, and rusty wagons. A mongrel-looking dog, chained to a sagging grey house, barked as they drove by. The former fire station, also made of Cream City brick, now held a pawn shop and a car repair business. Across the street Norm's hangout, the Thirsty Rhino, sported a parking area filled with motorcycles, one of which was Norm's Harley. And Norm, smoking a cigarette with another fellow, could be seen standing outside.

"I see Norm on the corner," Beatrice said. "Wasn't he supposed to charm Florence today? I wonder how that encounter turned out. Probably like SpongeBob SquarePants enticing Cruella de Vil."

"I suppose it's too late to back up and go around the block," Vlad muttered. "Maybe if you duck down, he won't notice us."

"I'm sure Norm won't be interested in joining us for a sundae."

"Not unless they make it with Budweiser."

As they rolled up to the corner, Norm began waving his arms wildly and gesturing for them to join him. He pointed to his companion, then held up the man's arm like a prizefighter who'd just won a match.

"Can we pretend we didn't see him?" Vlad said between clenched teeth.

"I'm not that good of an actress," Beatrice chuckled.

As they waited for the light to turn green, Norm threw his cigarette on the sidewalk and ran over to their car. He pounded on Vlad's window, yelling, "Hey, Doc. Beez, ya gotta hear this. Roll down your window, dude."

Beatrice quickly removed her hand and folded them demurely on her lap.

Vlad reluctantly held the button as the window slowly opened.

"We're heading to Cullin's for some ice cream. Can't it wait?" he asked.

"Nah, man. Yer gonna want to hear what my buddy has to say. It will knock yer socks off. Maybe even make ya soil your tighty-whities."

Beatrice leaned over Vlad and said, "Didn't you meet Florence today? How'd that go?"

"Just like you warned me. She's a bitch. I wasted my best pick-up lines and hardly got a smile. She ditched me at the café. When I got to the Thirsty Rhino, I started talking to Duane here, and he had some interesting shit to say. Park the car and come inside. Buy him a drink. It'll be worth your time. I guarantee it."

"Let's hear what he has to say. We'll have plenty of time for ice cream. We need to keep all our options open until we figure out what really happened." Beatrice smiled sweetly at Vlad.

Her smile was the only thing stopping Vlad from stepping on the accelerator and driving to the A&W on the outskirts of town.

"You're right. Cullin's doesn't close until ten," he sighed.

He made a right turn and parked the car halfway between the Thirsty Rhino and the ice cream shop.

"Besides, I've never been in the Thirsty Rhino. I've always wondered how it got its name," Beatrice grabbed his hand as they strolled down the sidewalk.

"We'll soon find out."

Norm tapped his foot as they approached. "C'mon, c'mon. Duane already went back inside."

The air conditioner in the bar was working overtime to dispel the warm July air. A scent of stale beer seemed to emanate from the walls themselves. The slightly sticky floor prevented any fast movements or sliding dance steps. As Vlad's eyes grew accustomated to the dim light, he could see a mural on the back wall of a cartoon-like rhinoceros in a biker jacket cozying up to the bar, waiting for a skimpily clad female bartender to fill a mug of beer from a tap. He pointed it out to Beatrice.

"Now I get it," she laughed. "Rather odd, but it fits the place."

Aging bikers in Harley vests over well-worn t-shirts crowded around the bar, accompanied by their female counterparts in pink camouflage tees or glittery biker shirts. Pinned to the ceiling above their heads hung an assortment of bras like a valance: lacy pastels, wild animal prints, and sexy black underwires. A poster tacked to the long mirror behind the bartender announced the monthly wet t-shirt contest. Winners of the contest donated their no longer needed bras to the overhead collection.

"Oh, my goodness!" Beatrice exclaimed. "Some of these bras probably cost fifty or sixty dollars at Victoria's Secret. I would never toss off expensive lingerie like that."

"I don't think these ladies shop there. More likely Frederick's of Hollywood or the Super Saver. Don't tell Sandra about this place. She'll hit the owner up for a burlesque gig."

"One of those bras might be hers. That one looks like the one she lent me for my wild night on the cruise." Beatrice pointed to a red push-up plunge bra dangling directly above them.

Norm shoved his friend in between them, putting an abrupt end to their conversation. "This here is Duane. He works part time at the Ho-Chunk Casino in Madison. These two are my detective buddies, Doc and Beezy. Maybe you read about them in the newspaper."

Duane had a squat nose, watery brown eyes, and thinning hair that was an unnatural shade of black. His orange and yellow Hawaiian shirt, unbuttoned to the waist, revealed a hairy chest and a slight paunch. Too much booze and late-night partying had taken their toll on whatever good looks he once had.

"Nah, I don't get no newspaper," he replied. "I just watch cable news if I'm home. Or whatever is on the TV at the shop."

"Anyway, they're on a case right now. You heard about that woman that got poisoned at the County Fair? They're working on that—better at grilling suspects than the cops. Plus they got Gaston the Wonder Dog helping them," Norm boasted.

"Keep your voice down, Norm. We don't want to broadcast our investigation." Vlad shot him a warning look.

"Hah!" Duane snorted. "Cops around this town don't know shit. All they're good for is busting up parties and giving out speeding tickets.

Not to mention harassing people with drunk and disorderly tickets. Right, Stevie?"

He gestured toward the bartender, a red-headed female dressed much like the server in the mural with a low-cut tank top and cut-off shorts. Her long hair was pulled into a no-nonsense ponytail while her pale complexion suggested an aversion to the sun.

Stevie sidled up. "Tell us some more about that dog. A poodle, right? I read the *Daily Times.*"

"Smartest dog in the world. Caught a terrorist right here in Crawford and smashed up a big diamond heist ring in Germany. The little fella gets big results," Norm continued with an expansive gesture.

"Heard he got some reward money, too," Stevie chimed in as she filled some glasses at the tap.

"Enough for Doc here to buy a diamond for his fiancée and take her to Europe." Norm jerked his thumb at Vlad and Beatrice.

"No shit. Wish I had a dog that smart." She glided away, hips swaying, with two full glasses of beer in hand.

"You said Duane had some valuable information for us," Vlad reminded Norm.

"I'm mighty thirsty," Duane said. "My mouth is so dry it's hard to talk."

"Hey, Stevie," Norm shouted. "Set us up with another round of beers. ALL of us."

"The same Nitro on tap?" she asked.

"That's the one. You guys gotta try this beer," Norm insisted to Vlad and Beatrice. "It's damn good."

Stevie filled four glasses and set two in front of Vlad and Beatrice.

"Anyhoo, Duane works at the casino, and guess what happened the other night?" Norm said after he took a swig. "Tell 'em who was there."

"No. first you tell 'em that joke about the old gambler and the cop," Duane insisted. "The little lady will get a kick out of that one." He elbowed Beatrice and winked.

"This old guy is stopped by a cop around two a.m. and asked where he's going this time of night. The old guy says, 'I was on my way to attend a lecture about gambling, alcohol abuse, and their effects on the human body, as well as staying out late.'

"The cop says, 'Really? Who's giving a lecture at this time of night?' And the old guy says, 'That would be my wife.'"

Duane punched Norm in the shoulder and laughed, "That's a good one. Almost as good as the horse betting one."

Vlad jumped in before Norm could speak. "We were on our way to Cullin's. We still want to get there before it closes. What's up with the casino?"

"I service the machines a coupla nights a week," Duane answered. "When I was there Wednesday, there was a big ruckus. Some guy was complaining. Seemed like he was mad because he just lost five thousand bucks. He was four sheets to the wind, too." This time he elbowed Vlad.

"Yer never gonna guess who it was?" Norm exclaimed.

"I couldn't see his face at first, just heard him begging for a line of credit from the manager. When he turned around I saw it was that insurance guy, the one with his face plastered over all the billboards going out of town. Earl Adams. The one whose wife died. The guy you're investigating. And I heard it ain't the first time he's lost big at Ho-Chunk."

"Earl Adams is a gambler? I can hardly believe it." Beatrice gave a little shake of her head.

"Well, believe it. He's there every Wednesday. Even before his wife passed. He's a regular." Duane took another gulp of Nitro. "He's dropped a lot of money at the poker table."

"Earl Adams! That explains a lot," Vlad said. "No wonder he needed extra insurance."

"Yeah. Security even had to escort him out because he had a chip on his shoulder," Norm guffawed.

"Chip on his shoulder. Good one." Duane punched Norm in the arm again and roared with laughter.

"Couldn't resist that one, Doc." Norm's expression grew solemn. "But the gambling is legit. Earl Adams is a regular at the casino. Wonder if the cops know that?"

Chapter Eighteen

After a night of tossing and turning, Beatrice woke with a blazing headache. Merlot, Nitro beer, and ice cream probably weren't the best combination to consume the night before a police interview, even though it had seemed good at the moment. Impromptu sex on the living floor with Vlad seemed even better at the moment.

He'd insisted on spending the night with her, even though she'd told him to go home.

"I know I'm not going to be able to sleep, and I'll be restless," she had said. "No sense in both of us having a bad night."

She found herself smiling remembering his reply.

"I don't care about sleep. I care about you. I'm going to stay. I'll be your cornerstone, your rock. Someone to lean on. Keep you calm through the night. We're in this together. I won't be a distraction in the morning. I promise. I love you."

She smiled and kissed him. "I love you, too. Thank you for saving me from myself."

Vlad had cuddled spoon-like until he fell asleep, sound asleep, with his arm draped over her waist. She arched her back against him, trying to comfort herself with his warmth, but the possible police scenarios played over and over in her head, all ending with the clunk of a cell door slamming in her frightened face. Beatrice propped her head on her elbow and watched him sleep, envious of his ability to lie there unconscious while she tried several positions with her pillow, punching it to various degrees of puffiness, none of them comfortable. When he said he was her rock, she had presumed he didn't mean sleeping like one.

When her leg began cramping, it was time to abandon all hope of sleep and crawl to the living room couch, where reruns of *The Waltons* numbed her mind to the point of drifting off into an uneasy rest. *Goodnight, Grandpa. Goodnight, Grandma. Goodnight, Ma. Goodnight, Pa.*

Goodnight, John-Boy. Goodnight, consciousness.

When Beatrice opened her eyes, there was Vlad standing over her with a fresh cup of coffee and an anxious expression.

Gratefully, she took the cup and tried to reassure him. "Coffee is just what I need after a restless night. Thank you. Please don't worry. We both know I didn't poison Alexandria Adams. I'm sure this interview is just a formality."

"I can clear my schedule for today. Get my fishing license this afternoon. I'll call Maria to let her know. Plenty of time to pick up the kids tomorrow. I can drive down to the station with you." He picked up his cell phone and began scrolling.

"No. Absolutely not!" She pressed her lips together in a firm line. "You're not changing your plans with Nicholas and Kaitlyn for me. I'll be fine."

"Tomorrow works better for fishing anyway."

"No. I need to do this myself." Her eyes flashed a warning look.

Vlad made one more pitch. "I still think you should have a lawyer with you. The police don't know you're innocent. They just want to solve the murder so the media get off their case."

"You watch too many cop shows. This is Crawford, Wisconsin, not New York. Go home and quit worrying about me," she said as she pushed him out the door.

Vlad grabbed her hand and pulled her to him in a warm embrace. "I'm only a phone call away if you need me. Stay strong. You'll convince them that you're innocent. I know you will." He kissed her fiercely before walking to his car.

As she dumped an aspirin onto her hand and gulped it down with a glass of water, her bravado began to fade. *What if the police consider me the number one suspect? With all of Earl Adams' questionable behavior coming to light in their investigation, the police have to be looking closely at him, too. Husbands are always the main culprit. Why am I worrying? Because Florence was actively promoting me as the villain and, according to Sandra, Earl Adams was more than happy to throw me under the bus. That's why.*

Beatrice dressed modestly in a light green shift with a matching cotton sweater, in case the police station was cold. A minimum of make-up. Hair neatly combed. She looked like a harmless librarian. Hell, she was a harmless librarian who somehow got sucked into these crazy investigations. First, the terrorists last year, then Norm and the jewel thieves, and now murder at the county fair. What next? Up against the mafia? Gaston would probably be willing to bite the boss of the crime syndicate without flinching. She shook her head. *Don't give Norm and Sandra any ideas.*

Fifteen minutes before her interview with the detective was scheduled, Beatrice walked into the Crawford Municipal Building. The brown brick structure squatted along the river, housing the fire and police department as well as the city government offices. The lighter tan accents were an attempt to make the building look less institutional, as were the green and blue wavy lines on the Crawford sign, symbolizing the river winding its way through town. She took a deep breath in the lobby, then headed toward the door with "Police" stenciled on it. The young officer manning the counter was absorbed in a manual and didn't notice her entrance.

She glided before him and said, "Hello. I'm Beatrice Krup. Here to see Detective Johnson."

He looked a bit startled to see her there, as if she had been suddenly pulled from a magician's hat, and blinked a few times before he spoke. "I'll let him know you're here." He spoke into a phone. "Miss Krup is here, sir."

The rest of the department was deserted. Gray dividers partitioned off empty desks. Officers who presumably occupied the desks could easily look over the top and see everyone else in the room. This department was a far cry from the bustling offices on cop shows. The only picture on the anemic yellow walls was a small seascape of a sailboat in frothy waves. Toward the back Beatrice noticed a warren of rooms used for private offices and interrogations. She wondered if she would be questioned in a room with a two-way mirror so the interview could be observed. Observed by whom? No one was around.

A man in a rumpled tan suit, probably in his fifties, emerged from one of the back rooms. As he bulldozed his way across the room, Beatrice knew he was definitely a man she wouldn't want to cross.

He stuck out a large hand and said, "I'm Detective Johnson. Thank you for coming in to talk with me."

They shook hands, her small one engulfed in his. His skin was rough like he jackhammered concrete slabs in his spare time. With a muscular frame trending toward obesity, his suit jacket wouldn't button, and his stomach hung over his trousers. He didn't seem like he cared about his appearance: no Keto diet for him. His thick dark hair, in a shaggy, uneven cut, hadn't seen any comb besides his fingers. When he gazed at her, his bear-like brown eyes made her feel as if she should confess something just to make him look away.

"Please follow me, Miss Krup." He led the way to a small room, just as dismal and monochromatic as the outer office: a few uncomfortable metal chairs under a large wooden table. A table recorder stood ominously in its center.

"Won't you take a seat?" Detective Johnson said as he gestured across the table.

An odor of stale sweat clung to the uncomfortable chair. Beatrice wondered how many shoplifters and car thieves sat in this same seat under the wilting gaze of the detective.

"I'll be tape-recording this conversation. I have to read you your rights. They're both routine procedures."

"Being questioned about a murder I witnessed is anything but routine for me," Beatrice said nervously, "but go ahead."

He turned on the recorder, then said her name and his, their location, and the time and date.

"You have the right to remain silent…"

Beatrice started to perspire as he droned on, adding her pungency to the previous occupant's lingering smell.

"Do you understand each of these rights I have explained to you?" he asked. "Having these rights in mind, do you wish to talk to us?"

Beatrice nodded her head, "Yes. I have nothing to hide. I'm innocent."

"Would you mind walking through your movements on the day of July 16?" His cold stare made her squirm.

"I woke up at five o'clock and started mixing up my pie crust. I was going to enter the Madison County Fair Pie Baking Contest, and I wanted it to be fresh out of the oven. I put the dough in the refrigerator to chill and began preparing the fruit. Peeling peaches, chopping cherries, measuring a cup of blueberries."

"Where did you get the fruit?" He fired questions at her like a machine gunner, giving her no time to think.

"I bought it at the Farmer's Market the day before."

"From a reliable vendor?"

"Yes. I've been buying produce from Gary for years," A nagging doubt popped up; *Was Gary really reliable?*

"So there's no chance some wild berries inadvertently were mixed in?" He raised one eyebrow quizzically.

"None at all. In fact, I ate some of the blueberries on my cereal for breakfast."

"So then what did you do?"

"I finished baking the pie. I watched the oven time very carefully because this was my one shot at making a prizewinning pie. It turned out perfectly."

His relentless stare made her feel like a third-grader tattling about who broke the pencil sharpener.

"What time did you arrive at the fair?"

"At nine o'clock, an hour before the judging was to begin."

"And the pie stayed in your possession the whole time?"

"Until I placed it on the table with the other entrants. Donna Kloostra checked me in, and then I left the pavilion for a while to find a cup of coffee." Beatrice's words tumbled out.

"So the pie was out of your sight while you went for coffee?" The detective's downturned mouth showed his disapproval.

"Yes. The other contestants were milling around. I needed to stretch my legs and clear my mind. Coffee helps me focus."

"How far did you go for coffee?"

"Um...there was a stand selling coffee and funnel cake nearby. Maybe three or four booths away." Uncertainty crept into her voice.

He shot the next question at her. "What time did you return?"

"About quarter to ten. Before the judging started. I was able to find two seats near the front." When Beatrice noticed his raised eyebrow, she hastily added, "For my fiancé and myself."

"Did the contest proceed normally?'

"Yes. Alexandria tasted several pies, made some comments. None were especially outstanding until Florence Heidt's chiffon pie. It earned the first blue ribbon of the day. Then she sampled my pie. She said the first bite was delicious. But then...," Beatrice faltered, remembering Alexandria's contorted face.

"Then you witnessed the victim's reaction to the pie?"

"It was horrible. I'll never forget the terrible sounds she made, the violent vomiting, the convulsions. It was a nightmare." Beatrice covered her face with her hands as a wave of nausea swept over her. She swallowed hard to hold it back. "Excuse me for a minute."

"Would you like a glass of water?" the detective asked.

Tears welled in her eyes. She blinked them away and looked up at his face, implacable as a stone gargoyle.

"No, thank you. I'm all right. I just need to take a few breaths." She slowly took a breath, counting to four on the inhale, then slowly letting it out. She felt the nausea begin to subside.

"Take all the time you need until you're ready to continue."

Detective Johnson turned off the tape recorder, made a tent of his folded hands on the tabletop, and watched her impassively. Beatrice wished she knew what was going on behind that expressionless mask.

"I'm ready," she finally said.

He leaned forward to turn the tape recorder back on, restating the time.

"Did you have any disagreements with the victim?" He gave her a pointed stare.

"No, not really. Just the usual occasional differences of opinion." Beatrice shrugged.

"Some witnesses observed a heated altercation between you and Alexandria Adams after a Garden Club meeting. Did she try to revoke your membership?" He picked up a pen from the table and began twirling it with his fingers as he waited for her answer.

She spoke carefully, clasping her hands together in her lap to keep them from shaking. "She scheduled meetings when I was working, then annulled my membership because I missed too many meetings. I thought she was being unfair and told her so. That's all."

"You were overheard to say, 'I could kill that woman sometimes.' Would that be accurate?"

Her face flushing red, Beatrice gulped, "Yes, I mean no. If I said that, I surely didn't mean it. She was just so aggravating!"

"Can you think of anyone who may have had similar conflicts with the victim?" He jabbed at the air with the pen.

"Alexandria was a difficult person to deal with at times, and several people had run-ins with her." Her voice grew strident. "Even her best friend, Donna, endured several tongue-lashings from Alexandria that were witnessed by many people. On the day of the pie judging, Alexandria berated her for not providing a comfortable chair for judging."

"Anyone else?"

"Earl had struggles in his marriage. Money issues."

"What kind of money issues? How do you know this?" Detective Johnson's eyes locked on hers until she looked down at his hand, still holding the pen.

"I can't say. I've just heard rumors," she deflected his question. *Dare she tell him about the gambling?*

"From whom? You seem to know a lot about the Adams' affairs."

Beatrice thought, *How reliable was a friend of Norm's?* Then she said, "It was idle gossip. I know firsthand how destructive rumors can be. I really don't know anything more." Beatrice clamped her mouth shut and lifted her eyes back to his.

The detective gave a curt nod. "Thank you, Miss Krup. We may call you back in to talk again as the investigation continues."

Chapter Nineteen

Vlad swirled the gin in his martini as Sandra gazed questioningly at him. He took a small sip, then set the glass down on the end table, smoothing both sides of his mustache, without speaking. Gaston snoozed comfortably on her lap, twitching his ears occasionally like he was deep in a pleasant doggy dream. She stroked his silky ears, and the dog let out a contented sigh.

"Something wrong with your drink, dearie?"

"No, your cocktail is excellent, as always. I just need to keep a clear head for what I'm planning to do next."

"What's that?"

"Since Beatrice is tied up with an AAUW meeting tonight, I'm going to work solo. I've got a plan to spy on Sid Fredricks. Something doesn't add up between Alexandria and him. Why would he buy a house next to her when she dumped him in high school? I'm going to need Gaston for my cover story, if I'm caught. He and I are going out for an evening stroll that just happens to take us down Larkspur Lane."

Gaston raised his head at the mention of his name. He shot Vlad a baleful look and tried to settle back down on Sandra's lap, but she nudged him off. He landed on all four paws and gave a low growl. Sandra stood up and shook her finger at him.

"You heard Vlad, Lovey Puppy. He needs you to swing into action. Don't be a cranky paws."

"Come on, Gaston. I've got Greenies in my car. You love Greenies, boy." Vlad reached for the leash hanging on the hall tree and waved it at the recalcitrant dog.

"If you're a good little detective dog, Mom will buy you a cheese Danish," Sandra cajoled.

The little dog's eyes grew brighter when he heard those words, and he gave his tail a little wag. He pranced over to Vlad, stood next to him in perfect heel position, and waited patiently while Vlad snapped the leash to his collar. Then he scratched at the door, eager to be off.

"It's a miracle what a bite of cheese Danish does for his disposition," Vlad drily commented.

"Same thing a good gin martini does for mine," Sandra laughed.

VLAD PARKED THE CAR on the street leading to the cul-de-sac, out of sight from the Fredricks' house. He hoped he had parked far enough away that none of his yoga classmates would notice his car if they lingered after class. He remembered to put a few dog treats in a plastic sandwich bag and stuffed it in his pocket. The promise of a cheese Danish might work for Sandra, but he needed something more immediate and tangible to ensure Gaston's cooperation.

Even at seven o'clock in the evening, it was still warm and humid. Some gathering dark clouds in the west threatened rain later that evening. Vlad hoped it was just heat lightning he saw in the distance. As they turned the corner onto Larkspur Lane, he noticed Earl's house was dark. No sign of life anywhere, just a sad-looking monument to Alexandria's extravagance. Fortunately, the Fredricks' house was well-lighted. No cars parked on the street meant no yoga classes or meditation classes for Sid. No prying eyes or suspicious neighbors.

Gaston sniffed happily at the flowers and bushes, lifting a leg occasionally to leave his calling card. Vlad decided to walk past the empty house first, trying to come up with some excuse to interrogate Sid. *I could ask him about his meditation classes. And somehow divert the conversation to Alexandria? That might be a stretch.*

Since no one was home at the Adams' residence, Vlad led Gaston to the backyard and the long white privacy fence separating the two properties. The poodle relieved himself near a giant blue hydrangea. How could such a small dog produce such a copious amount of feces? In his haste to leave Sandra's apartment, Vlad had forgotten to bring the plastic poop bags. Evidence of the dog's presence lay glaringly in front of the shrub so he kicked some mulch over the offending poop and hoped the rain would clear away all traces. Probably good fertilizer, in any case.

The fence had a gate on the side. Vlad stealthily lifted the latch and entered the Fredricks' yard. He crept from shrub to shrub, slowly drawing nearer to the house. A patio door faced the backyard. Shar and Sid sat at a dining table in clear view from where he and Gaston stood. Deep in a serious conversation, neither looked very happy with the topic. Sid was gesturing wildly with his fork while Shar looked driven to tears. Suddenly, Sid slammed the fork down and leapt up, grabbing her shoulder and giving it a shake.

She batted away his hand and shouted loud enough for Vlad to hear. "I never asked for your help!"

Since Sid was turned with his back to them, Vlad couldn't hear his response. He and Gaston had to sneak closer so he could catch what Sid was saying. Carefully, he crept up the stairs to the deck. A wooden bench surrounded the entire perimeter of the deck with its typical assortment of patio table, chairs, and a grill. A large wooden potting bench stood along the side of the house near the door. Vlad could see bags of potting soil and empty flowerpots on a shelf underneath a metal work surface. Garden tools hung from hooks on the side of a hutch-like top while small pots filled with blooming flowers lined the top shelf. A perfect place for hiding.

He picked up Gaston and whispered in his ear, "Not a sound, boy. We have to be quiet."

He held him tightly so there'd be no chance of his escaping. The little dog seemed to understand and snuggled silently, all the while watching the humans in the house with sharp eyes.

Shar wept into her hands. "I couldn't stand it anymore. I had to do something. It wasn't right."

"But why that? I don't understand. You waited fifteen years. Look at me." Sid grabbed her chin in his hands and made her face him. "Why now?"

She muttered so lowly Vlad could hardly hear. "The letter—"

Sid brought his face closer to hers and said in a softer voice. "What letter? I don't know what you're talking about?"

"I got a letter from…" Shar's voice dropped to a whisper.

Vlad couldn't hear so he moved a bit closer. Gaston leaned forward to listen better, too.

Sid dropped down to his knees and gently stroked her hair as she sobbed. "It came right before the anniversary. Every year I think it will get better, but it never does. Then when…"

Crash! Vlad didn't see the watering can next to the bench and kicked it over. Water seeped onto the deck and into his shoes. Gaston wriggled free from his grasp and ran over to the door, scratching at it with his front paws, barking all the while. The deck was instantly flooded with bright light from a motion detector

"What the hell was that?" Sid dashed over to the patio door and flung it open.

He glared at the barking dog. Vlad stood exposed in the blinding spotlight, holding up his empty hands.

Shar moved next to her husband and surveyed the scene with a puzzled expression. "Vlad, what on earth are you doing on our deck?"

"I was just taking my neighbor's dog for a walk. She just lives a few blocks away. I was admiring your beautiful roses in the front yard when suddenly Gaston must have seen a squirrel or something. He tore loose from my grasp and went running to your backyard. Somehow he ended up on your deck."

"That's a huge coincidence! You just happen to be walking past my house and your dog just happens to see a squirrel in the dark. You know what I think?"

Vlad swallowed hard. *The gig's up,* he thought. *He suspects I'm onto him for Alexandria's murder.* He spoke in a shaky voice. "What do you think?"

Sid quivered with anger. "I don't for one second believe that chasing a squirrel bullshit. I think you're stalking my wife. Don't think I haven't noticed how you're always finding excuses to stay after class. Always asking her questions. Trying to see if she's lonely." He made his voice sound high-pitched and ingratiating. 'Was Alexandria hard to get along with as a neighbor? Did she invite you to join the Garden Club? What about your kids? Did they get along? How did she react to them dating?' I'm onto you, asshole. Get off my property. Leave my wife alone. Take your mangy mutt with you."

Shar touched his arm and quietly said, "I don't think that's why Vlad is here. It's not like that."

But Sid shook off her hand and balled his hands into fists, looking like he was ready to pound through the door and punch Vlad. Suddenly, her eyes grew wide, and her mouth dropped open. She stared at Vlad with growing suspicion. She bit down on her forefinger and remained silent.

"I'm very sorry if I caused you any harm. The dog is ill-behaved and got away on me. I understand your feelings. Of course, I'll go. Shar, I wasn't stalking you. Please believe me."

"Don't come back. No more yoga classes for you, jerk!" Sid glowered fiercely.

Shar no longer protested Vlad's innocence, just continued to watch him retreat from the deck.

Chapter Twenty

Kaitlyn squealed with delight when Gaston hopped out of the car. His happy yip matched hers in intensity as he scampered around her. She dropped to her knees and flung open her arms so he could jump on her shoulders, giving her a big doggy kiss. Giggling, she turned her face to the side, clearly an invitation to keep on licking.

"Probably checking out the peanut butter and jelly toast she had for breakfast," Maria commented as she stepped outside. She watched as Kaitlyn disappeared in the garage and came out with an old tennis ball, which she proceeded to throw to Gaston. "Nicholas is in back, digging in the garden for worms. Erin helped him get down the fishing poles and tackle box. I found an empty five-gallon pail, if you catch any keepers."

Nicholas rounded the corner of the house, carrying a margarine tub. He opened the lid to show Vlad, "Look, Dad. I got at least twenty worms. Is that enough?"

"That should be plenty. I'll load up the gear so we can go." Vlad picked up the two poles leaning against the garage and the worn wicker tackle box.

"I'm serving notice, I don't clean fish," Maria continued in her disapproving tone. "Kaitlyn only eats hot dogs and chicken nuggets so fresh fish is wasted on her. Erin only likes salmon so you may as well keep whatever you catch at your place."

"We'll most likely only catch carp, but we may get lucky and catch some wall-eye that's the right size." Vlad tousled Nicholas's hair. "Ready, buddy?"

"Ready, Dad."

"Let's go, Kaitlyn. You can bring the tennis ball along. You and Gaston can play on the grass by the picnic area."

He fastened her in her car seat as Nicholas slid in the front passenger side. Kaitlyn chattered happily to Gaston, who positioned himself at her side in the back.

"Maybe we'll see some fairies today. I think it's a good day for fairies to be out. They like to ride on their pet dragonflies. I bet they will have a dragonfly race."

"There's no such thing as fairies," Nicholas scoffed.

"There is to. Mom read me a book about them. And I saw *Tinker Bell* shows on Disney," she argued. "You just have to believe. And I know where to look."

The argument continued all the way to Tripoli Island.

Vlad only weighed in once. "Kaitlyn has a great imagination. If she wants to see a fairy riding a dragonfly, just let her. When you were her age, you pretended your stuffed penguin had superpowers and could beat up bad guys."

"Yeah, but I knew Waddles wasn't really magic. I was just making stuff up," Nicholas scoffed.

"Please grant your little sister the same grace. End of discussion."

Vlad parked the car near the bridge to Tripoli Island, a historic two-span bridge with tubular iron arcs and wooden planks once used by horses and wagons to carry revelers to summer picnics and concerts on the island in the 1890s. The island had been ignored by the city council and the undergrowth allowed to run wild until about twenty years ago when the Izaak Walton League designated it a Wilderness Park and laid out hiking trails. Adventurous teens ignored the bridge and climbed the retaining wall near the dam to explore the island. Vlad left the exploring to them; the mosquito infested trails were unpleasant at best. However, fishing near the bridge often yielded worthwhile results. He hoped Nicholas would catch at least a few carp.

At the shoreline Vlad showed Nicholas how to get the worm on the hook and cast off. He got the second pole ready for Kaitlyn.

"E-ew. That's disgusting!" she said as she looked at the worm wriggling on the hook. "I'd rather play with Gaston." Then she grabbed the dog's leash, leading him to a copse of linden trees. There she accumulated a pile of sticks.

Not wanting to waste the baited hook, Vlad cast off and joined Nicholas on the bank.

"How was the new book?"

"Really good, but I'm only about halfway done. There are these twins, Sophie and Josh, who get mixed up in a battle of magic. Josh works in a bookstore, and this evil magician steals an ancient book of magic from Josh's hands, but he manages to hang onto two pages." Nicholas's face shown with animation as he recounted the story. "The bookstore owner is an alchemist and immortal and—"

A splash from the bridge nearby interrupted the conversation. Vlad turned quickly to see Kaitlyn standing near the bridge railing.

"What do you think you're doing, young lady?" he yelled as she ran across the bridge to the opposite side, Gaston yapping at her heels.

"I threw in two sticks. The fairies are riding the sticks. They're having a race in the water to see which stick is the fastest. I'm watching to see which one comes out from under the bridge first." She leaned over one end of the arc. "See. Here they come."

"You dummy," Nicholas shouted. "You're going to scare all the fish away if you keep throwing stuff in the water."

Vlad commanded, "I don't want you playing on the bridge. Get back on the grass right this minute. Play fetch with Gaston, and practice some of his tricks."

Kaitlyn trudged back to the tree area and picked up a stick, giving it a feeble toss near the water, saying, "Fetch, Gaston!"

"Throw the stick away from the river, please," Vlad said. "You don't want Gaston to fall in the water, do you?"

Gaston picked up the stick and trotted back to the little girl. "Good boy, Gaston." She started playing tug of war with the stick. "Let go. You're getting the stick all slobbery."

"Why don't you and Gaston find some pretty rocks? We can start a fairy garden in Auntie Sandra's flower planter when we get to my place," Vlad suggested.

Soon she was stacking up stones under the trees instead.

Nicholas saw the bobber disappear and immediately felt a slight tug on his line. "I got something!"

"Reel it in. You don't want it to get away, son."

Nicholas wound the reel methodically, trying to hold back his excitement. When he finally pulled in the line, a small fish dangled at the end.

"Oh, darn. It's too small," he said, disappointment clouding his face.

Vlad quickly took the hook out of the fish's mouth as it wriggled on the riverbank. Before he could toss it back in the water, Gaston emitted a low growl.

"Don't get upset, Gaston," Nicholas said. "It's only a fish."

Vlad threw it back into the river. Nicholas watched dejectedly as it swam away. Gaston continued growling, seemingly at an invisible fish.

"Better luck next time." Vlad patted his shoulder.

"There's a monster on the island!" Kaitlyn shrieked. "See him there in the bushes. A monster like Bigfoot." She pointed to the shadowy undergrowth.

"I don't see anything." Vlad shaded his eyes and surveyed the island. "The shadows are playing tricks on you."

"No, I saw it! A monster all black with glowing eyes and sharp teeth." She stared fearfully at the thick brush. "See! The bushes are moving!"

"Stop making stuff up. You're being a pest," Nicholas said scornfully. "I knew we shouldn't have brought you along."

"It's probably just a breeze blowing through the shrubs," Vlad added.

"Gaston saw it, too. That's why he's growling." Kaitlyn stamped her foot.

The little poodle growled even louder and began tugging on his leash.

"The monster was watching us," she insisted, her voice growing shriller. "Gaston wants to chase it away."

"Stop yelling. You're getting the pooch all worked up," Vlad frowned at her.

Suddenly, Gaston produced loud, frenzied barking. Pulling the leash out of Kaitlyn's hand, he dashed over the bridge and disappeared into the woods.

"Gaston, come back. The monster will eat you."

Kaitlyn sprinted after him, but Vlad grabbed her shoulder and stopped her from going any further.

"You stay here with Nick. I'll go after him." He firmly gripped the struggling child.

"No. I want to catch the monster." She strained to follow the dog.

"All you'll catch is a bunch of bug bites. If I brought you home full of ticks, your mother wouldn't be happy."

At the mention of her mother, Kaitlyn finally stopped.

Vlad turned to Nicholas. "Please watch her while I get the blasted dog."

"Here, you can use my fishing pole. Maybe you'll catch a bigger fish with mine." Nicholas cast the line and handed her his pole.

Kaitlyn began singing, "One, two, three, four, five, I caught a little fish alive. Six, seven, eight, nine, ten. Then I threw it back again."

Nicholas joined in with the next line," Why did you let it go?"

She sang her answer. "Because it bit my finger so."

Vlad silently thanked Nick for humoring his little sister as he left her singing happily on the riverbank.

Cursing under his breath, Vlad departed from the brilliant sunshine of the bridge and entered the tangled vegetation of the wilderness park with the scent of rotting wood and moldy leaves. Soon the main trail split into two paths, each one leading into gloomy darkness. He paused to consider in which direction the wayward poodle would go when he heard a sharp bark on the trail to the right.

"Gaston, you're in big trouble when I catch up with you, you damned nuisance!" Vlad shook his fist, wishing he was shaking the disobedient pooch instead.

Mosquitos started hovering around him like he was the last bargain picture book at a teachers' conference, and he slapped at the ones on his face and neck. As he strode deeper into the woods, small branches struck him in the face. Sweat started to sting his eyes. He glanced in alarm at a small dot that latched onto his bare leg. Was it a tick? He frantically brushed it off. He stumbled on a root and caught himself before he stumbled over another and fell headfirst into a patch of some plant with three leaves.

When he heard the roar of rushing water, he knew he was nearing the old dam. *Where the hell is that dog?*

A twig snapped behind him. He turned abruptly but all he saw was tangled shrubbery. Gaston's barking seemed close at hand so he pressed forward, the din of the plunging water drowning out the buzz of the mosquitoes. More rotting fallen trees covered with moss, but no dog.

Another crack of branches breaking. He pivoted, and this time caught a glimpse of a black glove wielding a thick tree branch. A hooded figure flashed into view. *Who's crazy enough to wear that get-up in this heat?* Vlad thought.

A menacing voice snarled, "Stop sticking your nose where it doesn't belong."

Then he felt an immense pain on the side of his skull and an explosion of shooting stars. Everything went black.

When he regained consciousness, Gaston was whining and licking his face. He tried to sit up but a wave of pain washed over him. He felt as if he was going to throw up so he lay back down. His head throbbed like an anvil had been dropped on it. Even the slightest movement caused excruciating pain.

He managed to utter, "Gaston, get help. Go, boy,"

The dog scooted away, hopefully, to channel Lassie and to not chase some damn squirrel. He gingerly reached to explore the source of the overwhelming pain. He felt a huge lump and something wet and sticky. The broken limb of a tree lay next to him. *What the hell happened? Who would attack me while I'm with the kids? My God! The kids! I hope they aren't in danger!*

Once again, he struggled to sit up but the crushing pain struck with such violent force it caused a tsunami of nausea. He vomited in the nearby vegetation and flopped back down. Closing his eyes, he hoped for the blessed darkness to flood over him again.

Soon he heard Gaston yipping. Footsteps were approaching.

"Dad! Dad! Are you all right? What happened to you? Your head is bleeding!" Nicholas cried.

"Daddy, did the monster get you?" Kaitlyn whimpered.

Vlad opened his eyes to a blur of color. When everything finally came into focus, he saw his children standing safely before him. A wave of relief swept over him. They were safe and unharmed. Gaston was licking his face again in between little yips. Kaitlyn stuck her thumb in her mouth, something she hadn't done in a long while. Her eyes, wide with fear, filled with tears.

"I'll be okay. Just had a little accident," he moaned. He rolled to his side. 'Nicky, please get the phone out of my back pocket and call 911. Tell them there's been an accident on Tripoli Island. I don't think I can walk out of here"

Nicholas's face drained to white as he knelt beside Vlad and gingerly reached into his back pocket.

"I'm scared, Daddy.' Kaitlyn shivered. "What if the monster comes back for you?"

Vlad's mouth seemed filled with cotton, and his tongue had a mind of its own. He hoped his words made sense. "No monster. Not coming back. Gaston'll protect me." He gave the dog a weak pat on his head. "Take Kaitlyn. Go wait on the bridge for the EMTs. Don't come back in here."

The effort exhausted him. He lay still and let the pain erase all thoughts.

Nicholas dialed 911 and talked to the dispatcher, "My dad's been hurt real bad. We're on Tripoli Island. Please hurry. He's bleeding."

When he finished the call, he protested, "I won't leave you alone. We're staying here. You can't make me go."

Nick's words broke through the pain. Vlad managed to lift his head once more. "Don't argue. Go. Show the EMTs where I am."

As his head dropped back down, he added, "And tell them to send the police."

Chapter Twenty-One

Gaston crouched down beside him as they waited for the EMTs. The little dog appeared ready to spring into action at the slightest provocation. Vlad listened intently for the scrunch of footsteps on the leafy path, fearing that Kaitlyn's "monster" would come back to finish him off. All he heard was the chirping of birds and a buzz of mosquitoes as they swarmed down to feast on his inert body. Lifting his hand to swat at them required more energy than he could muster so he just gave up and accepted his exposed flesh would look like he came down with chicken pox. Gaston whimpered once and shoved his head under Vlad's hand for reassurance.

"Good boy," Vlad muttered, then stroked his curly head.

He had no idea how much time had passed when a siren shrieked faintly in the distance. Shortly after, he heard Nicholas say "My dad is over here. Hurry. He's bleeding bad from his head." The rustling of branches and the sound of feet tramping through the woods accompanied the murmur of voices. Gaston sat up, yipped in greeting but stayed by his side.

"Kaitlyn, get back here," Nicholas yelled to the smack of flip-flops on the dirt pattering down the trail.

More swishing of boughs. A tiny hand tugged on his arm.

"Daddy! Daddy! We're back."

Vlad's eyes fluttered open. His little daughter knelt beside him, crying and clinging to his hand. Gaston thrust his face next to her and began licking her salty tears. She hugged the little dog, weeping into his fur.

Her father struggled to form the words, "Don't cry, Sweet Pea."

Nicholas and two burley EMTs closely followed behind, one

carrying an orange folding stretcher. He made quick work of unfolding it while his companion dropped beside Vlad and dug first aid materials out of a bag.

After checking the wound on Vlad's head, the EMT asked, "Can you tell me your name, sir?"

"Vlad Chomsky."

"Do you know where you are? What is your date of birth? What day of the week is it? Who is the president?"

As Vlad answered his questions, the EMT applied a pad of gauze to stem the bleeding. Satisfied with Vlad's answers, he explained, "I'm putting some direct pressure on your wound. We'll get you to the emergency room in a flash."

"Will my dad be all right?" Nicholas whimpered as he stood in the leaves, fearfully watching the ministrations of the EMT.

"Don't worry, son. There's always a lot of blood loss in a head wound like this. The doctor will run some tests, and then we'll know more soon," the EMT answered as he fitted some kind of foam-filled device around his father's neck.

"Sir, I'm fitting you with a C-collar to hold your head and neck in place when we lift you."

Vlad felt the EMT fasten some loops on the stiff collar so he couldn't move his head. Then four hands firmly lifted him onto the stretcher. The men carefully picked it up and carried him along the wooded path. Even though their movements were smooth, he still felt the nausea returning and fought down the bile. Each movement of the stretcher intensified the pain until his head pulsated like the worst migraine in the world.

"I'm okay, kids. Don't worry." Vlad made himself speak loud enough for his children to hear.

"You got the dog, kid?" an EMT called over his shoulder.

"Yeah, and I got my little sister, too."

Kaitlyn allowed her brother to take her hand and lead her on the trail. Her crying subsided to a snuffling noise as Gaston trotted along beside her.

"Good work, son," the EMT said. "Hang tight, sir."

"Call my ex. Number's in my cell," Vlad managed to mutter. "The kids can't stay here alone."

"Your son already took care of it. Called the police, too. Quite a kid, really on the ball."

Vlad closed his eyes and gritted his teeth as they moved down the trail so fast the mosquitoes gave up and left. Soon he felt the bright sunshine on his face. Footsteps clomped on the wooden bridge. He heard the motor of the ambulance before he opened his eyes to the flashing lights. Another siren blared from a police car, sending stabbing pains into his skull. He forced back a scream, determined to hold it together. He didn't want the kids traumatized any more than they already were.

As the EMTs whisked him into the ambulance, Vlad caught a glimpse of Officer Roberts emerging from the car.

The policeman asked the men, "What happened here? Why did you call the police?"

Nicholas piped up before they could respond. "My dad got hurt chasing the dog."

Kaitlyn interrupted, "There was a monster in the woods. I saw it. Gaston went after it."

"Quiet, Kaitlyn. We didn't see what happened. We found my dad bleeding." The boy voice quivered. "He told me to call you."

As he was closing the door, the EMT responded to the policeman, "This man was attacked in the wood, by an unknown assailant. There's a branch covered in blood on one of the trails. The boy can show you where. You'll have to save any further questioning for the hospital."

Then Vlad gave himself up to the ministrations of the EMTs. First, they applied a cold pack to his head; he was grateful for the little relief it provided. One checked his respiratory rate, pulse, and blood pressure, efficiently moving from instrument to instrument, while the other recorded his vital signs.

"He's breathing on his own, another good sign."

The first man then asked, "Can you move your fingers?"

The pain overrode coherent thinking. His fingers looked far away. He willed them to move. The song fragment *Ground control to Major Tom* popped into his head. *I'm in control. Move, fingers.* Much to his satisfaction and the EMTs', he waggled his fingers.

A few minutes later Vlad was wheeled into the ER. He handed over his wallet with his insurance information to the intake clerk. Answering questions made him feel like a cartoon character, his head expanding like a balloon with every "responsible party" query until it felt ready to pop. Finally, the EMTs rolled him into an examination room where the antiseptic smell permeated the room.

The ER nurse checked his vital signs once again, then drew a curtain around him, promising, "Doctor Sullivan will be in soon."

How long did he lay there, listening to the pounding of blood in his head and the ambient noise of footsteps hustling about in the corridor? Ten minutes? An hour? He couldn't tell. The footsteps grew louder. When he opened his eyes, the emergency room doctor and his nurse had entered. The doctor examined him more thoroughly, checking other parts of his body besides his head.

Next, the doctor shone a light in his eyes, then asked him to track the movement of his finger. "Pupils respond to light. Eye movement appears normal."

The nurse entered his comments onto a laptop.

"You're going to need a few stitches for that head wound."

He also repeated the simple questioning of his name, birth date, day of the week, and current president. Then he asked Vlad to move his fingers, raise his arm, flex his foot.

"You appear to have good motor function. Now can you tell me how the injury occurred?"

"I was attacked on Tripoli Island. I couldn't see who it was. The attacker wore a hoodie, which hid his face." Vlad shuddered at the memory of the distorted voice threatening him.

"Do you know what you were hit with?"

"I saw a huge tree limb before I literally saw stars."

"John said you must have vomited. Do you still feel nauseous?"

Vlad observed the concern on the doctor's face. "No. Maybe a little queasy."

"On a scale of one to ten, with ten being the worst, how would you rate your pain?"

"Definitely a ten. My head hurts like hell."

Did you lose consciousness?"

"I must have blacked out for a few minutes. I woke up when the dog licked my face."

"Just to be on the safe side. I'm going to order a CT scan. You seem pretty alert but I want to rule out a fracture and a brain bleed."

Next, Vlad was transported to radiology where the nurse helped him undress and put on a hospital gown. The last woman to perform these tasks was his mother. She then wheeled him into a sterile-looking room, brightly lit. A huge white doughnut-shaped machine dominated the room. He saw a computer screen hovering over it while a young female radiology tech warmly greeted him.

"Hello, Dr. Chomsky. I'm going to do a CT scan of your head today. Some patients suffer from claustrophobia in the scanner. We find music helps people remain calm. Do you have a preference—Jazz, Classical, Country, Pop Rock?"

"Classical, please," Vlad muttered.

He lay perfectly still on a motorized table while his head, positioned on a metal brace, was stuck into the machine. His eyes remained closed as the music provided a counterpoint to the throbbing in his head. The radiographer talked him through the procedure on the intercom. What would the images of his skull and brain on the computer screen reveal?

He struggled back into his clothes in the changing room, the nurse taking extra care when he pulled his t-shirt back on. Every movement took such great effort. Was his shirt wet from blood or perspiration? The ER nurse walked him back to the room where the doctor was waiting.

"You're a very lucky man. No fractures, no evidence of brain bleeding. Now I will suture the wound." He began cleaning the wound as the ER nurse brought him the necessary tools for stitching his wound.

"You'll need to be closely monitored at home for any evidence of a concussion. Or any worsening symptoms, like slurring of speech, more vomiting, dizziness, or loss of balance. Is there someone living with you who can keep a close watch on you?"

"I have a fiancée, Beatrice Krup. She'll stay with me."

"Can you call her to come and get you? I'll release you to her care. Can you get Dr. Chomsky a phone, please?"

She picked up on the first ring.

"Beatrice?" His tongue still felt thick and his brain fuzzy.

"My God, Vlad, are you all right? Nicholas told me what happened. I'm pulling into the emergency room parking lot right now." Her voice was tinged with fear.

"Will you be able to take me home? And stay with me? My condition needs to be closely monitored for the next twenty-four hours."

"I'll be right there."

She abruptly hung up, and Vlad handed the phone back to the nurse.

Just then a raspy voice growled from the outside the door. "Not so fast." An overweight bear of a man in a rumpled suit stepped into the room and announced,

"I'm Detective Johnson from the Crawford police. I have a few questions for this man."

Chapter Twenty-Two

The ER doctor faced off against the detective. "This patient has suffered a traumatic head injury. He's in no shape for lengthy interrogation. Please keep it brief. You can question him more thoroughly at another time."

"I have officers gathering evidence at the scene. Our police force is not large enough to tie up half the force finding forensic evidence when the victim can possibly shed some light on his attacker."

The intensity of Detective Johnson's stare made the doctor glance down at his chart and clear his throat.

"Ahem! I have a broken arm in the next room. I need to check on that patient's X-rays so I'll leave you to it. Don't take too long."

With that, he strode out of the room. Detective Johnson settled in an armchair in the corner and pulled out some paperwork

"Dr. Chomsky, your son, Nicholas, informed Officer Roberts you'd been fishing near the Tripoli Bridge when your daughter claimed she saw someone watching you. She called it a monster."

Vlad struggled to speak, "We-we didn't believe her. Thought she made it up. Likes to pretend."

"But the dog grew agitated. He growled at whatever was in the bushes. Then he started barking very loudly." The detective raised a quizzical eyebrow.

"Gaston often growls at the slightest disturbance," he said. "I-I didn't think much of it at first."

"Then he ran into the woods, and you followed him?"

"Yes. I didn't want the kids to go on the island. Lots of mosquitoes and ticks. Easy to take a wrong path and get lost."

"Your son waited for some time with his little sister. He grew worried when you didn't return right away with the dog. Then the dog returned by himself and led the kids to where you lay. It was obvious to them that you'd been attacked. Do you remember how it happened?" Detective Johnson waited, pen poised to write.

Before Vlad could shape the scattered thoughts in his head into a cohesive answer, Beatrice burst in.

"My God, Vlad. What happened?" She catapulted to his bedside, seizing his hand, and clutching it to her chest. "My darling, I was so worried when Nicky called. I can't believe you were attacked. Are you all right?"

"Miss Krup, so we meet again," Detective Johnson said with the kind of smile Lex Luthor might have just before he zaps Superman with Kryptonite.

She turned away from Vlad to see her interrogator sitting in the corner.

"Detective Johnson, what…what are you doing here?" Beatrice gasped.

"I'm investigating the attack on Dr. Chomsky. He was about to tell me what he remembers."

Vlad squeezed her hand, then dropped his arm back on the bed. "It's okay. The officer is just doing his job." He gazed at the detective. "I heard Gaston barking near the dam. I remember hearing the loud roar of the water. I thought I heard someone behind me, but when I looked, no one was there. Then I heard someone right next to me. Out of nowhere, in the bushes. I saw a gloved hand. He had a tree limb. Like a club. He hit me with it." The long speech cost him, he knew. Pain clouds were gathering.

"Did you see his face?"

"No. He had a mask, a hoodie pulled over his hair."

"How tall was he?"

"I couldn't tell. It happened so fast. Maybe my size."

"Body type?"

"Maybe average. Not overweight, for sure. But with the hoodie? It's all a blur." Vlad's voice was barely audible.

"Anything else?"

Vlad remembered the gravelly voice threatening him. He hesitated, "No. Not really. He mumbled something, like stay away."

The detective stood up and handed Beatrice his card. "I overheard the doctor say you'll be taking him home. Here's my card."

He stepped closer to Vlad. "If you remember anything else, call me immediately. There's a killer on the loose in this town."

"What about a killer?" Maria suddenly appeared in the doorway with Nicholas at her side. "Now what mess has that crazy old lady and her even crazier handyman gotten you into?"

Nicholas ran to Vlad's side and hugged him. "Dad, are you okay? I did what you told me to do." Worry lines were etched on his young face.

"I'm fine, son. You did great—a real hero." Vlad patted his son's head.

"He made me bring him to the hospital as soon as we got back to the house. Insisted you needed your cell phone. That's how worried he was about his father," Maria said to the detective. "I had to leave my little girl and that awful dog with my teenage daughter and rush up here. I'm his ex-wife, by the way, Maria Chomsky."

"I'm Sergeant Johnson, doing follow-up on today's attack."

"Attack! Then it wasn't an accident?" Maria's voice grew shrill.

"I'M AFRAID NOT. All the evidence points to a premeditated attack on Dr. Chomsky." The detective waved the papers he was holding for emphasis.

She took a step closer to Vlad. "Ever since you moved in with that screwy landlady and her lunatic handyman, you've been involved in all kinds of crazy activities. You think you're detectives and that bad-tempered mutt is some kind of super sleuth dog. You're all totally delusional."

"He's not a mutt," Nicholas sputtered. "He's a-a-a...."

"Highly trained show dog." Beatrice finished his sentence.

"Highly trained? Don't make me laugh. The little beast bit me when I tried to get him into my car. Someone needs to get him before bedtime or I'm taking him to the pound. I won't have him in my house for the night. He's a walking tick bomb!"

"Wait a minute!" Detective Johnson held up his hand. "What's this about a dog sleuth?"

"Isn't it the craziest thing you've ever heard? The old lady has them all thinking her dog is some kind of crime solving genius. Just because he got underfoot, tripped a few criminals, and earned some reward money."

The policeman stood up and glared at Vlad and Beatrice. "You mean to tell me you've been playing detective all this time? Dr, Chomsky, you of all people should know better than to interfere in a criminal investigation. A university professor, no less. And Miss Krup, you're a head librarian. Look how dangerous it is!"

"Dangerous? And the kids were exposed to this danger?" Maria joined him in the death stare. "I can't believe you're so irresponsible."

"Stop playacting at *Magnum P.I.*," the detective commanded. "I repeat, there's a killer on the loose in Crawford. Leave the investigation to the police. If you go around stirring up trouble, someone is bound to get hurt. Stay away from pretend crime solving. Do I need to recommend to the D.A. that you be charged with obstruction?"

Vlad looked up and met the man's eyes. "No." His head felt like it exploded. He lay back into the pillow and bit down on the inside of his mouth, determined not to let out a groan. He just had to close his eyes and endure the torrents of pain.

"That's enough!" Beatrice cried. "Can't you see he's in no condition for all this drama?" Her scowl, fierce as any Mama Bear's, caused the detective to look away. "I have your card, Detective Johnson. He'll contact you when he's better able to help with the investigation."

As the detective put the papers back into his briefcase, Beatrice shifted to Maria. "I'll pick up Gaston once I get Vlad settled at home. And Nicholas, don't worry. I'll take good care of your dad." She patted his shoulder reassuringly.

The ER doctor entered the room. "You all need to leave except for Miss Krup. I'll give you the instructions for home care. My patient has had enough excitement for today. Now he needs rest so his brain can heal. I'm sure any further questioning can wait for a few days."

Chapter Twenty-Three

Beatrice assisted Vlad to her bed, inviting him to lean on her as they slowly made their way through the house. He looked gray and shaken, dark bruising had already appeared under the bandaged wound. His wan smile, meant to be encouraging, filled her stomach with a cold dread. She stripped off his bloody shirt and shorts, leaving him swaying unsteadily in his boxers as she threw back the covers. He collapsed onto the bed.

After she adjusted the bedding around him, he managed a weak "Thank you."

"Would you like some Tylenol?' she asked. "The doctor said you could have some for pain."

"Yes, please. Maybe a cold compress, too."

His eyes fluttered shut, and he lay quietly while she dashed to the bathroom and got some pain relievers and a glass of water. Then on to the kitchen where she filled the ice pack for a cold compress, as the fact sheet from the ER recommended. Her hands trembled a bit as she scooped ice cubes from the container in the freezer, then added a little water to the pack. She made sure the lid was screwed on tight with no leaks, then found a soft hand towel from the bathroom to place under it.

Back in the bedroom, she applied the compress to his head, then pulled down the shades. The bright afternoon sunlight made a mockery of the day's dark events. The yellow coreopsis with their towheads bobbling in the breeze promised happier times, along with the tall pink phlox and the baby blue delphiniums. Beatrice wished she could step back into the early morning when Vlad had brought her coffee. She should have made him stay longer, drunk their coffee together on the patio, and enjoyed the flowers and each other while the moment lasted. Now the ominous signs the doctor warned her to watch out for—seizures, inability to wake up, saying things that don't make sense, vomiting, bleeding form the ear or nose—filled her with foreboding.

After setting her cell phone timer for four hours, her reminder to wake Vlad to check for a concussion, Beatrice dialed Sandra. "I have bad news. Vlad's been hurt. He was attacked on Tripoli Island."

"What? How bad is he?" Her voice cracked with alarm.

"Someone hit him on the head with a heavy branch. He needed stitches. They did a CT scan—no skull fracture or bleeding in the brain. The diagnosis is mild brain trauma but I have to monitor him for the next twenty-four to forty-eight hours to make sure there's no serious complications. I just put him to bed." After the long speech Beatrice's strength began to fade.

"Do you need some help? I'll have Norm drive me over."

"No, thank you. He's exhausted from the long wait in the emergency room. So am I," she said as she sank into the nearest chair.

"You poor dear," Sandra clucked

"Then the detective who interviewed me showed up and asked him a bunch of questions. Worse yet, Maria barged in with Nicholas and accused him of being irresponsible. What he needs most is twenty-four hours of complete rest."

"Where's Gaston?"

"Maria has him at the house. Could you and Norm please pick him up?" A hint of despair crept into the conversation. "She's threatening to take him to the dog pound."

"What a nasty woman!' Sandra exclaimed. "Of course we'll pick him up, dearie. Can we stop for some fast food and bring it over for you? We promise just to drop it off. We won't stay more than a minute."

"I'm not even hungry. I have some chicken soup in the freezer. I'll take that out for Vlad when he can eat. He's really not supposed to eat or drink for the first six hours and then just small amounts. Like saltine crackers and applesauce." She closed her eyes for a second before continuing. "If Vlad's strong enough, we'll need to regroup and talk. The detective made it very clear: Any amateur attempts at investigating Alexandria's death are forbidden. He seems to think it's all connected. He warned Vlad to back off. There's a murderer in town."

"I can understand why he'd feel that way—IF we were amateurs. But we're not. Gaston has proven himself to be a brilliant dog detective time and again. We must be getting close to solving the crime if someone is trying to stop us." She almost cackled with delight.

Beatrice imagined her rubbing her hands together and beaming with enthusiasm.

"Please don't do anything rash until we talk. I'll call you and Norm tomorrow." With that admonition, she hung up

Supper was a lonely, solitary sandwich and half a banana. Beatrice peeked in at Vlad several times throughout the evening. He barely stirred from the position on his back, the compress draped over his forehead. She crept close to him, brushed her lips gently across his cheek, and whispered, "You darling, precious man. I love you so much." She even dropped to her knees at the side of the bed and did something she hadn't done in a very long time.

"Heavenly Father, I know you haven't heard from me for a while. I'm a little out of practice. But your Son did say to ask. So I now ask that you spare this loving father and devoted man from further injury. I got him into this mess. He was trying to keep me from harm when evil befell him. Please lift him up and keep him safe in your hands. Give me the strength to handle whatever evil that comes our way. Thank you for protecting me thus far and bringing Vlad into my life." She rested her head at Vlad's side in silence.

When she rose to her feet, she felt a bit lighter. The dreadful cold feeling weighing her down loosened its grip on her heart as peace descended. Beatrice grabbed her pillow from the bed and a blanket from the closet and settled down on the couch. Rather than risk disturbing her patient, she resigned herself to watching TV. After flipping through several channels, she found some old sitcoms from the '60s and zoned out. When the infomercial came on exhorting the marvels of the Ped Egg, Beatrice wondered how she'd lived this long without this extraordinary tiny egg that substituted for a pumice stone. Clearly, she'd been missing out on sexier feet. The TV screen promised no more dead skin dropping in heaps on the bathroom floor, not with the Ped Egg's advanced microfiber technology. With smooth skin on her feet, she could glide on stiletto heels with ease. Unfortunately, Beatrice fell asleep before the tollfree number came on so she missed this opportunity of a lifetime.

The jarring alarm on her phone woke her with a start. Time to check on Vlad. Beatrice sat up and rubbed the sleep from her eyes. It was only ten-thirty. *I must have drifted off.* She stumbled down the hallway into the bedroom and turned on the overhead light.

He was still sound asleep, but the compress and towel had fallen to the floor. She gave him a gingerly shake. When he didn't respond, her breath caught in her throat, and she shook him harder. His eyes flickered open, but didn't focus right away.

Panic rose in her voice as she said sharply, "Vlad, wake up. It's me, Beatrice!"

He mumbled something indistinguishable.

"You need to wake up,' she nearly shouted in his ear.

"I'm awake," he muttered.

"What's your name?"

It took a few heart-stopping seconds before he answered, "Vlad …Vlad Chomsky."

"Where are you?"

"In bed."

"At whose house?"

"Yours, I guess, since you're standing there?'

"Who am I?"

"Beatrice."

"Who is the president?"

"Not this again," he groaned before answering correctly.

"Will this be on the final exam?" he mumbled, then closed his eyes and fell back asleep.

As relief washed over her, Beatrice made her way back to the couch. She set the timer for the next four hours and turned off the television. This time she slipped into a nighty and let a deep sleep overtake her. She dreamed she was in the campus liberal arts building, Merton Hall, looking for her English Lit. class. But she couldn't remember the room number, and all the classroom doors were locked when she tried to enter. A raggedy man with an unshaven face and long tangled hair started following her. The man drew closer and closer. She pounded on the nearest door but it wouldn't open. The creepy man reached for her, his dirty hands grabbing her blouse as she tried to squirm away. He tugged at her clothes as she was paralyzed with fright. Suddenly, the fire alarm went off. When she opened her eyes, the alarm was ringing in her living room. Beatrice sat upright with a start, panting with fear until she realized she was safe on the couch, not in a deserted hallway. It was the four-thirty a.m. wake-up call. Tossing the blanket aside, she shuffled to the kitchen for a clean glass of water, then to the medicine cabinet for more Tylenol. Bottle in hand, she went to Vlad.

A vigorous shake woke him the first time as she called his name. "I brought you some Tylenol," she said, handing him the pills. "How's your head feeling?"

He gulped them down before he spoke. "Still hurts like hell, but I think I'll live. Wasn't so sure when you brought me home."

The man patiently answered her questions: name, date of birth, where they were.

"Do you remember why I brought you here?"

"Someone attacked me. Hit me over the head."

"That's right. You were at Tripoli Island. You didn't get a good look at your attacker," she prompted.

"But he said something I didn't tell the cop," Vlad muttered.

"What was that?" She leaned closer to hear.

"He said, 'Don't stick your nose where it doesn't belong.' It may have been the killer."

Those words reawakened the mindless fear from her dream. "Dear God. What have we gotten ourselves into?"

"I can't think clearly right now. Need to sleep some more. Tomorrow. We'll think tomorrow." He couldn't stifle a small groan.

Beatrice tenderly kissed his forehead, then picked up the empty glass, turning toward the door. The chill she was feeling was not from wandering in the night air in her nighty. It was bone deep. Vlad reached out and grasped her hand, his warm clasp a morsel of comfort.

"Please don't go. Stay with me. I want to feel you next to me."

"What if I'm restless and elbow you in the night? I settled on the couch with my pillow."

"You won't disturb me, I promise. I'd feel better having you by my side."

"I'd feel better, too. Let me get my pillow and the cell phone. I'll be right back."

By the time Beatrice had collected both items, Vlad had fallen back to sleep. She hovered over him for a few minutes, watching the rise and fall of his breathing, once again thanking God he had come this far without serious aftereffects. According to the information sheet, he still could be susceptible to posttraumatic symptoms. Like Vlad said, "We'll think tomorrow." The heat of his body brought her some solace as she nestled under the covers. She stretched her hand toward him and rested it lightly on his hip. Her last thought before slumber was: *Whatever tomorrow brings, we'll face it together.*

Chapter Twenty-Four

Vlad woke to the sound of Beatrice breathing softly beside him. Judging from the light seeping in through the shades, he estimated the time was probably around seven-thirty. He'd slept around the clock. The pain in his head had diminished from the crush of an anvil to the battering of a sledgehammer. The bottle of Tylenol stood on the nightstand next to a half full glass of water. Thankfully, the cap on the pain medication was loosened so he could help himself to the next dose. The room temperature water reminded him how hungry and thirsty he was—so thirsty he gulped down the remainder in the glass. The last time he'd eaten was yesterday at breakfast. He and the kids never made it to the picnic lunch he'd planned to have after Nicholas got bored with fishing. Easing back down on the pillow, he watched his beautiful Beatrice peacefully sleeping until thoughts of food in the kitchen drove him to sit up and swing his legs over the side of the bed.

With great effort he managed to stand, tottering back and forth like a newborn foal. *Not a good idea,* he thought and flopped back on the bed. The motion woke Beatrice.

"What do you think you're doing?" she said sharply.

"I thought I'd go to the kitchen and get something to eat. I didn't want to disturb you."

"I'll get you something. You just stay there. Do you need more Tylenol?"

"I helped myself." He gestured to the open bottle and empty glass.

Beatrice flung herself out of bed and grabbed the glass. "I'll bring you more water. Do you think you could handle eating a piece of cinnamon toast and some applesauce? We'll start out with something light to see how you respond. The doctor said to go easy with eating at first."

Before she made breakfast Beatrice brought him a cold glass of water. "Would you like a fresh compress, too?" Bending down to pick up the ice pack and towel, she added, "You gave me a bit of a scare last night, but you're doing better this morning, thank God!" She kissed his cheek and swept out of the room.

Never had a simple glass of water tasted so good! The cool liquid flowed down his parched throat, reviving his spirits. He felt like he could drink a gallon without stopping to take a breath.

The aroma of cinnamon wafted into the room as Beatrice brought him a tray with two pieces of toast, a steaming cup of what he hoped was coffee, and a small plastic container of applesauce. A cold compress was tucked under her arm.

"The coffee is a little milky. I figured you'd need some caffeine but didn't want to upset your stomach. How's the toast?"

"Delicious! I'm so hungry I could wolf it down in two bites, but I'm taking it slow for you."

The cinnamon sugar mingled with the melted butter in a delicious spread. Vlad chewed slowly, savoring each morsel. The coffee temperature was most palatable, and the pain medication was doing its job.

"I feel almost human again," he said. "Human enough to need a trip to the bathroom when I'm done eating, if you'd be so kind as to help me."

Vlad was too woozy to manage the walk alone. Leaning on Beatrice, he made the mistake of looking at himself in the mirror as he walked into the bathroom. He resembled a zombie from a cheap horror movie: black and blue bruised face, yellow undertones, dark circles under his eyes. If Kaitlyn saw him, she'd think *he* was the monster. The continuous headache and the effort of walking and talking were exhausting. He knew what he wanted to tell Beatrice but when he tried to formulate a coherent sentence, the words shifted around in his head and refused to come out.

"Do you have one of those things?" he asked.

"Those things? What do you mean?" Beatrice looked confused.

"Things… for me to put on, besides this." He fingered his wristband from the hospital.

"Do you mean your watch? The ER nurse put it in a bag with your socks."

"That's it, my watch. Can you please take this off and get my watch instead? And some clothes? What happened to what I was wearing?"

"They're soaking in the laundry room. I'll call Sandra. Norm can bring you some clean clothes." Before she left with the tray, she asked, "Are you ready to get dressed?"

"I think I need a little more sleep." Her bed was so inviting while closing his eyes helped diminish the pain. Any bright light made his head throb. He needed to not think so much. He settled the compress on his head and dropped off immediately.

Vlad slept until noon. When he woke his head felt better. Just the stab of pain when he moved too quickly. Clean clothes lay at the foot of his bed. A shower would feel pretty good right now. He'd like to get rid of the bandage, get a clean one, or maybe he didn't need one at all. He called to Beatrice.

"Could you help me into the shower, Love? A shower would do me a world of good."

Entering the room, Beatrice laughed, "This is a role reversal, me helping you in the shower. Usually, I'm the one in trouble."

The warm water washed away the perspiration, the traces of soil, some of the pain of remembering lying in the weeds and dirt waiting for the EMTs. Her verbena scented soap lathered into luxurious suds. Vlad felt revived, grateful for Beatrice's tender care through the night. When he stepped out of the shower, there she stood with a soft, fluffy towel in hand. She wrapped it around him and kissed him, a lingering sweet kiss that revived him even more than the shower. He kissed her back, his gratitude spilling over into his lips, his hands, his heart.

"No strenuous activity for twenty-four hours," she teased, backing away. "You've got a few hours to go. Besides, you have visitors waiting quietly in the living room."

"The way my head feels I couldn't do much but lie flat on my back. I certainly can't move much. You'll have to do all the work."

"I'd happily take charge on top. Just say when." She caressed him gently.

"Not yet." He pushed her hand away. "I couldn't enjoy your

loveliness when my head feels like hell. What were you saying about visitors?"

"Sandra, Norm, and Gaston have been here since ten o'clock. I figured it's safer to keep them where I can keep an eye on them rather than let them go half-cocked on their own. Now let's get rid of that old bandage."

The wound was no longer bleeding. The doctor's handiwork was evident on his partially shaved head.

"There's still some seepage." Beatrice looked critically at the wound. "You should probably still keep a bandage on for a bit longer."

She cleaned the wound with an alcohol wipe and applied a clean gauze pad, gently taping it down Then she led him to the bedroom and helped him pull a clean t-shirt on carefully over the bandage.

"Thanks, Love. I can do the rest myself." Vlad pulled on his boxers and sweatpants, then sat for a minute on the bed. Norm had also brought his slippers and socks.

"I'll skip the socks for now." Vlad stood up and stepped into the slippers. "I'm ready to face the team."

"I'll heat up some chicken noodle soup. You need to eat first."

Gaston yipped when the bedroom door opened and Vlad first appeared. He leaped down from his spot on the couch and ran to Vlad, happily circling his feet.

"Good boy, Gaston. Lassie's got nothing over you when it comes to search and rescue."

The dog stood on his hind paws, front paws on Vlad's leg. Vlad reached down and patted the top of his head.

"How ya doing, Doc?" Norm said. "You gave the little lady here quite a scare."

"We were all worried about you, dearie. I'm glad you're back on your feet. You look like hell, though." Sandra rose and stepped closer to him. "You need a hug." She encircled him with her bony arms. "That's better. You're among the living now."

"He's still recovering from a nasty blow to the head. The doctor insists on rest and a day or two off work. No driving. No drinking. And certainly no vigorous activity that could reinjure the brain." Beatrice gave her a stare that brooked no arguments.

"Of course, dearie. We don't expect him to jump back in the saddle. Norm and I are going to pick up the slack." Sandra twirled the long string of glass beads she wore around her neck. "I'm heading to the casino tonight to meet up with Earl. And Norm's signed up for some meditation intro with that Sid fellow. We figure you can keep an eye on that bitch Florence at the library. All Vlad has to do is rest and recuperate."

"Besides, Doc, the way you look now you'd scare the suspects. They'd clam up for sure," Norm added.

Before Vlad could protest his cell phone rang. Beatrice picked it up from the end table and turned to Vlad.

"It's Maria. Are you well enough to speak to her? She called earlier but I told her you were sleeping."

"Maybe it's something about the kids. I'll take the call." Vlad reached for the phone. "Hello."

"So your personal bodyguard is allowing you to talk on the phone?"

"I've been sleeping until now, just like the doctor recommended. I'm feeling a little better, thanks for asking."

"I just wanted you to know I had a hell of a night, thanks to your foolish escapades."

"What do you mean?"

"Just a second." Vlad could hear Maria talking to someone else in the room." Yes, I'm on the phone with your father. He's obviously well enough to carry on a conversation with me. If you want to talk to him, I'll get you when I'm done. Now I'd like you to leave the room because this conversation is private."

She waited a few moments before she spoke again. "That was your son. He was up half the night worrying about you. He refused to talk about what happened but hung out in Erin's room until she convinced him to get a sleeping bag and camp out on her floor."

"I'm sorry to hear that. Is he better today?"

"I made him get out of the house and go to baseball practice. Yes, he's better, But that's not the worst of it." Her voice sounded ominous.

"What else happened?" Vlad dreaded to hear her answer.

"Kaitlyn was convinced the monster followed us home. She screamed her head off when that old dingbat picked up the mutt. She wanted the dog to sleep in her room to protect her. She threw a fit and hung onto his collar. The old lady said he could stay, but I had enough of the fleabag."

"Gaston loves Kaitlyn. He would've slept on the foot of her bed."

"No way! I told her she was a big girl and had her stuffies to protect her. But she insisted I check under her bed and check the closet for the monster. I had to open the lid of her toy box so she could peek inside. There was nothing there, of course, but that didn't satisfy her."

Vlad held the phone away from his ear, as her voice rose with anger.

"She kept wandering into my room, crying and whining, until I let her sleep with me. It was the only way I could calm her down."

"Did she finally fall asleep?"

Oh, yes. But I had her foot in the small of my back the whole time. She kicked like a kangaroo. And she yelled, 'Go away, monster,' in her sleep all night I barely slept a wink. I look like hell today, and I have to show a house."

"What a bummer! Kids are pretty resilient. She'll get over it. I'll talk to her, reassure her."

"That's why I've decided you need to make a choice. I'm not having the kids put in any danger again. You need to give up this ridiculous amateur detective stuff or I won't allow any unsupervised visits with the kids. I'll take you back to court if I have to. I'm sure that sharp police detective will back me up."

"You can't ask me to do that!" Vlad's horrified look brought Beatrice to her feet as she drew near to him.

"That's my ultimatum. Sleuthing or the kids. Until the police catch the killer, you can't take the kids on your own. Let me know what you decide." Maria hung up.

Vlad stared at the phone in disbelief. "She just delivered an ultimatum. Give up the investigation or give up seeing the kids."

Beatrice threw her arms around him. "Oh, dear! What a mess I've gotten you into. Of course, you can't stop seeing your kids. Nicholas and Kaitlyn, even Erin, would be heartbroken. They need their father, especially after what happened yesterday. I can't ask you to choose between them and me."

"All the more reason for us to solve this murder lickety-split. We're more than ready, right, boys?"

Sandra chortled as Gaston barked and wagged his tail and Norm flashed a thumbs-up.

"Eat your soup, dearie, so we can get this show on the road!"

Chapter Twenty-Five

"Please drop us off at the front entrance, dearie," Sandra said to Norm. "I'll call when I need a ride home. Are you sure you won't come in with us?"

She pulled down the mirror in the visor and checked her make-up. Her best Showgirl Red lipstick accentuated her slightly wrinkled but still pouty lips. Fake eyelashes held firmly in place when she blinked coquettishly. She had splurged on a hair appointment that afternoon so sexy wisps of silver hair floated above her perfectly made-up face. No denying it, Sandra Tooksbury could still stop wheelchair traffic on the way to Bingo.

"Nah! Gambling is like eating pistachios. If you get a good one, you want another good one. If you get a bad one, you want a good one even more. That's gambling in a nutshell. I got enough bad habits—I don't need to add gambling to the list."

"It's all undercover work. I've got to get Earl to crack. If he attacked Vlad, he's got to be stopped." Sandra slammed her fist on the dashboard.

"You got a vibe going with Earl. I'd wreck it if I was around. Just be careful." Norm's look showed his concern.

"Don't worry. I've got Gaston. He won't let anything happen to me, right, Lovey Puppy?"

Gaston sat up in the back seat and gave a little arf. He was back to wearing his service dog disguise—red harness and black strip with somewhat ratty lettering spelling out Service Dog. The eager look in his eyes matched the excited wag of his tail. This was no night on the town; this was canine detecting at its finest.

"I'm going to the movies but I'll keep my phone turned on. Call if you need back-up," Norm said as he reached across the seat to open her door.

The bouncer at the door cast a skeptical eye at her outfit, a glittering gold jacket embellished with sequins, red hearts and diamonds, black clubs and spades. She wore a gold lame jumpsuit underneath, hoping the new Depends underwear truly didn't show a telltale bulge. Sleuthing demanded her full attention, and she didn't want to be caught with her pants down literally while she was on this case. Sandra gave him her friendliest smile as Gaston obediently heeled at her side. The man shrugged, carelessly waving her in. She immediately scanned the room.

The kaleidoscope glass ceiling threw patches of colored light over the crowded casino floor. Sandra soon realized she was overdressed for the crowd. Most players were wearing t-shirts and shorts or jeans. Most sat mesmerized by the neon flashing lights of the slot machines, mindlessly pushing buttons. Smoking was no longer allowed anymore but the lemony cleaning products couldn't erase the ingrained stench of cigarette smoke. This modern casino differed a lot from the Las Vegas gambling joints of her youth. However, like Vegas, most gamblers swiftly lost their money.

Sandra searched in vain for a quarter slot machine, but there were only dollar signs plastered on the screens. She reluctantly pulled out a twenty and inserted it into some flashy thing called Cleopatra, featuring a green-eyed temptress in a gold headdress, reminiscent of her burlesque days. The spinning mixtures of playing card letters and numbers and symbols from Egyptian mythology made her feel a bit dizzy as they flashed by in multiple rows and columns. Her twenty quickly disappeared.

Gaston pushed his cold nose against her leg, urging her to slide off the stool and move around.

"I know. I know. We're here on business. Besides, loosing twenty dollars in a matter of a few minutes isn't much fun. I don't understand the appeal but I can understand how the money can disappear. It doesn't seem real until your wallet is empty or you get the credit card bill," she complained under her breath to the little dog.

As Sandra wandered through the canyons of slot machines and gamblers, mostly ordinary people out for a night of entertainment, she scanned the crowd for Earl. With his tall, gangly body and shiny bald head, he shouldn't be too hard to find. Unfortunately, she saw an abundance of balding men slumped over the whirring machines.

"Who knew there'd be so many receding hairlines tonight? That guy wearing the turtleneck looks like a giant roll-on deodorant!" She nodded in the man's direction.

Gaston sniffed the floor like a bloodhound on the trail of an escaped convict. He tugged on the leash without stopping in his push to a new room where slot machines gave way to poker tables. Again, Sandra hunted for the telltale shine of Earl's head. Nothing. Suddenly, loud voices from a corner table drew her attention.

"He's cheating. I saw him pull an ace from his sleeve!"

"You're crazy. You're just a shitty poker player."

"You're a damn liar! I play at Vegas all the time."

"Vegas, hah! You'd be out on your loser ass in seconds, you dickhead"

"Who are you calling a dickhead?"

A massive man in a casino shirt that barely covered his bulging arm muscles bulldozed his way through the onlookers gathering to watch the developing fight. Jet black hair pulled into a man bun exposed a face lined with scars and pock marks, a face that squelched arguments just by staring.

The poodle eagerly followed in his wake, hauling Sandra in the direction of the angry shouting. She elbowed her way through the throng.

"I need air," she said. "Please let me through. I feel a seizure coming on." To accentuate the seriousness, she raised a hand to her forehead and swooned, but no one seemed to notice.

Yip! Yip! Yip! The frantic barking drew attention.

An onlooker shouted, "Please let this old lady through! She's ready to pass out."

"Air! I need air." Sandra raised a hand to her throat and gasped loudly.

No one moved out of her way.

Then Sandra shouted, "Watch out, I'm getting ready to hurl!"

She emitted loud, gagging sounds, adding to the cacophony of Gaston's barking and the two men still swearing at each other. The imminent possibility of wearing an old lady's upchuck got their attention so people quickly stepped out of her way.

Sandra found herself face to face with Earl Adams, held at arm's length from a scruffy-looking twenty-something man by the huge casino worker. Earl's hands were balled into fists, flailing at empty air, and he shouted four-letter words at the empty space. The greasy haired younger man, eyes bloodshot and rimmed with dark circles, gestured with his middle finger, then sneered.

"Eff you, asshole," he said.

That made Earl flail all the more. A wry smile crossed the casino worker's face as he listened to the angry men spout off.

"Earl, did you forget your promise to meet me at the door?"

Her shrill voice overshadowed the display of testosterone. The large bouncer turned to her as she continued.

"I was hoping your kind offer to escort me around the casino still stands."

Sandra made an expansive gesture toward Earl as she addressed the crowd. "This dear man volunteered to treat me to a special night out. I have health problems, as you can see, so his kindness is much appreciated."

The bouncer said apologetically, "Sorry, lady, I had to break up a fight between these two card sharks. This one…" He pulled on the collar of Earl's shirt to slightly lift him off his feet. "…is about to be escorted to the parking lot."

 Earl stared at her with a dumbfounded expression and stuttered, "T-t-treat you to a special night?"

"Kind sir, if you let him go to a different part of the casino with me and my service dog, I guarantee we will keep him out of trouble."

"I don't know…." The huge man eyed Earl appraisingly. "It's our policy to kick any troublemakers out."

"I don't get out much. It would mean so much to me. I even wore my special gambling jacket. If I was your grandmother, wouldn't you want to see me have a little joy in life before…" She cast her eyes heavenward.

"We have rules I gotta follow."

He remained unconvinced as a voice from the crowd commented, "Bro, have a heart."

"I'm sure it was just a misunderstanding. This young man probably doesn't want to pursue the disagreement any further." She gave the scruffy younger man a hard stare. "He looks like a kindhearted fellow who'd prefer to get back to his card game. Am I right, sir?"

"Yeah. I want to go back to the table. I don't want to spoil the evening for the old lady." He hung his head contritely. "It was a simple misunderstanding. I didn't mean nothing by it."

"And you, buddy, have you cooled down?" The casino employee glared at Earl.

"Yes, sir. Like the young man said, it was just a misunderstanding."

"All right. Collect your chips and move on. Better luck with the slots."

The man folded his muscular arms over his chest and coldly regarded Earl as he collected everything from his spot on the table and offered his arm to Sandra. The gawkers quietly dispersed back to their games.

"I suppose I owe you a debt of gratitude. Thanks for getting me out of that nasty situation." Earl took a few uncertain steps into the next room.

"You can show your appreciation by buying me a drink in the lounge."

A few moments later, martini in hand, Sandra plunked herself across from Earl at a faraway table in the lounge. He threw a few nervous glances at Gaston, who bared his teeth menacingly before settling at his mistress's feet. Earl ordered a Scotch on the rocks and swallowed it in two gulps. He flagged down a waitress and ordered a second.

Sandra watched the waitress head to the bar before she spoke. "How did you happen to be at the casino on a Wednesday night?"

"Force of habit, I guess. I always told Alexandria I had a sales meeting on Wednesdays and we'd go for drinks and dinner after. But I came here instead."

"So you lied to her about your gambling?"

Earl cleared his throat like he was about to protest, but Gaston sat up at the noise and emitted a barely audible growl.

"May I remind you I just saved your ass? I think you can answer a few questions for me in return." Sandra held Earl's gaze until he looked away.

"Yes, I lied about the gambling. I needed my night at the casino. It was a kind of stress release for me. Alexandria wasn't the easiest woman to live with."

"Rumor has it you owed a bit of money to the casino."

"I put my losses on my business credit card, not my joint one with my wife. I've taken care of it." He tapped his chest with one finger. "I always managed to come up with the money without her finding out."

"Was there anything else you kept from her?"

"You should be asking about if Alexandria kept anything from me."

"What do you mean?"

"She had secrets, too. Destructive ones. Ruined our family, but I didn't find out the whole truth until after she died."

The waitress returned with the second drink. This time Earl put both hands around the glass and slid it back and forth for a few minutes before he drank. Sandra waited patiently for him to swallow, her blue eyes softening at his obvious distress.

"What kind of secrets?" she asked gently.

"Oh, hell. I have to tell somebody. It's been eating me up inside ever since Gillian told me. You're safe, I guess. You don't live in the neighborhood. You came from church with the food after the funeral. A good Christian woman. I can trust you, can't I?" He searched her face for an answer.

"Oh course, dearie. I only want to help."

Earl sighed with relief before he continued. "Gillian is our daughter. She lives in New York now. She hasn't been home, really, since she left for college. Not even on holidays. When she called home, she always asked for me, never her mother. That should have been a warning that something was wrong, right? I should have picked up on it."

"Maybe you were in denial?"

"Yes, definitely in denial. Alexandria wanted the perfect image. The perfect wife, perfect mother. What a joke!"

"The truth can be hard to face."

"The truth. Yes. The truth is Alexandria was an evil bitch who ruined our daughter's life. Gillian told me all about it in a letter." His hand gripped the glass so hard Sandra thought it might break.

"How did that happen?"

"Gillian dated our next-door neighbor's son, Justin, a nice young man. They were high school sweethearts. She was only seventeen. So much in love, puppy love, I thought. But tragedy struck. Justin died in a car accident."

"I'm so sorry. That must have been terrible for your daughter." She oozed sympathy in her voice.

"Gillian never recovered. It was the night of their senior prom. I wasn't home at the time. I had to present at an insurance agents' institute. She got into a fight with her mother over what I thought was some dumb argument. Little did I know the real reason was so awful. Justin came to pick her up for the prom and somehow got involved. Alexandria kicked him out of the house and grounded Gillian. If only I'd been there to stop her!" Earl slammed his fist on the table.

"Was Justin angry at your wife?"

"So angry he drove too fast on a back road. Missed a curve and was killed. Gillian was heartbroken. She didn't speak to her mother for months. I tried but I couldn't reach her. She grew so despondent. I was afraid she'd do something rash," his voice cracked. He paused for a minute, then went on. "She went away to college at the end of summer, got some grief counseling there, and got back on track."

"Did Gillian resolve her issues?"

"No. Here's the secret. Gillian kept it from me all this time until she sent the letter. She had an abortion. Her mother, the bitch, made her have an abortion. Told her 'I'm not going to let you ruin your life getting married so young like I did.' She told our daughter marriage ruined her life. She never really loved me. What a lying phony bitch!" He spat out the words.

"What about your poor daughter? That's an awful burden to carry all by herself all those years."

"She had Shar Fredricks, Justin's mother, to console her. They both were grief-stricken with the loss. Gillian had to turn to a neighbor for comfort, not her own father. I'm trying to make it up to her now. I'm trying to undo all the harm her mother inflicted on her. I'll never get over the lies. I hate Alexandria. I'm glad she's dead. With her gone I can pick up the pieces of our ruined lives. I'm in complete control now." He drained the second glass of Scotch. "Now you know what a lie I've been living all this time. Appeased my bitch of a wife instead of standing up to her. Failed my daughter. I'm a horrible person. Your dog doesn't even like me."

"You certainly had your share of trouble. It'd make any person feel horrible." Sandra commiserated.

As she gazed at him, she thought, *Do you feel horrible enough to have killed your wife?*

Chapter Twenty-Six

The throbbing headache from the attack paled in comparison to the ache of missing his children. Maria issued no idle threats. His only contact with Erin, Nicholas, and Kaitlyn was by cell phone. Erin was openly defiant.

"I don't care what Mom says," she said. "If I want to see you, I'll ride my bike to your apartment. She can't make me stop seeing you whenever I want."

Nicholas worried and said, "What if you get attacked again and we aren't there to call 911?"

Kaitlin cried, "When are we going to have another sleepover at your place? I want to see Gaston and Beatrice and Auntie Sandra. And Norm promised to teach me to whistle with my two fingers."

His only answer: "It's just for a short while. I'm fine. My head is better. Everything will turn out all right in the end. You'll see. It always does."

Then he took a selfie of himself, no longer needing the bandage, and sent it to Erin to show her younger siblings, captioned: "Look, I'm back to normal." He took the photo from his uninjured side.

Neither could he escape Beatrice's apprehension. "You've given up so much for me. I love you for your sacrifice, your loyalty, but what if we never solve this? A killer on the loose knows we're on his trail."

"We must be getting close if the killer is threatening us to stop."

"Florence Heidt is scheduled to come in today. I'm going to confront that bitch. I should have done it long ago, instead of sending Norm to do my dirty work." Her eyes gleamed in anticipation.

"Could you please drop me off at home on your way to the library? I'm going to check in with Sandra and do some catch-up. The new semester is starting in a month. Time to look over my syllabi and brush up on my lectures."

As Beatrice pulled up to his driveway, she asked, "Shall I pick you up after work for dinner together? We could spend some quality time together now that you're feeling better."

"I'd like that very much."

Her goodbye kiss offered a promise of renewed relations of the highest quality. In fact, Vlad almost urged her to go into work late and venture up to his apartment for a little foretaste of the evening activity, but then he remembered what the patient information sheet had said about resuming vigorous physical activities, about how it could cause a relapse.

"Maybe we'd better take it slow," he said with a melancholy sigh.

"I like slow, the slower the better. Slow and easy is pleasurable, too. We'll be in no rush. I promise I won't tax the limits of your recovery. You just lie back and enjoy." She gave a sexy laugh.

He leaned into the car before he shut the door. "I love you, you incredible woman."

"I love you, too. Don't overdo it today. Save some energy for us." She blew him a kiss and drove off.

No sooner had Vlad settled down at his desk than he heard a knock on his door. He turned on the laptop, then rose to answer it. Sandra barged in and planted herself on the loveseat, with Gaston hopping up beside her. While the little dog curled up and closed his eyes, Sandra leaned back into the cushions. She gestured to Vlad.

"Pull up a chair."

With a wistful glance at his laptop, he grabbed the armchair and slid it closer to her. "What's up?"

"You won't believe what I found out last night, dearie. Not only was Earl Adams at the casino, he spilled his guts about Alexandria and their daughter. Seems she wasn't the perfect wife and mother like we were led to believe. She forced the poor girl to have an abortion, broke up her relationship with her high school lover, and basically told the girl getting married was a mistake. She didn't love Earl, maybe never really did."

"Wow. That must have been a cruel blow to his psyche." Vlad ran a finger along his mustache. "Did he say the boyfriend's name?"

'Yes. Justin. The neighbor's kid. He died in a car accident shortly after Alexandria stepped in."

"I knew it.' He snapped his fingers. "I knew there was something secretive about their relationship. Donna, the bookstore lady, was about to give me the lowdown but she clammed up. I saw a picture of the two kids at the Fredricks' house. Only I can't go back there since Sid kicked me out."

"Not to worry. Norm's got it covered. But there is one more thing I just found out." Her blue eyes glinted bright and intense. "The toxicology report."

Vlad jerked up in surprise. "How in God's name did you get access to a confidential police report?"

"I got friends in high places. Right, Gaston?" She nudged the little dog with her elbow, and he yipped.

"Don't tell me you're friends with that overbearing police detective?"

"That plug-ugly bastard whose mug is plastered all over the newspapers? Don't be ridiculous, dearie. I got better taste in men. But my friend Juanita's daughter—you remember the one who works in the hospital? It seems she's shacking up with a cop, and he leaked the toxicology report over a little pillow talk."

"What did it say?"

"Alexandria Adams was poisoned all right. The crime lab said it was a tincture of aconite, probably from the root of a monkshood plant. One of the most highly toxic plants."

"A tincture? What exactly is that?"

"In Beatrice's pie it could go practically unnoticed because aconite is very hard to detect. Luckily, the state crime lab has sophisticated equipment that can do a proper toxicology analysis. The local forensic lab never would've found it."

"My God! Now I've got to talk to Donna." Vlad stood up abruptly. "I'll head down to the bookstore to return her yearbook. Somehow I'll get her to tell what she knows about the Fredricks and Alexandria."

"You shouldn't be driving by yourself yet, dearie. I can't let you go alone. You better take Gaston with you."

Vlad ignored the dull ache in his head as he drove. His thinking felt fuzzy as if his brain was filled with cotton instead of gray matter. He stopped keeping track of how many times motorists passed him, beeping their horns and flashing him the middle finger. Gaston sat in the front passenger seat, watching him with alert eyes.

"No snoozing this time, Buddy."

He took the slow route across town, choosing to stop at controlled intersections or right turns, even if it meant going a bit out of the way.

"I don't trust myself to cut across lanes or turn into oncoming traffic," he told Gaston.

After narrowly avoiding a door opening from a car parked at the side of the street, Vlad felt sweat beading on his forehead. Another car turned abruptly in front of him with no signal. He slammed on the brakes, then clenched the wheel tightly and slowed even more. Gaston yipped, and put a paw on his leg.

"I'm okay, boy. Just a little out of it. We'll get there in one piece. Don't worry."

The bookstore sign brought a sigh of relief as Vlad parked in front, hands shaking. He managed to snap the leash on the little dog, keeping it short. "You need to behave in the bookstore. Donna has a cat, who is hopefully taking a nap somewhere."

Then he tucked the yearbook securely under his arm and headed for the store.

Cool Beans and Books opened at seven o'clock, and they arrived two hours later. Hopefully, all the customers stopping for morning coffee were well on their march into their day, and the lunch crowd hadn't yet appeared. The timing was perfect; Donna was situated on her stool behind the cash register. Her friendly hello with a big smile dissolved into an expression of concern when she saw Vlad's face.

"What on earth happened to you?" she exclaimed.

"Just a little mishap. Looks worse than it feels," Vlad lied. "Hope you don't mind if I bring my dog in with me. He watches out for me. He can tell when I'm starting to fade and makes me sit down to catch my breath."

"Of course, I don't mind. Can I get you something to drink? Fresh brewed coffee? A latte? I have a nice herbal tea that some customers find invigorating."

"Actually, that tea sounds rather pleasant. I'd like to try a cup."

"Please sit down. I'll brew some and bring it to your table. It's specially made for my store."

Vlad collapsed into the nearest chair, grateful for something solid and unmoving after the harrowing drive across town. Gaston sat on his haunches, swiveling his head to scan the new environment: rows of bookcases, a table with the newest offerings for the start of school, but not much of interest to a dog. He flopped down, resting his head on his paws.

When Donna brought the cup of tea to the table, Vlad asked, "Won't you join me for a minute? I'm retuning your yearbook, and I still have a few questions if you don't mind."

She checked her watch before she answered. "I have a few minutes to spare. What would you like to know?"

"I noticed Sid Fredricks standing next to you in the National Honor Society picture." Vlad struggled to choose his words carefully. "Did you and him—I mean he and you—ever become friends?"

"Not after Alexandria dumped him and started dating Earl. We'd say hi to each other in the hallway, but that was about it."

"When did he meet Shar?'

"After he went away to college. He met her his freshmen year, and they got married a few months after Earl and Alexandria. Alexandria liked to tell everyone Sid married on the rebound, just to spite her and Earl. She could be vengeful that way. Shar was slightly older, a single mom with a toddler. She worked at UW-Whitewater in the Registrar's office. That's how they met. She basically put Sid through school."

"The toddler was Justin, who later dated Gillian Adams."

"Yes. Sid got a job as a school psychologist, and they bought the house next to Earl and Alexandria. For a while they were all friends. Let bygones be bygones. At first Alexandria pretended all the high school drama was forgotten but she never failed to badmouth them behind their back. Called Shar a 'Sugar Mommy' and Sid a 'freeloader.' Made fun of their 'hippie' lifestyle. I hope she wasn't as two-faced when I wasn't around."

"Then Justin was killed in a car accident."

"A tragic car accident, on the night of Senior Prom. Alexandria didn't have much to say about it, only that Gillian got sick and couldn't go to the prom with him. She was so thankful Gillian wasn't in that car with him. But…" Donna paused, tightening her face muscles.

"Is there more to it?" Vlad prompted.

The words came out in a rush. "Alexandria never confided in me. Sid and Shar were too devastated by the loss of their only child to speak about it. But something went on the night of the prom. Something went down with Gillian. I think…"

The black and white tuxedo cat suddenly appeared from behind the bookcase. He stretched his paws in front, raised his hindquarters, and yawned. The cat lazily surveyed the room. Gaston jumped up on red alert and barked loudly. Then he skyrocketed across the room toward the cat, leash trailing behind him like a jet plume. The cat hissed and arched his back, fur standing on end. The poodle drew near, still barking, when the cat lashed out, claws extended like knives. One paw slashed the dog's nose, and Gaston yipped in surprise. Then he growled, and the chase was on.

"Gaston! Come back!" Vlad shouted.

"Max, behave yourself!" Donna ordered.

Both animals ignored the humans. Max ran under the display table, Gaston in hot pursuit. As the animals headed past the glassed-in bookcase filled with the vintage books, Vlad held his breath.

"Don't knock that case over," Donna shrieked.

Max swerved around the bookcase, but Gaston brushed too close, the door popped open, knocking a few children's books to the floor. Donna scurried to pick them up, examining them for damage. Oblivious to the books falling behind him, the poodle persevered. The cat zigzagged around bookcases and a rotating wire display rack of popular series books. Faced with a wall blocking his escape, Max vaulted to the top of the nearest bookshelf, toppling a row of self-help books. He perched on his safe sanctuary, hissing at the frenzied dog below him.

Vlad jerked on the poodle's leash and dragged him away, saying, "I'm so sorry. He's never behaved like this before. I'll lock him in the restroom and help you pick up the books."

He picked up the squirming dog, ignoring his scratched and bleeding nose, and unceremoniously deposited him into the men's room, As Vlad slammed the door shut on him. Gaston barked loudly in protest.

"Bad kitty. You know better," Donna scolded as she picked up how-to manuals.

The cat calmly licked his paws, green eyes coldly watching the two humans working below, flicking his tail back and forth.

Vlad handed her books as she reshelved them, all the while apologizing profusely. One title caught his attention: *The Herbal Alchemist's Handbook: A Complete Guide to Plants and Herbs and How to Use Them*. When he flipped it open to check out the Table of Contents, he discovered a whole section had been ripped out.

"Donna, did you know one of your books has been vandalized?"

"Oh, dear. Which one?" She pushed back a frizzy strand of hair that escaped from a banana clip at the back of her head and drew near to better see.

"*The Herbal Alchemist's Handbook.* Some pages have been torn out."

"That book's been on the shelf forever. I ordered it when the New Age stuff was popular. Why would someone tear out pages?"

"Looks like a whole chapter has been removed." Vlad once again turned to the Table of Contents and scanned the page numbers. "The whole chapter titled 'Tinctures, Philters, and Elixirs' is gone."

"Who on earth would be interested in that?" she exclaimed.

"Perhaps someone interested in experimenting with potions who doesn't want to be discovered. Or poisons, like what killed Alexandria. Do you recall anyone browsing in this section?" Vlad looked unwaveringly at her.

Donna wrinkled her brow in concentration. "I seem to remember someone over in the herbalist section a few months ago. Now who was is?'

"Think hard. It could be important," Vlad urged.

"Was it….?' Her face clouded for a second. She whispered. "No, couldn't be… Got to check…"

Vlad watched her struggle. "Anything you can recall would help. My fiancée, Beatrice Krup, is under suspicion for Alexandria's death. Her pie contained the poison. I know she didn't put it there. I'm trying to clear her name."

She shook her head sadly. "Sorry. I can't remember."

"Not as sorry as Beatrice and me, I'm afraid." He handed her his university business card. "If you should happen to think of anything, please call me."

Not meeting his eyes, she said 'I will," in a quivering voice.

Chapter Twenty-Seven

Norm studied the ad on the web page: *Start your meditation journey today and let Sid Fredericks, Soul Life Coach, guide you toward self-love, spiritual healing, and relaxation.*
Welcome Orientation
First Saturday of every month
9:00-9:20 a.m.
He read it aloud to Sandra, then added, "This is my chance to question Sid. I'm going to attend this meeting and then try to find out more about him and Alexandria Adams."

"How do you propose doing that, dearie? I don't mean to throw cold water on your plans, but you don't look like the mindfulness type."

"I am a veteran, and I did suffer from PTSD for a while until you hired me as your handyman. I can say I'm hitting a rough patch in life. I need some of that spiritual healing."

Sandra studied him for a minute. "Are you sure you're up to this? You're our last hope of cracking the case with Sid. No funny business."

"If I could flirt with Florence Heidt, I can spend twenty minutes listening to a meditation guru. Trust me. I can handle this," Norm insisted. "I'm at the top of my game. I didn't even have a lite beer last night. I'm sober as a...as a church mouse."

The meditation room was sparsely furnished, its main feature being a large wall hanging that depicted a tranquil scene: a full moon shining on hazy blue mountain ridges, its silvery light reflected in a nearby lake. A few inspirational posters adorned the uncluttered walls with sayings such as *The breath is a door to rejuvenating the body* and *Meditation is the way for nourishing and blossoming the divinity within you.* The tinkling music in the background made Norm wish he'd used the men's room before stepping into the cascading sounds while little lavender scented candles seemed to float on the floor in the dim light. The barefoot man wearing a pale orange shirt over loose orange pants greeting people must be the meditation master Sid.

"My name is Norman Clodfelder." He grabbed Sid's hand and gave it a vigorous shake. "I'm here because yer ad said new to meditation or in need of healing. That's me! I decided to take up meditation. It beats sitting around doing nothing all day."

Sid gave him an annoyed look, then a forced laugh. "I see you have a sense of humor. Welcome to this brief orientation."

Four other newcomers nervously laughed following Sid's lead. The only other male in the group, an older man, well-dressed in his Tommy Bahama shirt and khakis, frowned at Norm and glanced impatiently at his fancy gold watch. Norm felt glad he'd borrowed a name brand athletic shirt from Vlad instead of wearing his usual thrift store bargain. The three prospective female students, all middle-aged and garbed in colorful athletic wear, went back to their side conversations

"Seriously, I'm a veteran. I've been in a shitty place for a little while now. My brain jumps all over. I can't seem to focus, like my mind's lost in a dark cave and I can't find the light. It's starting to affect my job and my love life. My lady friend is getting tired of broken promises. I'm hoping some meditation classes will help me with spiritual healing, like yer ad sez," Norm said apologetically.

"You've come to the right place. Welcome." Sid faced the entire group. "Welcome to all of you. I'm Sid Fredricks, your meditation guide. Please find yourself a comfortable seat."

He sat down on a puffy round cushion that looked like the top of a mushroom. Other pastel cushions were scattered about along with a few low cushioned reclining seats. Norm grabbed one of the recliners, as did the other man who ignored Norm's friendly wave.

As Sid described what would be covered in the eight-week beginning course, Norm puzzled over how such a serene man could have ever been friends with Alexandria Adams, if what Vlad discovered from the bookstore lady was true. The man described scattered thoughts as clouds and the true self as the sky.

"We will learn to not hold onto negative thoughts, for that only creates storms in our lives. Holding on leads to suffocation. You will learn to let go and free your mind. Focus on the now, not the past, which we can do nothing about. Rid yourself of the illusion of the past and the illusion of the future. Step out of habitual thinking into an open mind. This focus begins with the breath."

At the end of the ten-minute session on breath work, Norm did feel more relaxed. A sliver of awareness crept in as he put his hand on his abdomen and took in some deep breaths. He almost regretted when the introductory session ended and a beautiful woman in a plum-colored tunic and yoga pants entered the room carrying a tray with cups of tea.

"This is my lovely wife, Shar. Some of you know her from her yoga classes."

The three ladies happily nodded.

"This is her herbal tea, her own energizing concoction. Please try a sample as you fill out the registration forms on the clipboards. We urge you to join us next Monday night for our first session."

"I'm not usually a tea drinker, unless it's Long Island tea at the bar, but what the hell, I'll give it a shot." Norm said to the woman.

She watched as he took a sip and smiled when he smacked his lips.

"This is pretty damn good," he said, "kinda fruity tasting, a little sour, but good."

Shar drifted over to the ladies and warmly greeted them, complimenting them on their decision to give Sid's class a try.

"Meditation will change your life. Try to envision the possibilities. You'll find a new inner strength. I found myself full of courage—able to focus on my purpose. More willpower, less distractions." Her eyes glittered as she pontificated. "Once you align your purpose with action, nothing can stop you from achieving your potential."

Taking their paperwork, she ushered them out into the hall.

The well-dressed man paused on his way out to ask Sid, "Would you be willing to work with me privately? I'm quite able to pay more for your services. Monday nights aren't good for me. I'd prefer Thursday. I think I'd make faster progress alone. I find the distraction of less motivated people to be a hindrance."

He stared pointedly at Norm, while Sid drifted over to check schedules on a handheld device. After perusing it for a minute, the guru agreed to a Thursday night time slot. He made a note on the man's registration form.

"Please give this to Shar on your way out. Your first class will start in a week."

Norm slowly sipped the tea, even after it grew cold, ostensibly studying the form. He cleared his throat as if to speak while Sid entered some items on his device. Soon just he and Sid were in the room.

Sid set the device down and walked over to Norm. "Do you have any questions? I'd be glad to answer them. You appear to be stuck in a negative self-narrative. Meditation can help change that. It's possible to transform your mind set through repeated practice."

"I'm thinking about it. Can I take the registration form with me?' Norm asked. "Monday night is my gun club night. We go out to the shooting range and raise a little hell. I'd have to find another night for going out with the guys."

"Do you want to transform your life? Leave the dark places behind? The decision is yours."

"I notice you live next to a big house, almost like a mansion. Kinda dwarfs this house. Who owns that monster house?"

"That house belongs to Earl Adams."

"The guy whose wife just croaked? Ya know anything about that?"

"We aren't really that well acquainted. Mr. Adams doesn't really confide in me. He keeps pretty much to himself, I'm afraid."

"I heard the wife was a mover and shaker around town. She never came over to shoot the breeze?"

"I'm afraid not. I didn't know her very well. Alexandria Adams and I moved about in different social circles. Our interests were poles apart."

"No yoga or meditating for her then. Her loss, I guess. How did ya become this meditation guru? Did ya go somewhere and climb a mountaintop to see the Zen Master? Like in the pictures, some guy with a beard in a robe sitting with his legs crossed on a cushion?"

"No. I had a very painful experience in my life. I had to learn how to survive the pain and the fear—to stop lying to myself. I realized we are all going to die so we have no time to waste. You have to be courageous enough to tell yourself the absolute truth and then follow where the truth leads you."

Shar came back into the meditation room, "I'm sorry to interrupt but Sid, you really must get going if you're going to make it to the airport in time to catch your flight. Your carryon bag for the conference is sitting by the hall tree."

"Please excuse me. I must cut this conversation short. I have a prior engagement. Perhaps if you sign up for the class, we can talk again." He moved over to the table and picked up the device again.

Shar turned to Norm. "Did you enjoy the energizing tea?"

"I did, thanks. I'd like to buy some, if ya have it for sale."

"I'm sorry. We're all sold out. We had a run on it at the fair."

"At the fair? Were you at the county fair a few weeks ago?"

"We were there all five days. We had a booth in the commercial building, selling some of our natural health supplements. We completely sold out of this tea, and I haven't had time to make another batch."

"Were ya at the fair when yer neighbor's wife died?" Norm watched her face carefully.

"No!" she blurted out.

"Yes, Shar, we were but in a completely different building," Sid gently reminded her.

"That's right, Sid." She snapped her fingers. "We heard the siren but didn't find out until the evening news that it was Alexandria who'd taken ill. Poor woman!"

"A tragic loss for Earl. Now I really must go. Please excuse me. Shar, can you show Mr. Clodfelder out?"

Sid gave him a little bow, a *namaste,* and exited the meditation room.

Chapter Twenty-Eight

The text message from Donna Kloostra came two days later. When Vlad checked his cell phone upon rising, he read: *I remembered something that may help your fiancée. I did some checking last night to be sure. Could you please stop by the store after five? Ignore the Closed sign and come in.*

He shouted "I can't believe it!" so loudly that Beatrice came running from the kitchen

"What's up? I heard you two rooms away."

"I thought Donna was a dead end but apparently I was wrong. She remembered something—something she thinks is important. It must be concerning the stolen pages from the book. She had a strange look when we found the damaged book, as if she was hiding something. She wants to talk tonight after she closes the shop."

"Maybe she was protecting someone but changed her mind," Beatrice said.

"Whatever the reason, her change of heart breathes some new life into the investigation." Vlad strode over to the dresser and began putting on his pants.

"Especially after Norm's failure with Sid Fredricks on Saturday." Beatrice shook her head.

"It wasn't a complete failure. Sid did lie to him about not knowing the Adamses that well. There were pictures at the funeral to the contrary." Vlad buttoned the top button of his shirt.

"Do you have to get dressed right away?" Beatrice glided over to him. "I have a half hour before I need to get to the library. Plenty of time for a quickie," she teased as she opened her bathrobe to reveal her filmy negligee. "Now that you're on the road to recovery, we should take advantage of your improved health."

She slid her arms around his neck and drew him to her, dropping the robe to the floor. Her almost bare skin against his chest felt warm and inviting. She kissed him long and hard; he felt his breath quickening. He moved his hands to her buttocks and pulled her closer when the phone rang.

"Let it go," she moaned. "We're just getting started."

"Let me check who it is. It may be important."

Vlad saw Maria's name. "It's my ex."

"It figures," said Beatrice, picking up the robe. "She may as well have thrown a bucket of ice water over us. That woman has a sixth sense about butting in when she's not wanted."

"What's up? Is everything okay with the kids?" he asked as he took Maria's call.

"The kids are fine. I'm just checking in to see if you've given up the detective boondoggle yet. It's time for the baseball tournaments and Nicholas's final game of the season. He'd like his father to be there."

"I can come. What time is the game?"

"If you're still playing Sherlock Holmes, forget it. I'll tell him you're busy," Maria snapped.

"I'll just show up at the ball field. I won't take him anywhere. I'll just be there to watch."

"You're useless then. I wanted you to give him a ride there, but never mind. I'll call one of the other player's moms."

The cell phone went dead. Vlad stuck up his middle finger at it, then slammed it down on the dresser. Beatrice came up behind him and slipped her arms around him, resting her head against his back.

"I'm sorry." Her voice sounded sad. "I couldn't help but overhear."

"It's all right. But she's totally wrecked the mood." He covered her hands with his but didn't move.

"True that. I'm getting dressed and going into work early." She reluctantly drew away and began rummaging in her dresser for undergarments.

"Me, too. I'm heading over to my office—lots of planning to do for the fall semester. It will keep my mind off Maria." He finished buttoning up his shirt.

Beatrice stopped searching in the drawer and faced him. "You should just show up at Nicky's game. Stay long enough to let him see you so he knows you care."

"I'll check out the Parks and Rec website to find out when and where it is. Screw Maria and her demands."

Vlad had just enough time to catch a few innings of the late afternoon game before heading over to the bookstore. As he walked over to the bleachers, he observed Nicholas standing in right field, The boy's eyes were on the batter but occasionally he glanced over to where the parents were sitting. He held his glove upright, ready to spring into action should a ball head his way. Other parents were chattering and yelling encouragements to their sons. Vlad settled at the end of the row nearest the parking lot for a quick getaway. The batter made the third out, and Nicholas jogged over to the bench, stealing one last look at the crowd. When he saw Vlad, he smiled broadly and gave a little wave. Vlad signaled thumbs-up and flashed a matching grin.

Vlad stayed through two complete innings, long enough to see Nicholas hit a little blooper toward the third base line and get thrown out at first. But he did advance a runner and earned some claps from the spectators for getting a teammate in scoring position. When that boy scored on a base hit, Nicholas's team pulled ahead. Vlad checked his watch. Time to leave for the bookstore. Nicholas was taking the field as Vlad waved good bye. No slumping on the bench in this game; his bouncy step revealed the boy's growing confidence.

During the sluggish drive through downtown in rush hour traffic, Vlad wondered what he'd find out from Donna. It had to be about Earl or Sid. Florence didn't seem to be more than an acquaintance from the Garden Club and the pie baking contest. Considering what Sandra learned about Alexandria and her daughter, nothing would surprise Vlad about the dead woman's malice.

Checking the clock on his dashboard, Vlad noted it was quarter after five, plenty of time for Donna to be rid of any closing time customers. Although the head wound still looked ugly, his headache had nearly disappeared. The stitched-up gash made him look like an authentic hardboiled detective, a mustached Humphrey Bogart as Philip Marlowe. He jangled his key ring in his pocket as he sauntered down the sidewalk to Cool Beans and Books.

Mrraow! Mrraow! Mrraow!

Vlad heard the loud cries of the cat half a block away. *Is there an amorous feral cat on the loose?* He glanced down an alley as he passed by, but no cat was in sight. *Sounds like the noise our Bootsie made when she was in heat.*

As he approached the bookstore, he realized the incessant yowls were coming from inside. It must be Max wanting to be fed. The noise was so frantic the cat must be starving.

Ignoring the Closed sign as directed, Vlad pushed open the door. He saw the tuxedo cat on the counter, caterwauling as he paced back and forth, whipping his tail in annoyance. No Donna in sight. Perhaps she was in the restroom.

"Donna, are you here?" he called as he stepped into the room.

At the sound of his voice, the cat jumped down from the counter and dashed over to him. Max rubbed against his legs, meowing even louder, sounding like a foghorn on a stormy night. He almost tripped Vlad with his frantic motions.

"What on earth is wrong with you, cat?"

Max gave his ankle a little nip.

"Are you that hungry?"

"Donna!" Vlad shouted again. "Come and take care of your cat. He's so desperate for some food he tried to take a chunk out of my ankle."

An unpleasant odor drifted from the back room. She must be using the restroom. No sound of a flushing toilet, a door handle turning, or nearing footsteps. The store was completely silent except for Max.

Vlad's head felt tight, like it was caught in a vise. The atmosphere in the store felt oppressive, slightly off-kilter. A throbbing pain tiptoed at the edge of his consciousness. He picked up the cat to calm him down, but the animal hissed, bit his arm, and squirmed out of his grasp. He pushed off against Vlad's chest, back claws digging deeply into his shirt, and bolted toward the back of the store with Vlad scurrying after him. A tiny prick of blood appeared where the cat dug in, staining his shirt.

Damn you, cat. His anger at the cat was short-lived.

The second he saw the books scattered on the floor in the back room Vlad knew something was very wrong. Donna would never leave behind such a mess. His heart seemed to explode in his chest, and his mouth grew dry with fear. A heavy wooden bookcase had been upended, books heaped in a pile. A foot clad in a purple canvas shoe stuck out from the pile.

Scarcely able to breath, Vlad inched closer, alarms going off in his head as the nasty smell grew stronger. Like an electromagnetic force, the motionless foot drew him forward. Next, he saw a hand, fingers curled upward, an arm lying limp, encircled by a gold watch. So strange to see a body buried in books like a sand dune made of paperbacks.

He moaned, "Oh, my God," and jumped backwards a step, his legs ready to crumble at the sight.

Donna Kloostra was lying on the floor, weighed down by the clumsy bookcase resting on the lower half of her body. Her brown eyes were staring sightlessly at the ceiling, blood pooling beneath her head. Her frizzy hair was set free from the green claw clip that lay in pieces at her side. He wanted to look away but her open mouth and her pale bluish face transfixed him.

Vlad dropped to his knees at her side and picked up her wrist, icy to the touch, his fingers pushing aside the gold watch, but there was no pulse. He gently set her arm back down and stared in horror at her dead body. Her thin ankle jutting out from rainbow striped capris gave him a sense of unreality. When Donna dressed that morning in her bright cheerful colors, was she thumbing her nose at Death? *Because I could not stop for Death, he kindly stopped for me.* The fragment of Dickinson's poem echoed in his mind, but Death had not been so kind to Donna.

The cat reappeared and began to meow piteously, breaking the spell. Vlad rose and stumbled out of the room, Max's plaintive cries giving voice to his own feelings of alarm.

With trembling fingers, he dialed 911. "I just found a dead body… at Cool Beans and Books. I think the owner is dead. A bookcase fell on top of her."

"We'll send the EMTs right away."

"She's dead, I tell you. Donna's dead! I couldn't find a pulse." His voice rose to a shriek.

"Take a deep breath, sir, and talk slowly."

"There're books scattered all over hell. The woman is lying there, not moving. Her cat's yowling like he's demon possessed. It's terrible."

"Stay calm, sir. Help is on the way. What's your name?" The woman's monotone voice gave little reassurance.

"Vlad Chomsky. Please tell them to hurry."

The same two burly EMTs who carried him off Tripoli Island soon burst in through the door. Vlad pointed them toward the back, scarcely trusting himself to speak. The cat hissed at the two strangers and disappeared under the front counter. Vlad heard them call in.

"The bookstore owner is dead. It looks like foul play. The place is a mess, giant bookcase on top of her, books tossed all over. You better send the cops."

The older man walked over to Vlad. "You're the one who made the 911 call?"

"Donna asked me to stop by after she closed the store. She said she had something to discuss with me. When I walked in, the cat was making an earsplitting racket, yowling loud enough to wake the dead."

Vlad realized how ridiculous that must sound to the two men, but he couldn't stop talking. "She was nowhere in sight. Then I found her. I found her like that, just lying there under the massive bookcase, covered in books." Vlad felt bile rising in his throat. "I think I'm going to be sick. I don't want to go back there to the restroom."

He searched frantically for a garbage can. One of the EMTs handed him a blue recycle bin from behind the counter. Vlad was still emptying his stomach when he heard a raspy voice.

"Not you again. Trouble seems to stick to you like flies on a pile of roadkill."

Vlad looked up to see Detective Johnson frowning at him, hands on his hips. "Where's the body?"

The EMT answered, "In the back room, Detective."

Vlad heard the policeman swearing as he walked around the next room.

"Sonovabitch! Another body on my watch," he said to the EMTs. "You didn't touch anything, did you? This is a potential murder investigation. I'll call in my forensic team and the medical examiner. It looks like an accident, but I have some doubts about a bookcase of that size just tipping over on her."

The burly detective shuffled back into the showroom, talking on his cell phone to a dispatcher. "Send in the usual team and Doc Walters. Stat. I got a potential witness here—the guy who found the body and called it in. I got a few questions for him."

Detective Johnson loomed over him, glaring at him with his bear-like eyes. Vlad didn't need to look up. He felt those eyes drilling into his back as he suffered from the dry heaves. The policeman snorted as he pulled a small notebook and pen out of his rumpled suit jacket.

"Now that you're done puking, how about pulling up a chair and telling me why the hell you're at another crime scene?"

Chapter Twenty-Nine

By the time the detective finally finished grilling him about Donna Kloostra, Vlad's head pounded like a demolition crew was inside his skull. He told him about *The Herbal Alchemist's Handbook* with the missing pages and how strangely Donna acted when he asked if she remembered anyone in that part of the bookstore.

"Why were you at the bookstore that day?" the detective asked, his face pinched with suspicion.

"I was returning her high school yearbook. I was looking at some old pictures of Alexandria and Earl, trying to fill in some background on their relationship."

"You didn't think that background info was important enough to share with the police?" Detective Johnson said sharply.

"No, not really. People change a lot after high school. I was just trying to understand how it all started. They were an unlikely match back then. Different social classes, different interests. I was just trying to discover if there were any skeletons in the closet." Vlad rambled on, careful to maintain a look of innocence.

"Were there?"

"No. Not in high school anyway."

"I'd like to know exactly what Donna Kloostra told you." Johnson's eyes penetrated Vlad's innocuous façade.

"Alexandria was a very domineering woman. Vindictive if she was challenged. Relentless when she went after a perceived enemy. Any idiot who spent two minutes with Her Highness could figure that out."

"Damn it, man! Don't be so flippant!" The detective exploded. "I shouldn't have to remind you this is an ongoing murder investigation. Your fiancée is in it up to her neck. And now you turn up with a dead body. It isn't some damn Clue game—Colonial Mustard in the kitchen with a poisoned pie!"

"I'm sorry. I'm just trying to help Beatrice clear her name," he said in a small voice.

"I'm ordering you to stop! You may think the police are slow and plodding, but we have to build an ironclad case against a killer. Our methods get results that stand up in a court of law. We can't have amateurs muddying up the waters. We'll get the job done. If your fiancée is innocent, the evidence will point to the real killer. Your continued interference is making our job a lot more difficult. Stop! Cease! Desist! Have I made myself clear?" His forefinger stabbed Vlad's chest with each new command.

"Yes. Crystal clear, sir."

"Good! Now get out of my crime scene." Johnson waved him off dismissively.

Vlad stood up to leave. He slowly walked to the door but the vision of the black and white fur ball darting under the counter nagged at the edge of his consciousness. The cat's yowls were so heart-wrenching. *I don't even like cats.* He glanced down at the spot of blood and the hole in his shirt. *The damn cat ruined my shirt. Let Detective Johnson tackle the beast. Not my problem.*

His hand was already pushing the door open when the words spilled out, "But what about the cat?"

"The cat? I don't know what the hell you're talking about?" the detective growled at him, tapping his foot impatiently as he checked his watch.

Vlad thought, *Why didn't I make a clean getaway?*

"Donna has a cat. It ran under the counter and hid when the EMTs came in."

"Oh, for Christ's sake. A cat is the least of my worries. I have a dead body in the next room, and my forensic team seems to have taken a detour." He looked at his watch again.

"He's probably scared and hungry. He was very agitated when I came in. I don't know how long he'd been in such a state of distress."

"Yeah, we saw it, too. A cat took off like a bat out of hell when we went into the back room," the older EMT said.

The detective lashed out. "Can't you men handle it? Call the animal control officer."

The EMT reminded him, "There is no animal control officer. That position was axed in the last round of budget cuts."

"Let the cat fend for itself. I've got enough on my plate without trying to deal with a damn cat!"

"Do you want us to call the Humane Society?" the EMT suggested. "They're closed for today, but maybe we can get someone to meet us there after we catch the cat."

"Watch out. He's vicious with those claws. Look what he did to my shirt." Vlad pointed to the hole.

"I can get a towel from the ambulance and throw it over him once we lure him out," the younger man said.

"Nah. That won't work. You have to grab him by the nape of the neck, like a mother cat carries her kittens." The older EMT shook his head.

"The cat's been through a lot. He just witnessed the death of his owner. That's traumatic enough without scaring him more," Vlad implored.

"If you're so concerned, why don't you take him?" Sarcasm colored the detective's response.

Vlad shook his head in alarm. "Animals don't seem to care for me. I already have a friend's dog that is as likely to bite me as lick my hand. I don't need a cat that bites and scratches, too."

"Then butt out and let these guys handle it."

Vlad pictured Max dangling helplessly from the ham-fisted grip of the burly EMT, meowing frantically. *I can't just leave him terrified at the rough handling.* He sighed. "I'm probably going to regret this but I'll take the cat. I can contact the Humane Society tomorrow."

"Go ahead. Adopt him. Turn him loose on the streets. Do whatever. Just get the hell out of here." The detective jerked his thumb toward the door.

Vlad remembered where Donna kept the cat food. He opened the cupboard to fetch the bag of cat food and Max's bowl. He poured some out and knelt in front of the counter. "Here, kitty, kitty, kitty. Come here, Max, and get your kitty food."

He gently shook the bowl. The cat cautiously stuck out his nose and sniffed, then out came his head. He looked around. When he saw it was just Vlad, he slowly ventured out and approached the food. Vlad let him gobble a few mouthfuls, then snatched him up. Max hissed a few times, squirming and clawing to break free.

As he firmly grasped the animal, he scolded, "Stop it, Max. I'm on your side, cat. Probably the only friend you've got."

The young EMT observed the struggle for a few seconds, then said, "Let me help. I'll bring the bag of food and his bowl to your car."

The two men hurried down the street with Max complaining all the way. Vlad clicked open the door, and the younger man held it for him until he was securely inside with the cat and all his paraphernalia.

"Good luck with that beast," the EMT said.

"Thanks," Vlad replied. "I need more than luck—maybe a whip and leather protective gear."

Vlad watched a police van pulled up to the curb. Several officers poured out and entered the bookstore, along with the retreating EMT. He could hear the detective's thunderous reprimands from a block away.

"What the hell took you so long?"

Vlad called Beatrice the second he released the cat and dug his cell phone out of his pants pocket. His hands finally stopped shaking but his stomach still lurched whenever he recalled Donna's face distorted by death.

"Donna Kloostra is dead!"

"What! How can she be dead? You were going to meet with her after work," she exclaimed.

"When I got to the store, I found her body. It looked like a bookcase had tumbled onto her. But I'm sure it was no accident. She knew something. Somebody wanted to shut her up."

"Oh my God, Vlad. I can't believe it. Poor sweet Donna." Her voice cracked with sorrow.

"It gets worse. Your favorite detective was on the scene. He read me the riot act and told me in no uncertain terms to stop. Plus I took her cat. He was totally freaked out. They were going to capture him and haul him to the Humane Society. He's hiding under the passenger seat of my car right now."

The tip of the cat's tail stuck out, moving back and forth like a hopped-up metronome.

"This investigation is getting too dangerous. Maybe we should stop." He could picture the way her brow knotted when she grew worried.

"Not yet. Especially since Sandra got a line on the toxicology report.

It was poison. One of the plants you researched—monkshood. There's one more thing we have to do. I'll tell you when I come by. After I dump this cat off at my apartment."

"The poor frightened thing. First, he witnesses his owner's murder. Then he's taken away from the only home he knows and is dumped in an apartment by himself. What happens if he sees Gaston?" Beatrice offered. "Why don't you bring him here where he'll be safe."

Chapter Thirty

After locking the cat securely in his car, Vlad clambered up the steps to his apartment and changed into a black long-sleeved t-shirt and black pants. A can of ginger ale kept in the fridge for digestive purposes settled his stomach. He drank half the can before brushing his teeth, fully ridding himself of the lingering vomit taste. When he knocked on Sandra's door to check in with her, he felt somewhat restored. As Sandra slowly made her way to the entry, Gaston raced ahead of her and jumped on him as he stood waiting. After a few loud yips, the little dog pointed his nose at the hook holding his leash, scratching his front paws on the wall.

"Not now, Gaston." Sandra scolded. "We'll go for a walk later."

She turned to Vlad. "Won't you come in, dearie. I'll mix us up a quick drink. We can catch up on the case."

"Something terrible has happened." He told her all about finding Donna and the grilling from Detective Johnson. "Beatrice and I are going to check out some gardens for monkshood. If we find the plant, we find the killer."

"If he hasn't destroyed the evidence by now," the elderly lady bemoaned.

"Unless he's friends with Juanita, too, he won't have a clue what's in the toxicology report. Remember, aconite is supposed to be nearly impossible to detect without specialized equipment. I have a feeling our killer still thinks he's pretty safe."

"Do be careful. Whoever killed Alexandra and Donna won't hesitate to kill a third person." She wrung her hands as she spoke. "Maybe you'd better take Gaston for protection."

Gaston let out a woof when he heard his name, still eyeing his leash and wagging his tail so hard his whole rear end shook.

"I can't. I have Donna's cat in my car. Beatrice said she'd take him. Remember, last time Gaston's 'protection' ended up making a mess in the bookstore. Besides, Beatrice knows her plants, probably even better than the cops. She'll be the one to identify the monkshood if anyone can."

"You never would have found the book with the missing pages if not for Gaston. He led you straight to that clue."

The little poodle woofed in agreement.

"And to a death warrant for poor Donna Kloostra, I'm afraid. I won't be able to close my eyes for a long time without her face haunting me." His voice quivered. "I don't want to think about that now. Best not to go down that path."

"You poor man. What a dreadful experience." Sandra slowly shook her head and clicked her tongue.

"It's just Beatrice and me tonight. We have a lot of territory to cover. A dog will only slow us down." Vlad clamped his lips together firmly.

"Suit yourself." Sandra shrugged. "Gaston is here when you need him."

Just then Norm came into the entry. He took off his greasy baseball cap and fanned his sweaty face with it. "I just got done trimming those shrubs like ya asked. That lilac is on its last legs. Looks kinda spindly to me."

He gave Vlad a quizzical stare. "Hey, Doc, ya going to another funeral? Or is it Johnny Cash night at the karaoke bar?"

Vlad briefly related his discovery of Donna's body at the bookstore and his encounter with Detective Johnson.

"That sucks, bro. I seen enough of that shit when I was in combat. It takes a lot out of ya, take it from a guy who's been there. If ya need to talk…"

"I'll keep that in mind. But tonight Beatrice and I are investigating some gardens. Sandra can fill you in on the toxicology report. We don't want to be noticed in the dark, especially by the police. That ham-fisted detective gave me the word to drop the case immediately."

"So yer going in yer burglar duds. Ya want some help? I broke into lots of joints when I was young. Or I could act as a lookout. Let ya know when the coast is clear."

"Thanks for the offer, but the fewer people on this caper, the better. If we get busted, it'll be just us two. The police have us on their radar already. You and Sandra will be in the clear."

"Okay. But we're waiting up for ya. If ya run into trouble, give us a holler. We'll be there quick as a flash."

"That's right, dearie. I won't be able to sleep a wink until I hear from you," Sandra added.

"We'll call the minute we head for home," Vlad promised

While making a quick stop at the Super Saver for a cat box and litter, Vlad picked up a better flashlight and long-lasting batteries. Max finally settled down and crept out from under the seat, only voicing an occasional weak meow. He allowed Vlad to scoop him up and carry him to Beatrice's front door, although his ears were flattened back and his tail began twitching again. No need to knock, Beatrice was watching from the window. She flung open the door and took the quivering cat from him.

Stroking the cat's soft fur, she cried, "Poor kitty. I'll take care of you. You've had a terrible time of it."

Once Vlad was certain the cat wouldn't tear Beatrice to shreds, he went back to the car to retrieve all the cat necessities, piling everything into the empty litter box. By the time he returned to the house, Beatrice had the cat purring in her arms.

"Shall I set up his cat box in the laundry room?" Vlad nudged the door shut with his foot.

"Yes, please. I'll fix up some food and water for him in the kitchen."

She set the cat down and took the bag of cat food and bowl from him. Max followed at her heels into the kitchen, still purring and rubbing against her legs all the way.

Once the cat had eaten and used the litter box, Beatrice turned her attention to Vlad. She enfolded him in her arms and murmured, "You poor man. Finding Donna like that must've been so horrible. I still can't believe it."

"Like my worst nightmare. I'm not going to get any sleep tonight so I may as well do something useful."

"What do you need me to do?"

"We need to check out to the gardens. Earl's. The Fredricks'. Even Florence's. If we find a monkshood plant in one of them, we'll know who the murderer is. We can tell the police what we've found, and they can get a proper search warrant." Vlad's eyes blazed with determination.

"We've got to be damn close."

"But Detective Johnson told us to stop."

"We are stopping. No more talking to suspects or witnesses. We're just taking an evening stroll and admiring the flowers."

"An evening stroll at two o'clock in the morning all dressed in black." She ran her eyes up and down Vlad's dark clothes. "Isn't that just a tad suspicious?'

"I have insomnia. A walk in the night air makes me sleepy. You're along to make sure I'm safe. I just got over a concussion. You don't want me to relapse."

"I'm the dedicated fiancée. That's for sure. I can't allow you to go gallivanting around by yourself. At least not until after we're married. Otherwise, I won't inherit your marital property when you expire."

"That's the spirit." Vlad flashed her a thumbs-up.

"We still have several hours to kill. I've got some good ideas how to do it. It'll take your mind off Detective Johnson," he added.

He grabbed her hand and led her to the bedroom. "You can change to your burglar clothes when we're done."

Chapter Thirty-One

First stop at two o'clock in the morning was Florence Heidt's backyard.

"Monkshood needs a lot of sun this far north. They can grow to a height of four feet so they are usually planted in the back of a flower bed. Look for a cluster of purple flowers that resemble a helmet or a hood. Darn, the flower could be yellow, too. Just look for a tall plant like in the picture I showed you," Beatrice advised in the car.

Parking several blocks away, they cautiously approached the property. Florence's house, bathed in the light of a full moon, stood completely dark. No lights shone in neighboring houses, either. Mature maple and oak trees insured a shady environment, with hostas growing around the base of the trees and beds of feathery astilbe and showy double impatiens lining the house. Vlad swept his new flashlight over the vegetation.

"It's very unlikely monkshood can grow in this much shade," Beatrice whispered. "Let's check the sides and the front."

"Shrubs, roses, and lilies galore, but no monkshood," Vlad observed after they'd walked around the house. "On to Larkspur Lane."

Neither spoke as they drove through the deserted streets. Vlad kept his eyes moving as he drove, on the lookout for a police patrol car. Beatrice also surveyed their surroundings intently and clasped her hands firmly in her lap to keep them still. He appreciated her efforts to project an appearance of calm when he knew both of them were on high alert. A curious policeman, a neighbor with insomnia, a high-strung dog chained in the backyard—any of these could sandbag their last chance at finding the killer. The full moon was a bonus, shedding enough light to help them find their way without shining the flashlight too soon.

Vlad parked on a quiet street several blocks away from both the Fredricks' house and Earl's.

"Follow me. I've traveled this route before."

The chirping of crickets filled the night air. Moving shadows of tree branches flickered under the streetlights as Vlad and Beatrice walked past. He half expected something to leap out at them from the depths of the darkened yards. When a small animal rustled through a shrub, he pivoted sharply toward the sound; his heart was beating faster than a gerbil on an exercise wheel. Beatrice gave a little squeal and grabbed his arm. They froze until his heart slowed to a normal beat again, then he gestured for her to move on.

The Fredricks' house was nearest. Vlad knew to avoid the deck area where the motion detector had turned on the floodlight in the back. They crept along the privacy fence that couldn't keep the Fredricks truly separate from the Adams. Their children bound them together forever, despite what each parent desired. Vlad shone the flashlight on the ground, skimming over the flowers in full summer bloom. Beatrice could probably name them all, but he categorized them as short and medium height, with daisy-like, powder-puff, or feathery blooms. No tall ones with a bunch of purple helmets on a stem so far. He illuminated the tall flowers near the fence with little pink flowers on their stems, carefully examining the blossoms. *Garden phlox,* he thought. *Maybe some zinnias.*

"Ouch! Damn it!" he cursed softly as he twisted his ankle on a newly dug hole. He stepped back and shone the flashlight on the black earth. A small shovel leaned against the fence. "Somebody's been digging back here. Must be Sid or Shar."

Beatrice tiptoed next to him and stared at the hole. "We may be too late. Whatever was here is long gone."

"Wait. I see something still in there. Please hold the light." Handing her the flashlight, he noticed a dark colored horseradish-like fragment. He bent down to pick it out of the hole, his finger reaching for the small tuber.

"Don't touch it," Beatrice hissed. "If it's monkshood, even touching the root can make you sick. It's extremely toxic."

Vlad swiftly rose to his feet. "We need to get out of here fast and call the police. Hopefully, they can get a search warrant before Sid destroys all the evidence." He grabbed her arm and pulled her back along the fence.

"You're not going anywhere."

A harsh voice reverberated through the evening quiet. A flashlight beamed in their eyes. Holding the light in one hand and a small revolver in another, Shar Fredricks stood menacingly in their path.

Chapter Thirty-Two

It was three o'clock in the morning. Sandra and Norm were drinking coffee, trying to keep awake until Vlad and Beatrice returned. Gaston stretched out at Sandra's feet and closed his eyes. In his sleep he made a little huffing noise and jerked his paws like he was chasing something. After several dozen hands of poker, which Sandra repeatedly won, Norm slapped down his cards.

"Ya got anything to eat?" he said. "I need a bite to keep up my strength."

"I can make you a ham sandwich. Do you want cheese and mayo or mustard?"

As she rose to her feet, Gaston woke with a start and began barking wildly. Then he jumped up and scurried toward the outside door.

"What's wrong with Gaston?" Norm asked.

The poodle scratched at the front door with his paws so frantically that Norm feared he'd mar the wood.

"He's barking so loud he'll wake up the whole joint. The renters will be bitching in no time."

"Gaston, stop it. You know better than to act like that, you bad boy!" Sandra chided.

The little dog's agitation showed no signs of subsiding. If anything, he grew more overwrought, jumping on Sandra, then dashing to Norm, and pawing at his leg. He even nipped Norm's ankle before grabbing the edge of his pant leg and dragging him over to the leash dangling down from the hook.

He gave three sharp barks and bared his teeth, growling ominously.

"I think he wants to go outside," Norm said, reaching for the leash.

"I just took him out a little while ago, and he did his job. He can't be ready to poop this soon." Sandra threw her hands up in consternation.

"Maybe he's got the runs. I'm not about to argue with the little feller."

"I suppose not. Better safe than sorry."

The second Norm snapped the leash on him, Gaston stopped growling. He yanked the handyman out the door so hard it felt like his arm was lifted out of the socket.

"Easy, boy. I need to use my arm for mowing the lawn tomorrow."

The dog didn't head for the nearest bush as Norm expected. Nor did he squat down on his favorite patch of the lawn for relieving himself. Instead, he made straight for the garage, with Norm almost running to keep up. Then he clawed at the closed door and fixed a gaze as fierce as an angry wolverine, urging Norm to open the garage door, which, of course, he did immediately. As soon as the door was lifted, Gaston jumped against the car door and barked.

"Ya want to go for a ride?" Norm asked. "I left the keys in the car so hop in."

Turning on the Buick's engine brought on another fit of barking.

"I know yer trying to tell me something. What is it, little buddy? I wish ya could just come out and say what ya want."

Norm started backing out. "I feel kinda stupid cuz I have no clue where we're going."

The little dog picked up something from the floor, something scattered among the empty fast-food wrappers.

"Are ya hungry? There's nothing there for ya to eat. Sorry, pal. But we can head to Mickie D's if that's what ya want. The drive-through is open all night."

Gaston dropped the lavender scented paper on his lap and started to whine. His bright eyes were glued on Norm, following his every movement with as much intensity as when doggy treats were coming his way.

"What ya got there?" Norm stopped at the end of the driveway to look at the tooth-marked paper. It was the registration form from Sid's meditation class. He stared at it blankly for a second, then the sudden realization hit. "Ya want me to see this?"

Gaston gave an excited yip.

"Ya want to go to the Fredricks' place. That's where Vlad and Beatrice were headed."

Two more excited yips.

Norm said just as excitedly. "All right, little buddy. Hang on to your collar. We're on our way"

Shar surveyed the two of them, her eyes glittering with hatred.

"I could shoot you right now and claim the castle doctrine. I can see it all now. Sid was away on business. Whenever I'm alone, officer, I sleep with my gun nearby. When I heard a noise in the backyard and found two intruders, I panicked and shot them."

"You don't want to do that. You'd bring that pit bull of a detective down on you, and he's relentless. He'd never give up until he found you out. I should know. He's been on my case since Alexandria dropped dead," Beatrice warned.

"Precisely why I shot you. You poisoned Alexandria, and you were covering your tracks. You gave me a delphinium to plant at the Garden Club. I put it in my flower bed. I didn't know it was really wolfbane or monkshead or whatever you want to call it. I noticed something had been digging it up, but I thought it was chipmunks destroying my plants again."

"That story has more holes in it than a macramé plant holder. Alexandria kicked me out of Garden Club last year. Detective Johnson won't buy it," Beatrice retorted.

"So maybe you two will have to suffer a fatal accident like poor Donna Kloostra," Shar declared in a sarcastic voice.

"You killed Donna Kloostra! Why did she have to die?" Vlad asked pugnaciously.

"She knew too much. When she called me today, asking if I ever made elixirs like my herbal teas, she had to be silenced. She was aware Alexandria had tormented my son, drove him to suicide. Oh, I know the police ruled it an accident, but Justin was a good driver. He'd driven down that road a hundred times. He'd never miss that curve unless it was intentional. Only I didn't know why Justin was so upset. It was only a freaking high school prom. He'd been to dances before. But I didn't know the whole truth. Alexandria let me believe for years that Justin was mentally ill. That Sid and I had failed as parents somehow. But then I got the letter."

"What letter?" Vlad asked.

"Gillian wrote us a letter. Wrote one to her father, too, telling us both what really happened that night when Alexandria found out Gillian was pregnant with my son's child. They wanted to get married, keep the baby. They were that much in love. But Alexandria said no. She wasn't about to let her daughter ruin her life with a loser like she'd done with Earl. She called my son a loser. Said Sid and I were nothing but trash." Her voice trembled with emotion so she halted, then spat out the next words. "She told Justin to never come back. Since he was eighteen and Gillian was only seventeen, she'd have him arrested for having sex with a minor if he dared to show his face around their house again."

"So your son committed vehicular suicide?" Beatrice said incredulously.

"What's worse, she forced Gillian to have an abortion. One of her rich doctor friends was so obliging. She killed my grandchild and my son. She nearly drove Gillian to suicide, too. The doctor prescribed medication to keep Gillian compliant until she managed to break free from that evil woman's clutches." Shar's fingers tightened around the revolver as she ranted.

"Sid doesn't know, does he?" Vlad interjected. "You didn't tell him what you did. He never would have told my friend Norm you were at the county fair the day of the pie contest if he was trying to cover up for you."

"That idiot Norm is your friend?" Shar let out a harsh laugh. "I should have guessed he didn't come to meditate. He stood out like a scruffy mongrel at the Westminster Dog Show. Making dumb jokes. Asking stupid questions."

"There's going to be a trail of bodies leading straight to you," Vlad warned.

"A quiet little yoga instructor like me?" Shar mocked in an innocent voice. "No one will believe I'm capable of murder. Half the time no one even notices I'm in the room."

"A quiet yoga instructor with a handgun," Vlad said. "Won't the police find that slightly suspicious?"

"With a killer on the loose? A woman alone at night. I need my gun for protection. They'll believe me. After all, you're the ones trespassing in my yard. Now, Dr. Chomsky, please grab that shovel. I need your fingerprints on the handle. And Beatrice Krup, move along next to him." Shar waved the gun toward the freshly dug hole. "I'm tired of talking. Let's get this over with."

Vlad took one slow step in the direction of the shovel. He considered picking it up and flinging it at the crazed woman. He could knock the gun out of her hand before she pulled the trigger. If he moved quickly enough, she'd be caught off guard. But it was as if Shar read his mind. She stepped back, out of the reach of the shovel, and kept the barrel of the gun pointed firmly at him. He felt Beatrice's hand clutching the back of his shirt and thought, *At least we'll die together.*

Without any warning Vlad saw a fur covered torpedo explode out of the darkness. No warning sound as the rapidly moving projectile struck the back legs of the woman with such force she was propelled forward, and her gun hand flew up wildly. A shot rang out in the air. Then a snarling dervish sank his canines into her bare ankle.

Shar screamed, "What the hell? My leg! A damn dog just bit my leg."

Gaston held a death grip on her ankle in his best pit bull imitation. She twisted her body away from his relentless attack, all the while recklessly brandishing the gun.

The dog created a small window of opportunity. Vlad sprang into action. He seized the shovel and lunged at the woman. Swinging the shovel like he was batting a grand slam homer, he brought it down hard. Thwack. The shovel connected with her gun hand, and the weapon plummeted into the grass. Beatrice dove for it.

Shar shrieked, "Ow! Goddammit! You broke my wrist."

Gaston finally released her bleeding leg. The poodle stood at attention, baring his teeth and growling like the canine apocalypse. Shar's wrist bent at an angle that looked impossible to straighten. Dropping the flashlight, she cradled the injured hand with her good one and wailed, "It hurts like a sonovabitch! Look what you've done to me."

Vlad thrust aside the shovel and picked up the flashlight, holding it steadily on Shar's face, rendered grotesque as a gargoyle's with pain and hatred. "What we've done to you is nothing compared to what you did to Donna and Alexandria."

Beatrice raised the revolver and pointed it at the cursing woman. "The police will be very interested in the monkshood root left in that hole. You should have been more thorough when you were destroying evidence. I suppose you had to wait until Sid was gone to conceal your tracks."

The crackling sound of a body plunging through the shrubbery interrupted her comments. Beatrice looked with alarm at Vlad. Had Sid returned home? Would he defend Shar thinking they attacked her? They didn't need any more complications in an already fraught situation. A voice called out from the darkness.

"Where are ya, little buddy?"

The dog answered with some excited yips.

The voice continued, "Slow down, pal. I can't run as fast as you. I only got two legs."

Vlad's flashlight resting in the grass shone on a pair of beat-up athletic shoes and frayed pant legs. It was Norm. Huffing and puffing, he put his hands on his knees, bending down to catch his breath. When he straightened up, he let out a loud whistle at the sight of Beatrice with the gun.

"I never knew ya wuz a gun totin' mama! Only ya should be holding a Glock instead of that little sissy gun"

"It's not mine, it's Shar's gun. She was going to use it on us to shut us up. We found evidence that she poisoned Alexandria." Beatrice kept the revolver aimed at the moaning woman

"Please call the cops. Tell them we've captured Donna's killer," Vlad said. "She confessed to everything."

Norm whipped out his phone and began punching 911. Gaston stopped growling but kept a watchful eye on Shar. Norm gave the dispatcher their location.

"Ya better call in the homicide detective," he added. "I think we caught us a murderer."

When he hung up he exclaimed, "Holy shit! This is just like being in an episode of *Law and Order: Criminal Intent.* Only I never would have suspected Shar Fredricks of being the criminal."

"Shar was very clever," Vlad commented with a hint of admiration in his voice. "She ripped the pages out of *The Herbal Alchemist's Handbook* so no one could trace it to her. If she had bought the book, she knew Donna would have a record of the sale. She avoided any connection between the toxic plant and herself. But Donna remembered Shar acting weird in her store."

"If you fools had stopped your meddling, no one would have found me. I tried to warn you to stop," Shar growled.

"You attacked me at Tripoli Island. You scared my kids. My little girl thought you were a monster. She was afraid to sleep at night. Afraid you were going to hurt her, too." Vlad felt anger building. "You caused some big problems with my ex-wife. She had to deal with the kids and calm their fears. She took it out on me."

"Collateral damage. It was nothing compared to the harm Alexandria did to me." Shar gave an unrepentant glare. "I lost everything important in my life. What's a few sleepless nights compared to a lifetime of pain?"

Vlad heard a siren in the distance. As the shrill noise grew louder and louder, his muscles tensed, and he began rocking on the balls of his feet. He was more than ready to turn the whole mess over to the police and go home, pull the covers over his head, and sleep like a hibernating turtle. The flashing red and blue lights at the end of the street were a welcome sight, but the thought of seeing Detective Johnson tied his stomach in knots. He gripped the flashlight a little tighter to keep from shaking.

Beatrice met his eyes with a fierce look. Shar's whimpers only made her face harden with resolve while Vlad felt a twinge of pity for the woman who had lost her only son. He tried not to think of losing one of his children in a tragic accident, an accident caused by another person's cruelty. Cruelty begets cruelty unless one has the courage to break the vicious cycle and replace it with forgiveness. For all of Shar's high-minded intentions with yoga, she was unable to find any mercy in her heart for Alexandria.

A car door slammed. Gaston barked to signal their position in the backyard. As the crunch of footsteps drew near, a bright light from a huge flashlight nearly blinded Vlad. When his eyes adjusted, he could see the dim figure of a patrolman behind the light.

"What's going on here?" the patrolman asked.

"He hit me with a shovel and broke my wrist," Shar accused.

"She was planning on shooting us until I knocked the gun out of her hand," Vlad said. "She confessed to two murders—Alexandria Adams and Donna Kloostra. We've been holding her until you arrived."

"What's with the dog?" the patrolman thumbed at the poodle.

"Gaston saved us. He jumped on her from behind and distracted her so I was able to get the gun away," Vlad explained.

"The vicious mongrel bit me," Shar complained.

Just then another car pulled up. More doors opening and closing and the sound of another set of footsteps approaching.

"Not you again!" the familiar gruff voice exclaimed. "I had a sneaking suspicion I'd find you here. Now what happened?"

The patrolman blurted out before Vlad could craft a response. "They said this woman is a confessed murderer and the dog helped them capture her. Sounds kinda screwy to me."

Beatrice spoke up. "It's the truth, Detective Johnson. Shar Fredericks killed Alexandria because she threatened her son, Justin, with sexual assault charges. She forbade him to see her daughter, Gillian, again. Alexandria drove him to commit suicide."

"Alexandria forced her daughter to have an abortion. She killed her unborn grandson, too." Vlad added.

The detective shook his head. "Is this Crawford, Wisconsin, or some episode of a bad soap opera?"

"We found evidence, Detective." Vlad shone the flashlight on the partly exposed hole. "If you look inside there, you'll find a root left behind. Monkshood. The poison that killed Alexandria."

"How the hell do you know what killed Alexandria Adams? I just got the toxicology report. Are you psychic?" Johnson looked at him warily.

Vlad averted his eyes. He was grateful for the darkness so the policeman couldn't see his guilty expression.

"No, but the little feller is," Norm proclaimed.

"Who are you?" the detective turned to face Norm. "What are you doing here?"

"I brought the dog. We're kindova team. He's like Lassie, and I'm sorta his sidekick like Timmy. Gaston is a crime stopper," Norm boasted. "I had to drive him here. It was too far for him to walk, He's only a toy poodle. His little legs won't hold up for that distance."

"Now I've heard everything. A detective dog and his sidekick. I don't know whether to thank you or take you to the looney bin!"

Shar uttered a low sound like an injured beast, bringing the policeman's attention back to her.

"She does need medical attention," Vlad said. "I didn't mean to hurt her, but I had to save my fiancée."

"The woman holding the revolver? She looks like she doesn't need any help. She can handle pretty much anything." The patrolman gave Beatrice in her gunslinger stance an admiring glance.

"Oh, my goodness, here." Beatrice said with a start, realizing the gun was still in her possession. "You'd better take this from me. I won't be needing it anymore." She handed the revolver to the beefy detective.

"It's nearly four in the morning. We'll take over from here. You need to come down to the station tomorrow and give us your statements. Not before noon. In the meantime we'll take the accused woman to the emergency room before we book her."

"She confessed to killing Donna, too," Vlad added.

"Tomorrow. You can give us the details tomorrow," Detective Johnson said.

He gently grasped Shar's elbow and guided the dazed woman to the patrol car, saying, "Please come with me, madam. You have the right to remain silent. Anything you say can and will be used against you in a court of law. You have the right to an attorney."

Shar shot a look of pure hatred at Vlad as she was led away.

Beatrice drifted into Vlad's arms and clung to him, nestling her head on his chest. "You were so brave. Grabbing the shovel and knocking the gun from her hand. I thought we were going to die."

Vlad tilted her face upward, locking his lips onto hers. After a lingering kiss, he spoke. "Dearest Beatrice, you dove for the gun before Shar could try to regain it. You were just as brave. But Gaston was the bravest."

"Yep. He sure saved your butts. I think he deserves a reward." Norm rubbed the poodle's head.

"Come here, dog. We'll have a group hug." Vlad opened one arm to draw the dog to him., but Gaston didn't budge from Norm's side.

"I don't think he wants a hug. He'd rather have a cheeseburger from Mickie D.'s," Norm said.

Gaston gave a little yip when he heard the word *cheeseburger*.

"That dog knows what he wants," chuckled Vlad. "Apparently, it's not a hug." Vlad dug a twenty out of his wallet and handed it to Norm. "Please pick us up some burgers and fries, and we'll all celebrate at Sandra's."

Chapter Thirty-Three

Late the next morning Vlad was hauled into reluctant consciousness by the blip of a notification. *Damn, I forgot to turn my phone on silent.* Rather than checking the phone, he lay for some time just watching the beautiful woman sleeping beside him. Too exhausted to talk, they had barely managed to pull down the Murphy bed before tossing off their clothes and collapsing. Now the gentle rise and fall of her breathing filled him with a sense of wonder at her steadfastness. Sometimes when he woke, he felt a slight panic to reaffirm she was still with him, that she hadn't chucked it all and fled away into the night. However, there she was, his wise-eyed, passionate fiancée, a continual mystery for him to discover, loving and supportive as always. When her eyes fluttered open, she smiled sleepily at him. He bent down to kiss her but stopped short of touching her lips.

"I'm afraid I have a bad case of morning breath,' he muttered.

"So do I. Who cares?" She drew him to her, ignoring his protests.

Even her stale mouth was sweeter to him than a glass of Moscato. He kissed her so deeply and so long that soon they were panting to catch their breath.

Slipping beside her under the covers, he reached around her to slide his hands firmly along her petal soft skin. She tightened her arms around his neck and returned the kiss. Soon they were united in their desire to demonstrate their devotion to one another. All the terror of the previous night melted away in the heat of their passion.

Afterward, they shifted to their sides and lay as one, reluctant to break the connection.

"I love you, Beatrice Krup. You are the most exciting, amazing woman in the world. I could lie like this forever with you."

"And I love you, Vlad Chomsky." She kissed her finger, then gently traced his lips with it. "But you know, darling, we have a date down at the police station with Detective Johnson."

Vlad felt his body tense up at the mention of the detective's name, and suddenly they separated. Cold reality was worse than a bucket of freezing water to dampen his ardor.

"You're right," he sighed. "I suppose we should get dressed. Fortunately, you left a change of clothes here so you won't have to go home first."

Beatrice rose on one elbow. "I left plenty of dry cat food for Max, but we really need to check on him after our interview with the police."

His cell phone rang. He groaned. "Not Maria already."

He shuffled over to answer it. Sandra's voice crackled on the other end.

"Aren't you up yet? It's after one. Come on down. I've got something to show you.'

Vlad tossed on some clothes while Beatrice took a quick shower. Hopefully, Sandra would have coffee brewing when they got downstairs. Beatrice emerged from the bathroom fully clothed with damp hair and a bright smile. Vlad brushed her forehead lightly with his lips, almost giddy with relief that the cloud of suspicion was finally lifted from her.

Sandra eagerly opened her door to them, waving the afternoon newspaper aloft so they could see the headline: **Poison Suspect Goes to the Dogs.** Norm lounged in the armchair, looking a bit bleary-eyed after the long night.

"The phone has been ringing off the hook since the paper came out," Norm said. "I had to fire up the Buick and head to the drugstore to pick up a few copies."

"Sit yourselves down and listen to this." Sandra read aloud from the news story. "Toy poodle aids in the daring capture of an accused killer in a late-night encounter. A suspect in two recent murders is in police custody, thanks to the charge led by a dog named Gaston.

"Two more potential victims were able to disarm the suspect after the poodle's sneak attack. Owner Sandra Tooksbury extolled the capabilities of her highly trained dog, who has been involved in at least two other canine capers. 'Gaston thwarted a terrorist plot last year and helped to nab two international jewel thieves in May. He's an exceptionally smart dog with an almost prescient sense of timing and knowledge of criminal behavior. He has an uncanny ability to ferret out lawbreakers.' Detective Andrew Johnson, lead investigator of the high-profile case stated, 'Whether it was due to coincidence or superior canine ability, the dog arrived at the crime scene at a crucial moment and prevented another possible homicide. The suspect is in police custody, and a name will be released after further investigation by our department.'

"Gaston did it again. He's the cleverest dog detective in the world," she crowed. "Look how handsome you are in this picture, Lovey Puppy." She thrust the paper at the dog's face, then sat down on the flowered loveseat and opened her arms. "Come to Mama, Pretty Boy."

The poodle jumped up and licked her cheek, nuzzling her neck with happy throaty sounds. She turned her other cheek to continue the Puppy Love Fest.

"Mama loves you, doesn't she? Loves you to the moon and back."

"The little fella is sure smart. I once had a smart dog, too. He'd bring me the daily newspaper every morning." Norm paused to gulp his coffee.

"That's not so clever. Lots of dogs do that," Vlad protested.

"But I never had a subscription!" Norm guffawed.

Vlad smacked his forehead. "I fell for it again"

He caught Beatrice's gaze as she shook her head.

Then her face grew solemn. "When I think back to that first day when we brainstormed motives, how close we were to Shar's reasons for killing Alexandria. We wrote 'Revenge. Hatred. Greed. Crime of Passion. Love.' She tapped her finger on her chin. "Not passion like two lovers, but certainly the strong love a mother has for her child."

"And losing that love brought on hatred for the person that caused her loss. That led to revenge," Sandra added.

"Kinda like the famous saying: 'Hell hath no fury like a woman's corns.'" Norm jumped in.

Beatrice groaned. "No more bad jokes, please. Actually, the first part of the real quote fits Shar's motivation. 'Heaven has no rage like love to hatred turned.'"

"I was thinking Shakespeare fit more than Congreve. Shar reminded me of Lady Macbeth's advice: 'Look like the innocent flower, but be the serpent under it.'" Vlad mused. "She had everyone fooled with her serene persona, but inside she was seething with anger. We just witnessed a real-life tragedy that compares with any drama produced on a stage. Like William said: 'What's done cannot be undone.'"

"This talk about Shar is making me sad. Poor Sid just had his life upended again. Can we please talk about something else?' Beatrice said "You all helped to clear my name, and we should have a little celebration. Right, Gaston?"

When he heard his name, the poodle barked in affirmation. He jumped down from Sandra and moved to Beatrice on the couch. Promptly licking her hand, he wriggled between her and Vlad. When Vlad reached to move him, he gave a warning growl, forcing Vlad to quickly retreat.

"Let's have a picnic in the park. We can use the small pavilion at Riverview. We'll have a little party. Nicky and Katy and Erin can come, too." Sandra clapped her hands with excitement. "You can take a copy of the *Daily Times* to your ex and show her the case is over. She can't object to the kids coming with you anymore."

"One thing I don't understand," said Beatrice. "How did Gaston know he needed to be at Sid and Shar's?"

"I wonder if he's more than smart. He could be developing psychic powers." Norm scratched his chin contemplatively. "You hear about people having traumatic experiences—like near death—and coming back changed. Maybe when that cat attacked him in the bookstore, it triggered something within him."

"If that's true, I am definitely incorporating it into a new act," Sandra cackled. "Train him to guess the playing card. I'll call him Gaston the Psychic Pooch."

THE SUN SHONE BRIGHTLY on Saturday, a perfect cloudless day, with the happy buzz of insects flourishing in the August heat. Flitting from blossom to blossom, the bees were in overdrive. They weren't shy about crashing the picnic in the pavilion, causing Kaitlyn to shriek.,

"A bee! There's a bee in my root beer!" She ran to Vlad, ducking behind his legs. "Make them go away, Daddy. The bees are spoiling the party."

"I'll take care of it, Sweet Pea."

Vlad moved the garbage can piled high with rotting watermelon rinds and sticky soda cups away from their gathering. The bees obligingly followed.

Norm brought a tray heaped with burgers to the food table and announced, "Come and get it! The Scrum-delish burgers are ready."

Vlad stood behind Kaitlyn, helping her squeeze ketchup on her burger and making sure she put more than potato chips and pickles on her plate. Sandra stood behind a pan of congealed yellow and orange gelatin.

"This is my famous Sunshine Salad. People used to always ask me to bring it to the potlucks." She plopped a spoonful of shredded carrots, pineapple, and lemon Jell-O on Kaitlyn's plate. The conglomeration stood quivering next to the chips. "You'll love it, Katie. It's like taking a bite of summer sun. Try it."

Vlad was astonished when his picky eater took her plastic spoon and dug into the Jell-O. She stuffed a bite full in her mouth.

"This is the best salad ever," she said, then proceeded to shovel in more of the pile.

"I knew you'd like it, dearie. It's even better with whipped cream but I promised your mom I wouldn't load you up with sugar."

"I'll have a big spoonful, too," Nicholas said. "Your salad looks real pretty." He held out his plate.

Instead of the usual teenage disdain for all things old, Erin sweetly asked, "May I have some, too? I bet it's healthy with all the carrots. I'm a vegan, you know, so your salad is perfect."

Gaston positioned himself directly at Kaitlyn's feet, hoping for a morsel to drop from her plate. Vlad noticed she slipped him a chunk of her burger, but he let it go. No scolding today when at last he had all his children safely beside him with Beatrice beaming across the picnic bench at them. For a few awful moments in the past few weeks, he felt he was in danger of losing it all: the love of his life to the false accusations, and his children to his ex-wife's ultimatum, even his very life to Shar's murderous intent. Somehow he found an inner strength he never knew he possessed until it was sorely tested. And, of course, he had a little help from a certain French poodle that sat begging beneath the picnic bench.

"Dad, she's not eating her meat." Nicholas, ever the informant, pointed out the furtive movement under the table.

"Am so! Watch me take a bite." Kaitlyn opened her mouth wide but only broke off a nibble and noisily chewed it.

"I saw you sneak some of it to the dog," the boy accused.

"Did not!" the little girl declared.

"Did so!" Nicholas argued.

"Did not! You're lying." She stuck out her tongue at her brother.

"Stop it, the two of you," Erin ordered. "We're celebrating. We get to hang out with Dad again. And the police aren't investigating Beatrice anymore."

Vlad flashed her a smile of appreciation and thought, *My girl is growing up.*

"Ya know, it kinda reminds me of when the cop came out to my Uncle Bud's farm when I was working there. The cop pulls up to the barnyard and gets out of his car. He says, 'I mean to inspect this farm for illegal crops.'

"I tell him, 'By all means. Just don't go in that field over there.'

"The cop gets real mad and says, 'Don't tell me what to do. Don't you know who I am? I have the authority of the law with me.' Then he pulls out his badge. 'Do you see this shiny badge? It means I can go anywhere I want. Have I made myself clear?'

"I nod and say, 'Loud and clear, sir. I'm sorry if I butted in with your investigation.'

"A few minutes later I hear someone screaming. I see the cop come running across the field with an angry bull chasing him. He looks at me and yells, 'Don't just stand there watching. Do something!'

"I say, 'Your badge, sir. Show him your badge!'"

Norm chuckled and the rest of the party joined in except Kaitlyn. She screwed up her face and asked, "Uncle Norm, did the cop get away?"

"It's just a joke, honey." Vlad said. "There wasn't really a cop. Uncle Norm made it up to make us laugh."

"I like Beatrice's Knock-Knock jokes better. I don't think cops are very funny."

"Neither do I, sweetie," Beatrice agreed. "After everything that happened his summer, neither do I!"

Nicholas studied the food laden table for a minute, then remarked. "I don't see any dessert. Aren't we having something for dessert?"

Vlad playfully hit himself on the head. "I knew I was forgetting something. I can make a quick dessert run for some chocolate chip cookies. How about some fudge brownies from Sweet Talkin' Treats? Or maybe they'll have the Sea Salt Caramel cupcakes you like so much, honey," Vlad said to Beatrice.

She was quick to answer. "Brownies or cookies or cupcakes for dessert sounds great. Please, anything but pie!"

Cherry Berry Peach Pie

The murder weapon in my third Gaston Mystery Series is a pie. Not just any old pie, but a Cherry Berry Peach Pie. My character Beatrice enters a pie contest at the county fair, but instead of winning a prize, her pie kills the judge. Dessert pies were invented by American housewives, and my character Beatrice is following a long tradition of pie baking.

When I was growing up, no Sunday dinner was complete without one of Mom's pies. She mastered the art of a perfect pie. Not only Mom but all the church ladies at ice cream socials baked delectable pies. Still warm from the oven, with a scoop of vanilla ice cream melting on the side, dissolving in your mouth like a piece of heaven. Beatrice's pie could be no less.

I found the recipe for Cherry Berry Peach Pie in a little cook booklet, *Blue Ribbon Winners of the Wisconsin State Fair, 1860-1974*, that lay dormant in a china cabinet drawer for many years until I started the search for a catchy pie recipe. When my husband found a good deal on cherries on Facebook Marketplace, I knew this was the golden opportunity to create Beatrice's suspect pastry. I immediately bought blueberries and peaches and set about to bake a pie.

First, I called my brother-in-law, Paul, the pie guru. He gave me great advice for making a tender, flaky crust. Disclaimer: I did not make the pie crust from scratch. I cheated and purchased a refrigerated pie crust. But he did give me some hints for making the lattice top. For a murderer to sabotage a pie by adding poison, I figured Beatrice needed to bake a pie with an open top.

I assembled all the ingredients and reread the recipe. I noticed in the ingredients 3 Tbsp. of flour was listed, but there was no mention of flour in the directions. What does one do with flour if you're not making the crust? I consulted my go-to reference, *The Better Homes and Gardens Cook Book*, also from 1974. The recipes for both peach and blueberry pie called for that same amount of flour to be combined with the dry ingredients, then added to the fresh fruit. So that's what I did.

After I added the sugars, flour, salt, and cinnamon to the fruit, I was ready to tackle the lattice top crust. Watching a video on YouTube was a no-brainer for directions on forming the top crust. WRONG! The server was down. Back to my trusty cookbook. However, instead of the explicit video I was expecting to use, all I had was one small picture and a paragraph of directions: "cut pastry strips 1/2 to 3/4 inch wide." I got out my ruler and measured before I cut. "Lay strips on pie at one-inch intervals." Back with the ruler. "Fold back alternate strips to help you weave crosswise strips over and under." Huh? The picture showed the strips starting at the middle and working to the outer rim with every other one folded back. Easier read than done. "Trim strips. Crimp. Seal."

I tried using a knife handle to make a fluted edge, like the picture in the cookbook. My flutes went flat so I tried pinching them. They didn't cooperate. Some were bunched up and fat, some were skinny, and none were nice and even like the picture in the cookbook. Here is a picture of my finished pie with "killer's" hand. The pie was ready for the oven.

When I removed the pie to cool, the fruit did shine like jewels beneath the crust, just as I imagined when I described it in my book. How would it taste? I took it to a Fourth of July picnic to test it out on unbiased relatives. When I explained they were helping me test out the recipe for my latest book, I found some willing volunteers, including my husband. A slice of pie, a scoop of ice cream. No poison.

The results? The pie was delicious. Even though it wasn't as pretty as the fancy pastry described in the book, the flavors did not disappoint. All the flavors of summer in one bite—lush juicy peaches, tart cherries, and sweet blueberries. The recipe was a winner. I would definitely make it again but next time tackle the art of making a crust. As one cook describes it, it's a matter of "creating long, fine layers with streaks of butter between them." Light enough to melt in your mouth yet strong enough to hold the filling in place. My mom, Beatrice, and the church ladies would give me their blessing.

Cherry Berry Peach Pie (my version)

Ingredients:
3 cups sliced peeled peaches (about 6)
1 cup fresh blueberries
1 cup pitted halved fresh sour cherries
1/3 cup brown sugar
1/3 cup granulated sugar
3 Tbsp. flour
1/8 tsp. salt
¼ tsp. cinnamon
pastry for 2-crust pie
milk
granulated sugar to sprinkle on lattice top

Directions:
In large bowl mix together peaches, blueberries, and cherries. Gently stir in brown sugar, granulated sugar, flour, salt, and cinnamon. Line a 9-inch pie plate with half of pastry, trim overhang to 1 inch. Turn fruit into pie. Roll out remaining pastry and cut into strips. Arrange strips over fruit in lattice fashion. Fold strips under edge of pastry, make rim and flute edges. Brush with milk and sprinkle with sugar. Bake at 450 degrees for 10 minutes. Reduce heat to 350 degrees and bake 45-50 minutes, longer until pastry is brown and fruit tender. Serve warm or cool.

Note: Original recipe called for sweet cherries. If switching, sprinkle 1 Tbsp. fresh lemon juice on fruit and reduce brown sugar to ¼ cup.

Acknowledgments

Thanks to Karen Hodges Miller, my editor, who first convinced me my writing was publishable and continues to encourage and inspire, and to Wendy Loos, Jack Saarela and Sherri Lynn . Without your weekly support in our writers' group, I never would have finished this book in a year.

Special thanks to my long-time writer friends: Frances Milburn, Bruce Bentz, John Aschenbrenner, Paul and Kay Marose, Dan David and Kay Ferguson. You kept me motivated and laughing.

Thanks to Sherri Lynn, who shared her experiences as an EMT, to Tim Roets, who advised me on police procedures, and Dr. Charles Frinak, my medical consultant.

And of course, my unending thanks to Megan Detrie, who finished her edits of my book on the way to Portugal and to Michael Detrie, who always believed in me and supported my writing including taking many sacrificial naps so the house was quiet.

About the Author

Janice Detrie has been involved with books her entire life. "I've always loved writing and reading, even as a small child," she says. A former literacy coordinator, her reading tastes are eclectic, everything from biography to mystery to the classics to nonfiction.

Janice lives in Watertown, Wisconsin, with her husband, Michael, where she is active in community theater and distributing free books to children. She has two children and two grandchildren.

Book One in the Gaston Mystery Series, *The 7-10 Split,* can be purchased here: https://www.amazon.com/7-10-Split-Janice-Detrie-ebook/dp/B06XKJTGXS/ref.

Click here for Book Two in the series, *A Glint in Her Ice*: https://www.amazon.com/Glint-Gaston-Poodle-Mystery-Book-ebook/dp/B086VR8PPQ/ref.